Robert Grant

Jack Hall

Or the school days of an American boy

Robert Grant

Jack Hall
Or the school days of an American boy

ISBN/EAN: 9783337321550

Printed in Europe, USA, Canada, Australia, Japan

Cover: Foto ©Andreas Hilbeck / pixelio.de

More available books at **www.hansebooks.com**

JACK HALL

OR

THE SCHOOL DAYS OF AN AMERICAN BOY

BY

ROBERT GRANT

AUTHOR OF " FACE TO FACE," " THE CONFESSIONS OF A FRIVOLOUS GIRL,"
ETC.

ILLUSTRATED BY F. G. ATTWOOD

BOSTON
JORDAN, MARSH AND COMPANY
1888

The Riverside Press, Cambridge:
Electrotyped and Printed by H. O. Houghton & Co.

I Dedicate this Book

TO

MY THREE BOYS.

CONTENTS.

JACK HALL.

CHAPTER I.

IT was a bright February morning. The sun
was warm, so that the piles of snow in the streets
were in a perfect condition for snow-balling, much
to the satisfaction of a medium-sized boy of thirteen
who had just come out of the house and was standing on his doorsteps, drawing on his mittens. His
name was Jack Hall, and he wore a Scotch cap, a
reefer, and a pair of rubber boots.

As soon as his mittens were on he cleared the last
two steps with a jump, and, plunging his hands into
the nearest snow-bank, stood patting a ball into
shape while he looked around. The street on which
Jack's house stood was a long and tolerably steep
slope. There were houses on both sides. He lived

at the top, near the corner of an intersecting street, which ran at right angles to it down to Boston Common. Opposite to his house was a grocery shop.

Suddenly Jack looked animated as he caught sight of another figure, not unlike his own, on the way up the hill, and by way of welcome to the new-comer, who was still far off, he emitted a sort of shrill war-whoop, "Ehu — ehu — ehu!"

Immediately there came a faint reply from the distance, "Ehu — ehu — ehu!"

After each had twice repeated this salutation, Jack continued contentedly to make snow-balls. He had finished two, tucking one under either arm, and was moulding a third, when a man appeared on the further sidewalk of the intersecting street.

"Give me a shot, mister?" shouted Jack.

The man, who was going towards the Common, looked back over his shoulder and grinned, which Jack recognized as a sign that he might blaze away, which he did accordingly. The first snow-ball went a little wide of the mark, and struck the wall beyond with a thud; but the next hit the man plump in the middle of his exposed arm, and evidently convinced him that discretion was the better part of valor, for he gathered his coat collar about his · neck, and fled with precipitation until the corner shut him out from view, pursued by Jack's remaining snow-ball and derisive scoffing.

This put Jack in high humor. But before he had fully re-supplied himself with ammunition, the area door in the wing of the grocery shop opened, and the grocer's clerk, a young man of about eighteen, appeared, carrying some baskets and bundles, with which he proceeded to load a wheelbarrow belonging to the establishment, that stood beside the big window, paying no attention to Jack, though he perceived him very well. For there was perpetual war between the boys in the neighborhood and "Mustachio," which was the name applied by them to the grocer's assistant on account of a feebly sprouting down on his upper lip.

Jack had equipped himself amply with snow-balls by the time that the clerk, with his barrow-full of eggs and flour and other groceries to be delivered in the neighborhood, was ready to· start down the street, and stood leaning against a tree watching the enemy. Before Mustachio had proceeded

twenty feet, Jack let drive, not at him, but at the
. area door, having made sure by a glance that the
grocer himself was not looking out at the big window. Now the area door contained a pocket about
a foot square, cut in the panel and concealed by a
swinging cover, which opened inwards, and shut as
soon as pressure was removed. Through this the
baker dropped his rolls in the morning into a
basket in the cellar of the store, and one of the
never-tiring amusements of the boys was to try to
do the same with snow-balls. From across the
street this required some dexterity. As a consequence, the grocer had cause to complain bitterly,
both of the influx of snow into his bread basket,
and the dents in the woodwork of the door, which
was apt to need a new coat of paint as soon as the
spring came.

On this occasion Jack's first shot hit the woodwork with a plashing sound, for the ball was
slushy. The noise affected the grocer's clerk as a
red rag affects a bull. He stopped and, setting
down his barrow, turned towards Jack just as that
young miscreant's second ball hit the target and
disappeared. . The clerk muttered something under

his breath and made a dash as though to run across the street. Jack, divining that this was a feint, retired alertly as far as the corner, where he stood ready to beat a more hasty and prolonged retreat if necessary. But the clerk, thinking better of his first impulse, took up the handles of his barrow and started off again, trundling smartly.

This was Jack's opportunity. He regained his former post and, aiming with precision, sent a ball whizzing within an inch of the clerk's head, accompanying the shot with a vituperative cry loud enough to arouse the neighborhood.

"Mustachio-o-o! Mustachio-o-o!"

Dignity was the *rôle* which the victim assumed this time, for he paid no heed to either insult. Yet he was doomed to be discomfited. The second shot hit his barrow without doing any damage, but the next struck a paper bag containing eggs and broke two, a misadventure which would require the poor fellow to make another trip by-and-by. He turned and glared at Jack, realizing his helplessness and yet reluctant to be unavenged.

So absorbed was he in righteous indignation that he had failed to observe another small figure creep-

ing up on the opposite sidewalk in the shadow of
the houses and obscured by the trunks and branches
of the row of trees which grew along the street.
Mustachio stooped to gather some snow which he
was compressing with relentless vim into ice with
his bare hands preparatory to hurling it at Jack
with all his might, when of a sudden a ball from a
new quarter and at short range struck him with
stinging force in the side of the head, plastering his
ear like a poultice. For an instant he was dazed
by the shock which gave time — but only just time
— for the reinforcement over the way to shoot past
him and dive into the alley way of Jack's house
a few yards above. Mustachio plunging into the
snow had crossed the street and was at his new
antagonist's heels in the twinkling of an eye, but
too late. The heavy back door was slammed in his
face and double-bolted, and simultaneously from
behind it and from the street corner where Jack
had again sought shelter arose another triumphant
cry, " Mustachio-oh-o-ho! Mustachio-o! "

A few minutes later, a peculiar undulating whistle given vent to by Jack assured the prisoner
that danger was passed, who, accordingly, reap-

peared on the scene. The unhappy grocer's lad, having come to the conclusion that retribution at the moment was out of the question, was visible down the street trundling his wheelbarrow, but out of range of the parting snow-balls which the boys sent after him.

"That was a beauty, Dubsy," said Jack, by way of compliment to the shot which had struck Mustachio's ear.

At that moment a booby-hut swung round the corner. As it went by each of the boys sprang lightly on to one of the hind runners unseen by the driver. Away they swept down hill, passing their late enemy, at whom they grinned exultingly, and delighting in the jounces which the sleigh made at the uneven places. It turned into the next street, and soon they were spinning over the smooth, well-trodden snow of the milldam, amid a host of sleighs and a gay jingling of bells. Presently the driver pulled up the horses and they stopped before a house where a lady got out. But they were in luck for the time being; there was another lady to be left further on; then the booby turned and carried them back again, which was what they had hoped for. They held on firmly, still as mice, and well sheltered by the back of the sleigh.

All of a sudden, just as they had reached the foot of their own street, a voice abreast of them cried loudly, "Cut — cut behind!"

Simultaneously, a snow-ball aimed at them skimmed along the top of the booby and hit the driver. But the driver needed no additional stimulus; the cry was enough. Before the snow-ball struck him he had reached for the whip. Swish! swish! went the lash, curling round the back of the sleigh. But the boys were quicker than he; at the first note of danger they had let go their hold.

Instantly they darted after the urchin who had betrayed them, a ragged shaver, who had taken to his heels the moment after discharging the snow-ball, and was now running like greased lightning. Their rubber boots impeded them, and though they panted after the fugitive through a number of streets they paused at last, pretty well winded, and had to content themselves with firing a few harmless shots at him. He returned the fire from the brow of the hill where he stood, and one of his balls, which were very swift, hit Jack's Scotch cap, although Jack dodged, and nearly knocked it off; whereupon the enemy set up a jeer, and exclaimed before vanishing over the hill, —

"I 'll bring a crowd down this afternoon and knock the stuffing out of yer!"

Jack and Dubsy, looking rather sheepish, turned towards home. Their pride had received a downfall. Moreover they were heated and rather tired.

The vicinity of Ma'am Horn's struck them, accordingly, as providential, for it seemed as though "pickle-limes" were the only things in creation which could relieve their outraged feelings. They began by flattening their noses against the window-pane of the little shop. A goodly array of small wares delighted their vision, — peg-tops, of all sizes; marbles of every sort, from the common clay variety known as the "twoser" and blood alleys up to wonderful mottled agates; knives, jack-stones, jew's-harps, and valentines. There were caramels, pop-corn balls, cream cakes, and cocoanut cakes, and, most tempting of the whole in the way of sweets, was a tin tray of black looking sticks of molasses candy, each about the length of a short cigar, but rather thicker. On the counter, under the eye of Ma'am Horn, who did also a thriving business in tapes, needles, and haberdashery, stood a dish not unlike the bowls used for holding gold fish, half full of dark greenish yellow spheres: these were "pickle-limes."

Jack had seven cents in his hand, in copper coin, as he entered.

"Give me two pickle-limes, please, Ma'am

Horn," he said. Ma'am Horn, a thin and rather severe looking lady, fished out the dainties called for, one of which Jack handed to Dubsy, who had been gazing at them despairingly, having no money of his own, and who exclaimed with effusion, "Oh, thank you, Jack." Together they popped them into their mouths, and as they munched interchanged glances of rapturous congratulation.

Jack had five cents left; what should he buy? His eye lingered fondly on almost every article in the store. He was sorely tempted by a jew's-harp, a compressible snake, and by some fascinating striped marbles known as "Chinees." But his appetite was far from satisfied. Then, too, there was Dubsy, and Dubsy was out of cash; though, of course, if he bought marbles Dubsy would not expect him to share them with him.

"How much is a cream cake?" he asked.

"Five cents."

Jack sighed. He knew well the price of those luscious articles, but the desire to have one made him perhaps imagine that it might have gone down.

"Give me two cocoanut cakes."

Cocoanut cakes were a cent apiece. Jack put one into his mouth and munched it thoughtfully; then with a sigh he held the second out to Dubsy and exclaimed monosyllabically, " Here ! "

" You 're a brick, Jack ! "

Jack licked his fingers. " I took the brownest one," he said, apologetically.

There were still three cents remaining. With two of them Jack bought some " Chinees," but the expenditure of the last cent perplexed him. He finally selected one of the sticks of black molasses candy; these when fresh were so adhesive that it was common to transplant them directly from the tray to the purchaser's mouth, for if put in paper the paper was sure to cling to them. Jack's eyes closed with satisfaction as his teeth shut down on one end of the delicious morsel. When he looked again, he perceived Dubsy gazing at him with a manly resolve to exhibit no envy, and yet with dis-appointment, or let us rather say resignation, writ-ten on his face.

Jack could not speak, but he grunted and held out his mouth; Dubsy understood the signal. A moment later his teeth had hold of the other end of the stick of candy. Now began a struggle. The two boys, chewing vigorously and soon convulsed with laughter, tried to draw away from one another, but the tough and ropy compound balked them. In a moment or two, however, it began to yield, and presently the point of ambition with Jack and Dubsy was to draw out as long as possible the strand of stringy molasses which bound them together. At last, after they were separated from one another by the width of the shop, the strand became a thread. When this broke the fun was over. But, needless to say, the mouths of the participants were a sight to behold.

The corner from which they had originally started was the regular meeting-place for the boys who lived within the radius of half a mile from Jack's house. Thither they now returned only to learn that the other fellows had gone coasting on the Common. Accordingly, they went into Jack's back yard by way of the long alley already referred to, and soon reappeared devouring an apple apiece obtained from the cook, and dragging a double runner called "Never Say Die," made out of Jack's single sleds, "Star of the East," and "Reindeer," with

which they proceeded to the long coast, so called,
which ran from a point opposite the State House
diagonally across the Common to the West Street
gate. The coast was in fine condition and crowded
with sleds of every description, from the most di-
minutive type to huge double runners capable of
holding eight or ten big boys. Some of these last
named, elaborate with carpet laid over the main
board and a bell which sounded at intervals to warn
people to get out of the way, seemed to Jack and
Dubsy the most desirable things in the world, and
made their own double runner appear very insignificant by comparison.

However, theirs went tolerably fast, quite fast
enough to be safe for such small boys as they.
Jack went down in front " belly flounders," or
"belly bumps," — the phrase used to denote lying
flat on one's stomach ; little Bill French, whom
they had picked up on the way, came next in the
same posture, grasping Jack firmly by the legs just
above the tops of his rubber boots, and on the end
squatted Dubsy, " butcher " fashion, with one foot
hanging out behind for extra steering purposes.
The coast was like glass. They positively flew ;

and it was no easy work to guide their course so as to avoid running down the small sleds ahead of them, to say nothing of getting safely over an ugly rut half way from the top, which jounced and was apt to upset the unskillful. At the bottom of the hill, where a crowd of spectators was collected, another jounce was caused by a plank walk which crossed the coast. This passed without mishap, the sleds sped along the smooth mall so long as their velocity could hold out. Thanks to Jack's cleverness in handling, the " Never Say Die " made an excellent showing the first time down, being landed by dint of strenuous coaxing and nursing three inches ahead of a considerably larger competitor, to the great satisfaction of our trio. Then came the climb up hill with the prospect of another glorious descent to deter them from lagging.

It was great sport, and a boon to the hundreds of boys of every size and class who could thus spend their holiday out of harm's way in healthful exercise.

Jack and his friends went down half a dozen times without a mishap, and even beat their first record, running to a point on the path which none but the very largest double-runners had succeeded in reaching. But on the seventh trip they came to grief, though the fault was scarcely theirs. Jack was in front as usual, and with both his hands clasped over one of the iron-shod points of " Reindeer," was urging the " Never Say Die " on for all she was worth in point of speed, when, of a sudden, a lady started to cross the coast about half way down. You boys who know the Common do not need to be told that there is a more or less traveled path which intersects the long coast at this point.

The lady had been waiting on the edge of the coast for several minutes for a chance to cross. She was very nervous and at the same time in a hurry to catch a horse-car. There were a number of other people standing in line as spectators and what with so many sleds on the way down, and the stream of boys coming up hill dragging sleds behind them, she doubtless got confused, lost her head, and started just at the wrong time. It was too late to help her before the bystanders realized her danger. Jack was seized with horror as she loomed up on the track just ahead of him. The " Never Say Die " was going like a locomotive.

"Clear the lulla! Clear the lulla-a-a!" Jack shouted, as loud as he was able.

He made one frantic effort to wrench "Reindeer" aside, but to no purpose. The lady turned her head at his cry, and just then the points of the foremost sled struck her amidships, as sailors would say, and she fell with a despairing shriek on to Jack's head and shoulders, her legs flying from under her. Her clothing blinded Jack's eyes so that he could perceive nothing ahead. At the same moment, the hinder part of the "Never Say Die," as a consequence of the check in front, slued violently and swung nearly at right angles across the coast, a certain target for those coming after. Bump! Crash! Another double runner and a single sled struck them simultaneously, and the wreck of all three, mingled together and twisted awry by the ugly rut which by this time they had fallen into, flew asunder. Somehow or other Jack got free from the lady in time to dodge his head just as "Reindeer," torn apart from her mate, smashed into a tree and upset. The unhappy cause of the catastrophe was tossed a few feet behind him into the gutter. "Star of the East" darted off to the

other side of the coast, but, handicapped by the
remains of the board which ordinarily united her
with "Reindeer," capsized immediately and rolled
over and over with poor Dubsy.   Little Bill French,
being light and small, was lifted like a shuttlecock
off the "Never Say Die" by the prow of the "Iceland Queen," but only to be thrown a moment
later into the middle of the coast by the violent
slueing of that semblance of royalty, from which
dangerous predicament he managed to crawl away
unharmed.   "Iceland Queen" wobbled about for
a few minutes longer, but upset at last into the
gutter ; while the boy with the single sled, violently
thrown out of his path, shot between the trees over
the crust of the adjacent field, where he succeeded
in coming to a halt without further mishap.   Altogether it was a dire experience.

Fortunately the lady was merely shaken up a
little though a good deal frightened.   The injuries
to the three boys were also slight, consisting of
a scratch on Dubsy's cheek, a lame shoulder received by Jack from contact with the tree, and a
general wetting and begriming of them all.   Jack's
chief concern, after being satisfied that neither the

lady nor either of his companions was dead, was
for the " Never Say Die," which, to tell the truth,
was pretty far gone ; for not only was her main
board splintered, but one of the runners of "Star
of the East " was nearly twisted off. Nothing was
left, therefore, but to convey what was left home,
which was done by the boys ruefully, inasmuch
as such an occupation on Washington's Birthday
seemed the essence of misuse of time.

Jack, in common with the other boys of the
city, was rejoicing in the consciousness that there
would be no school until Monday, this being only
Friday morning. Washington's Birthday was to be
followed by some civic celebration on the morrow,
thus affording them two days of vacation in succession, with Sunday to boot. But though there
was so much time at his disposal, every minute of
it was precious to Jack. Accordingly, as soon as
the " Never Say Die " was reëstablished in the
back yard preliminary to sending her to a carpenter for repairs, the question arose, what to do during the hour and a half left before dinner.

To begin with, the three boys sauntered into the
grocery on the corner and were weighed, a process

which they were apt to inflict upon its long-suffer-
ing proprietor whenever there was nothing else in
particular to do.   For after getting off the scales it
was rather pleasant to wander about the store peering into the barrels, stroking the cat, and perhaps,
when there was a chance, "hooking" a dried apple or a handful of beans.   On this occasion, Bill
French stood treat to figs, which he charged to his
father with an audacity that seemed admirable to
Jack.   Bill, though the smallest of the three, was
their equal in age, and more than their equal in sly
ways; for whereas Jack was full of animal spirits
and very mischievous, and Dubsy (as the boys
called him, for no reason that was ever discovered,
his real name being Samuel) Perkins was not a
model of obedience, they were both straightforward
boys.   But they looked up to Bill as knowing a
thing or two, and accordingly listened with avidity
when, after they had pretty well exhausted the
resources of the shop, he suddenly exclaimed in
a confidential whisper, "I know what let's do, fellows."

"What?" they asked together.

Without disclosing his purpose, Bill led the way

out of the store, up the intersecting street, into one parallel with that on which Jack lived, and up the back stairs of his house into the garret, stopping on the way at his own room for a minute, from which he reappeared with some pieces of stick and a box of matches which he exhibited with a wink to his companions.

"What are they for?" Jack asked.

"I know," said Dubsy, after an instant.

"Mum's the word," answered Bill, putting his finger on his lips. Thereupon he mounted a short ladder leading to the skylight, pushed open the skylight, through which he crawled on to the flat, graveled roof, followed immediately by the others. This was a lark in itself. To be able to look over the tops of the houses and to discern the harbor and the forts and the shipping, or to see the horses and people in the streets below looking pigmy-like, was a genuine treat.

"Swanny!" cried Jack, with a burst of enthusiasm; "I can see Nahant!"

"And there's Bunker Hill," said Dubsy, who was looking in another direction. "The flags are flying everywhere. That's because it's Washington's Birthday."

Their attention was suddenly diverted by seeing
Bill light a match under cover of the chimney wall
and apply it to one of the pieces of stick which pro-
truded from his mouth ; then he drew in his breath,
puffed, and blew out a little smoke.

"She's going," he said, gleefully. "Have a
weed?" He pointed to the other sticks which lay
near by.

Jack looked a little awestruck. "What is it?"
he asked, "sweet-fern?" He had, sometimes, while
skating on the ponds, seen older boys when it was
dusk flying about with lighted cigarettes in their
mouths, which he had been told were made of
sweet-fern.

"No," said Bill. "Rattan, greeny."

Jack hated of all things to be considered green.
"Oh," he said, doubtfully.

Dubsy had already taken one of the sticks and
was lighting it.

"It's bully," said Bill. "Charley Buck has
smoked real cigarettes and says they're no better.
Don't be stumped by Dubsy, Jack! How is it,
Dubsy?"

"First rate," said Dubsy. "But mine does n't
draw very well, Bill."

"I'll fix it all right," answered the master of ceremonies. Whereupon he took his knife and worked it a few times in the unlighted end of Dubsy's cigarette. "There! try that."

The operation acted like a charm; Dubsy was enabled to emit a cloud of smoke which filled Jack's doubting soul with envy. To be stumped by Dubsy was more than he could bear, though he felt very sure that his mother would disapprove of his smoking.

"It's better 'n hay-seed," said Dubsy, who had seated himself on a ridge of the roof beside Bill, and was swinging his foot jubilantly.

"I never smoked hay-seed," replied poor Jack. "Which end do you light?" he asked defiantly, taking up one of the pieces of rattan.

"It makes no difference," said Bill. "Bully for you, Jack."

A moment later they were all three seated side by side, puffing like little Turks.

"Yesterday was my birthday," continued Bill. "See what father gave me." He drew out of his pocket an open-faced silver watch, which he exhibited with pride.

" My eye ! " exclaimed Jack. " Does it really go ? "

" Go? I guess she *does*. You ought to hear her tick at night. Father says I shall have a hunter when I 'm fifteen, and a gold repeater when I 'm twenty-one."

The other boys were silent with envy.

" My father 's got lots of money," went on Bill. " He could buy both your fathers out, I guess, and have a pile left."

" My father 's dead, you know," answered Jack.

" So he is ; I was n't thinking. Well, then, he could buy your mother out."

" Let 's see the works," said Dubsy.

Bill opened the inside cover with his thumb nail in response to this request, and the three heads were immediately in close proximity studying the internal arrangements of the watch.

" That 's a jewel," said Bill, indicating a colored spot among the cogs and wheels.

The heads went lower in mute admiration.

" It is n't a very big one, anyway," said Jack, glad of what seemed an opportunity for criticism.

" There are fourteen, mostly rubies," replied Bill.

"Don't breathe so hard, Dubsy. Father says it hurts the works to breathe on them."

"Wind her up," cried Jack.

Bill fumbled in his pocket and produced a key. "She's mostly wound," he said. "I wound her last night and again just after breakfast." One or two turns was all the watch would stand at the moment without danger to the mainspring; so this exhibition was unsatisfactory.

"My father has a stem-winder," said Dubsy, after a moment; "I've heard him say that a watch with a key was more bother than it was worth."

"I shouldn't care for one that *wasn't* a stem-winder," said Jack, stoutly.

"Sour grapes," said Bill, with a sneer.

"You feel awful big, don't you, because you've got a watch," retorted Jack.

"Oh, come off," said Bill, contemptuously. This was a phrase unfamiliar to the others, which Bill had picked up in the streets. The interest awakened by its use induced a pause, during which Jack cooled down. He did not wish a row, and was conscious of having been unwarrantably aggressive. But, as he would have said, he was sick of hearing Bill blow.

Bill, having by this time exhausted the delights of his cigarette, had taken his knife and split the rattan open down the middle.   "That's dried

blood," he said, holding out the pieces for inspection.

The boys looked, and there, sure enough, running down through the pith was a fine red thread, which resembled very much what Bill said it was.

"Every time one smokes, blood is sucked out of the lungs and collects like that," he said.

"How do you know it's blood?" asked Jack in rather an awestruck voice.

"Charley Buck says so." This was strong evidence. Charley Buck was nearly fifteen.

"I was awfully sick the first time I smoked," went on Bill, but his words were not regarded by Jack, who was deep in the process of dividing his own piece of rattan. There the red thread was, just as in Bill's piece. His lungs seemed all right, but his head was a little dizzy; he coughed once or twice and patted his chest without uncomfortable results; however, he felt grave. What would his mother say if she knew the truth! He put the pieces of rattan carefully in his pocket, and recollected that it was dinner time.

Just then Bill exclaimed in a tone in which pity and satisfaction were blended in about equal proportions, "I guess you're sick, Dubsy."

Dubsy was; the poor fellow looked very white and doleful, and was sitting still. "I feel faint, that's all," he answered.

But it wasn't all; moreover, it was a good quarter of an hour before Dubsy was able to lift his head from the roof and be helped down the ladder. Meanwhile, Jack and Bill sat on either side of him and tried to cheer him up. Bill, who was able to speak from experience, assured them that the sickness would soon subside, and that he had been much more miserable after his first smoke. But to tell the truth, Jack and Bill also, despite his former experiences, felt rather squeamish themselves and not much inclined to talk. Besides, the remembrance of what he supposed to be his dried blood haunted Jack's mind. Altogether, it was, on the whole, a bad quarter of an hour, as the French say.

CHAPTER II.

THE SNOW-BALL FIGHT.

As soon as Dubsy Perkins felt all right again, Jack and he left Bill French's and went home to their dinners. Jack lived alone with his mother; he was her only child. Her husband had been killed in the Civil War ten years before, and Jack was all she had in the world to care for and be proud of except the memory of Jack's father's gallant services as a soldier, which she was never tired of talking about to Jack. His name had been John Hall, just as Jack's was, and he had fallen at the head of the regiment of which he was Colonel, in one of the last battles of the war, when Jack was a mere baby.

Back of Colonel John Hall was a long line of Halls, running very nearly into Mayflower times, a good many of them John Halls or, as those who knew them best called them, Jack Halls, though John is a good name for any boy or man to be content with and not to wish to change. They were a hardy, thorough-going set, these Halls, Massachusetts folk who in Colonial times, when the days were gone by for shooting Indians, tilled their farms and made sure that their liberties were not interfered with by King James or King William or King George. When this was impossible without taking arms, they were equal to the occasion. Israel Hall, Jack's great-great-grandfather, was one of the raw recruits composing the Continental Army over which General Washington assumed command under the famous old elm at Cambridge. He followed his commander through thick and thin, became a sergeant, then a captain, was wounded, but got well in time to be one of those who made the memorable passage of the Delaware when our army, reduced to a forlorn band of four thousand, fell upon the Hessians at Trenton, routed them, and plucked up spirit and hope once more. He was shot dead, however, at the battle of Brandywine, and, as will be the case with many brave fellows so long as wars last, left a wife and some wee bits of children to get along as best they could.

It would take too long to give an account of the

lives of Jack's ancestors in detail, but you may be
interested to learn something of the career of Israel
Hall's eldest son, — also named John, — who, having to make his own way in the world, left the
family farm and came to Salem town in search of
something to do. Now, at that time Salem was a
famous commercial port, little as one would imagine it to-day. Forty years later its prestige was
usurped and overshadowed by its near neighbor,
Boston, but from 1770 until 1820 the maritime supremacy of Salem was unquestioned. Prior to the
Revolution, the inhabitants of the town had been
noted for their commercial energy, and when war
was declared they fitted out their trading vessels
with guns, and built others to the number of over
one hundred, which made great havoc among the
enemy's commerce in the English Channel and the
Bay of Biscay, so that the rates of insurance went
up amazingly among the British underwriters.
The patriotism and enterprise of the old Salem
merchants is a glowing chapter in the history of
our country.

But as soon as there was no more fighting to be
done, the merchants turned their fleet of privateers

into trading-vessels again, and as the vessels were
too large for mere coasters, sent them out laden
with Spanish dollars to every nook and corner of
the Oriental world, — to Calcutta and Madagascar,
and Batavia and Java, and the Celibes, and all the
chain of islands in the Indian Archipelago which
you have read about in your geographies. There
the silver freight was exchanged for pepper, spices,
gums, coffee, or other Eastern products, with which
the captains would either return or would bear
away to some European port, like Marseilles, where
part of the cargo was sold at a profit, and its place
supplied by wines and silk to be brought home.
It was an adventurous, exciting life for those who
sailed; and meanwhile the owners sat in their
counting-houses casting up figures and waiting for
their vessels to arrive. It was often two and even
three years that they had to wait, but the ships
came back at last, freighted with merchandise,
which their owners sold to their fellow townspeo-
ple at a snug profit. Or, if by chance the ships
were lost and never returned, the underwriters re-
imbursed the merchants so that they were able to
buy new ones.

It was into the counting-house of one of these merchants that Jack's great-grandfather, John Hall, chanced to stray one morning in search of employment. Probably the head of the firm liked the looks of the boy and divined that he would make a sterling sailor; at all events he took him into his service and sent him on a long voyage in one of his ships, which turned out very successfully for the merchant, and for John Hall too, inasmuch as everybody had a pleasant word to say in his behalf. From this time forward his life was one of marvelous experiences for many years to come. One thing leads to another when a young man is efficient. Before he was nineteen John Hall was a mate, and on his twenty-first birthday he found himself in command of a three hundred ton ship, which was a large one for those days. If it were his career I was narrating, it would be easy to keep you awake many hours with thrilling tales of what happened to him. He fought with pirates, and had hair-breadth adventures with savage tribes, was twice shipwrecked, and barely escaped being eaten by cannibals, only to be imprisoned in a South American dungeon instead. But in the end he passed safely through his perils, and settled down in Salem for the rest of his days with seventy-five thousand dollars in hard cash, which was quite as much as a million is now.

Very possibly some of you may be thinking that you would like to have lived when a career similar to that of Jack's great-grandfather was a natural one for an ambitious boy to follow. But though the glamour of such adventures as his does make the blood even of those of us who are grown up tingle as we read, it will not do to shut our eyes to the truth. We see only the glory and forget the hardships. We forget, too, — and their many virtues make us forget, — that resolute, noble fellows as were the men whose enterprise and pluck built up fortunes for themselves while supplying their country, starved and draggled by the Revolution, with the necessities and even the luxuries of life, these old merchant captains and their crews were rough, ignorant people compared with what some of your fathers are to-day. They had but little knowledge except of a practical kind acquired by bitter experience; their one absorbing interest was the accumulation of money, and, let us say it under

our breaths, the standards of morality by which
they did business were not the highest. How
could it be otherwise? The population of the strip
of seaboard States which then composed our country had to begin existence as a nation bankrupt,
and chiefly dependent for its wants on the products
of other lands. Our great-grandfathers were down
to hard pan, as the saying is, and life meant for
them a struggle for the means of existence unre-
lieved·by any but the most homely pleasures and
tastes. There were no mills and factories then to
compete with the manufactories of Europe, no
great west with its fields of waving grain and developed mines of gold and coal and iron, no cotton
gin, no splendid libraries and broad institutions of
learning, no railroads, no telegraph. All these
were yet to come, and it is to such men as John
Hall that we are indebted for having laid the foun-
dations of that prosperity which affords to their de-
scendants opportunities for usefulness and culture
such as our forefathers never dreamed of. Let us
admire their courage, grit, and perseverance; let us
applaud their successes and recognize the sterling
virtues by which they won them, but their lot

should no more arouse our envy than should that
of those later pioneers in the struggle of reclaiming
our west from the forest and the savage, inspired
by whose adventures as scouts and trappers so
many boys have run away from home and been
very sorry afterwards.

We left Jack going home to his dinner, for which
he did not feel very hungry at first. But a fine
piece of beefsteak with potatoes and macaroni, followed by cold rice pudding with bits of cinnamon
in it, of which Jack was especially fond, brought
his appetite back again, so that when he had finished his second plate of pudding, cleaning the
plate with his spoon until it shone, the thought
occurred to him that he would have a third help;
but the well-known " Ehu — ehu — ehu " resound-
ing from the street told him that the fellows were
beginning to collect again, and he started up.

Jack dined in the middle of the day, and his
mother had her dinner at night; but Mrs. Hall
made a point of taking her lunch at the same hour
as Jack dined, and after he had finished eating she
always tried to beguile him into sitting still for a
while, for he had a tendency, when anything inter-

esting was in prospect outdoors, to scurry through his meals and leave the table with his mouth full the instant the last course had been served. Sometimes he would bolt from his chair as soon as he had finished his meat, crying, — merely by way of explanation for his hasty departure, — as he seized his cap and just prior to slamming the front door, "Don't want any pudding." On such occasions his mother did not always have the heart to detain him.

But this day he dined alone and there was no one to put a check on his movements, for Mrs. Hall had been called away out of town to see an old friend who was sick, and would not be back until after Jack's bed hour. Deeply as he loved his mother and fond as he was of having her with him, Jack felt a certain pride in being his own master for once. As an indemnity for being left alone for the day, he had obtained permission to order whatever he liked for tea, and to have whomever he chose among the boys to share it with him. He had already exercised the second privilege by inviting Dubsy Perkins, Bill French, and Harry Dale, another of his friends, and it was now neces-

sary to decide upon the viands before he went out
again.   This was no easy task, as he had a number
of dainties in mind which ranked very evenly in
his estimation.   He felt pretty certain as to one,
however.   "We'll have cream cakes, Hannah," he
said with decision to the maid.

"Very well, Master Jack, I'll get six; that'll be
one and a half apiece."

"How much are *éclairs?*" he asked, presently.

"I don't know, Master Jack.   Your mamma,
when she has company, buys those at the confec-
tioner's."

"They're bully," he said.   "I like the chocolate
ones best.   I guess, though, the fellows would
rather have cream cakes."

"Cook has a Washington pie ready."

"That's hunky!   Mother said that we could
have quince jam and raspberry jam, and — and — I
know what we'll have," he cried with a wave of his
arm, — "waffles."

"I don't know as the cook has a waffle-iron,
Master Jack," answered Hannah, despondently.

Jack looked downcast a moment.   "We had them
at Bill French's, you eat them with butter and
nutmeg," he said, with a sigh.

"Cook makes those puff cakes very nicely," said Hannah, who had been thinking.

Jack clapped his hands. "They 'll do first-rate," he said. "I guess that 'll be enough, with the spread bread and butter and some muffins; don't you, Hannah?"

"Goodness sakes! yes, Master Jack. If you 're not all sick to-morrow, I shall be very much mistaken."

At the mention of sickness Jack was pensive a moment. Then he felt in his pocket and produced one of the pieces of rattan. "See there, Hannah, that 's my blood," he exclaimed.

"Your blood! Mercy on us, what does the child mean?" she added, as she examined the charred stick.

"It 's dried blood out of my lungs."

Hannah put the rattan up to her nose, then gave a start. "You don't mean to tell me, Master Jack, that you 've been smoking?"

"What if I have?"

"What will your mamma say?"

"I guess she won't mind."

Jack knew that this last statement was not true,

but as he intended to make a clean breast of it to
his mother, he felt justified in assuming a bold front
before Hannah.

Hannah shook her head prophetically. " It 's that
Bill French, I 'll be bound ; he 's always getting you
into some sort of mischief. Had n't you anything
better to do than go smoking that nasty stick ? "

" I only smoked a little piece," Jack answered.
" Besides, it is n't a stick, it 's rattan."

" I 'd just like to get my hand on that Bill French,
that 's all," said Hannah. " Blood out of your
lungs, too ! We 'll have you sick abed next, and
your mamma crying her eyes out."

Jack, as he went out of the house, was conscious
that he had not derived much consolation from Hannah, whose view seemed to confirm the fearful testimony already in his possession. But on closing
the front door his attention was at once absorbed by
what was going on outside. Some half-dozen boys,
including Dubsy Perkins, Bill French, and Harry
Dale, were engaged in building a huge dam. It
had grown milder since morning and was melting
fast. Underneath the piles of snow on either side
of the street, the water was beginning to flow rap-

idly along the gutters down hill. The boys had
selected a spot a hundred yards or so below Jack's
house, across the way, and had formed a basin by
digging up the snow until they came to the paving.
The curbstone constituted one bank, and the other,
or rather the whole remaining bulwark of the dam,
was made of snow piled up and mashed with shovels until it became firm. While constructing this
they had made a temporary dam a few feet further
up, to catch the water; but just as Jack joined
them Dubsy cut a big hole in it, and the accumulated torrent poured with a rush into the large res-
ervoir. When the smaller dam had emptied itself,
they closed it up again in order to strengthen the
resistance of the main one.

Most of the boys were armed with shovels obtained
from home, and they worked diligently as beavers,
building the walls higher and higher as the water increased in depth. Soon it was necessary to fortify
the curbstone with a layer of snow to prevent an
overflow on to the sidewalk. Every few minutes
one of them would test the depth by wading, and it
was not long before the water came up to within
half an inch of the top of Jack's rubber boots, so

that any careless movement on his part would be
sure to let some inside.   Their number was rather
smaller than usual, as some of the "crowd" which
ordinarily collected in front of the grocery shop had
gone down to the Frog Pond on the Common to see
if there were any "tiddledies," which, as all Boston
boys know, are cakes of floating ice formed during
the first stages of a thaw ; the sport being to jump
from one to another, until *terra firma* is reached,
without tumbling in.   This was one of the favorite
pastimes of Jack and his friends.   The water of the
pond was only deep enough to give one a thorough
ducking, and though whoever was so unskillful or
unlucky as to fall in was sure to be greeted with a
jeer of derision, it may be fairly doubted whether
the most miserable participants were not the boys
who went home dry.

But Jack considered himself very well employed
as it was.   He felt pretty sure that if there were
tiddledies to-day there would be tiddledies to-morrow, and he was interested in making the dam as
high as his waist, if it were possible.   There was
such a volume of water in the basin now that most
of their active force was employed in pasting snow

against the back of the lower wall, through which
there was a steady leakage in spite of their best
efforts. Two or three of them, Jack among the
number, had already gone in over their boots and
wet their trousers more or less above their knees,
so that now they stood along the sidewalk, or in the
street, gazing contentedly into the enormous pool.
Perhaps they realized that there was not much
more to be done, for there began to be some fooling. Bill French introduced it by dropping a bit
of ice down Harry Dale's back, gliding away in
time so that Harry could not get at him. Harry
was just about Bill's size, but a little more chunky.
He knew that Bill could outrun him, so he nursed
his wrath for the present, and, keeping his eyes
open, bided his time.

The spirit of playing tricks upon one another
proved contagious, so that the dam was almost forgotten in the interest of several flights down street
and subsequent tussles. Only Jack and Dubsy
still worked away at the walls now and then, piling fresh snow on top and stopping the leaks. All
of a sudden, as Jack was standing leaning on his
shovel trying to understand how a fine stream of

water trickling through the solid wall of the dam had thus been able to defy his labors, Harry Dale made a dive at Bill French, who was just behind Jack, and who was off his guard at the moment. Bill gave a shriek, and, to protect himself, tried to interpose Jack between his pursuer and himself by seizing Jack roughly by the shoulders. Jack, who had been already annoyed by Bill several times, and had contented himself with exclaiming, "Quit your fooling, Bill," or, "Let up, Bill," goaded now by what he supposed to be a fresh attack, dropped his shovel, seized his tormentor, and suddenly pulling him forward by a quick movement brought him to his knees; then picking up a handful of snow he rubbed it freely over Bill's face.

"That's the sort, Jack; give him some more for me," cried Harry.

Bill, who was struggling with all his might, sprang to his feet the moment he was let free, and launched himself with rage on Jack's neck. In an instant Jack had grappled with him in self-defense. Bill, who was thoroughly angry and bent on upsetting his adversary, twisted one of his legs inside of Jack's, and being lithe and active, though small, made it incumbent on Jack to exert himself to avoid being thrown. The pair swayed violently for several moments, then Jack, taking advantage of a failure of Bill's to trip him up, retaliated in the same fashion, and over they went with Bill undermost. They struck against the wall of the dam, which gave way before them with a slump. Jack, realizing what the catastrophe promised to be, tore himself by an effort of strength from Bill's grasp just in time to avoid more than a severe splashing, although he fell on his hands and knees, and had a lively scramble to get away from the deluge which came pouring down upon him as soon as the flood-gates were removed. But poor Bill, accelerated probably by the effort which saved Jack, fell with the wall backwards into the deepest part of the dam, so that his head and the upper portion of his body were completely submerged. For an instant his struggling black legs only were visible, then these were drawn under him as he reappeared head first above the surface, wallowing as he staggered to his feet. But Bill was doomed to still further discomfiture, for scarcely had he gained a footing when he slipped and fell sideways again into the dirty, slushy water, his head this time striking the curbstone.

The pain of the concussion must have been tolerably smart, but anger and mortification were sufficient to explain Bill's facial expression as he lay on the sidewalk after his companions had dragged him out. His eyes were shut and his mouth was wide open, but from it at first no sound issued. It seemed to the others as if the expected bawl were never coming. But it came at last, — a terribly vociferous cry, preceded by a noise like the humming of a large top, which increased in volume until it was a yell, — bursting on them as a thunder storm bursts in wind and rain after the silence which goes before. "Boo-ooo-ooo!" Then it seemed as if he would never stop. Jack and the other boys, who were rather frightened, bent over him with anxious faces, but it was soon apparent that Bill was more mad than hurt.

"I'm very sorry, Bill; I didn't mean to send you into the dam," protested Jack.

This attempt at consolation only induced a fresh fit of crying on the part of the victim, which was redoubled when he saw his cap trimmed with astrachan fished out with a shovel from the bottom of the now largely depleted dam by Dubsy Perkins.

"It was an accident; Jack did n't mean to," said one of the others.

"Served you right for fooling so, Bill," exclaimed Harry Dale. "We 'd all told you to quit." Then turning to the rest, Harry said, "He ought to go home or he 'll catch cold, fellows."

Bill sulkily allowed himself to be lifted to his feet. He stood shivering and dripping like a soused pup, sobbing and snuffling, and eying ruefully his bedraggled cap. "I 'll make you pay for this, Jack Hall," he blurted out.

But Jack scarcely heard him, for just at the moment he gave a start, and shading his eyes with one of his hands gazed intently down the street.

"Here come the muckers, fellows," he cried, with excitement.

His companions turned eagerly at his words and looked in the same direction. Sure enough, a gang of other boys, twenty to twenty-five in number, had suddenly emerged from a cross street at some little distance below and was advancing up hill. As the

invaders perceived that they were recognized, they
set up a derisive, triumphant yell, and dashed onward at a rapid dog-trot, preparing snow-balls and
waving sticks.

"There's a regular posse," cried Jack. "Who'll
go and tell the other fellows?"

"I will," cried Harry Dale, and suiting the action
to the word he started off to warn their friends,
who were running tiddledies.

Meanwhile, Jack and the four other boys, who
were all there were, for Bill French had slipped
away to change his clothes, retreated slowly as

their adversaries advanced, Jack having first, with the instinct of destroying anything that the enemy might find pleasure in, swept away with his shovel the remaining rampart of the dam. They were outnumbered for the moment in the proportion of four to one, and though to retire was ignominious, it seemed necessary under the circumstances. The vanguard of the invading army now began to discharge their snow-balls, the shower of which fell slightly short, but served to whet their ardor.

With another cheer and a yell the " muckers "
rushed forward, headed by a powerful - looking
butcher's boy, close by whose side ran the raga-
muffin who earlier in the day had threatened this
invasion, and who could be heard pointing out
Jack and Dubsy as special objects of vengeance.

" Them 's the chumps, go for 'em ! " he cried.

The little band, reluctant to run, wavered and
hurled back a volley of snow-balls, which were returned with vigor. The butcher's boy was well
known in that quarter of the city as a terror.
His balls made solely with bare hands were hard
as ice, and whizzed like bullets. One of them took
Jack in the cheek and stung like mischief, so that
the water ran out of the eye on that side of his
face.

" Clean 'em out ! " yelled the little instigator.

The consciousness that the protecting alley was
close at hand nerved the boys to hold their ground
for a moment longer, and the courage displayed by
them, supplemented by several skillful shots, caused
their opponents to halt and advance more deliberately. Just then there came flying round the corner Harry Dale, at the head of the detachment of

whom he had gone in search, and whom he had
found in the next street peppering the passers-by
in a listless fashion, and only too glad to come to
the succor of their friends.

" To the rescue ! " cried Dubsy, waving his arms
above his head ; and the reinforcement of a dozen
boys swept down upon the combatants.

This sudden turn of affairs was too much for the
backers of Joe Herring, — that was the butcher
boy's name, — who turned and fled precipitately,
although Joe and one or two others stood their
ground manfully and tried to rally them. But the
counter cheer was disheartening to an army with
victory in its very grasp. They broke and ran
helter-skelter, followed closely by Jack and his
comrades. Jack kept his eye especially on Joe
Herring, whom he longed to pay back for the blow
on his cheek ; but even Joe did not wait for the
new victors to get too near, but ran at last. As
for the youngster who had been the guide of the
raiders, he had taken to his heels at the earliest
sign of danger, and was among the first to reach
the halting-place, where the rout finally paused, not
far above the cross street from which they had

emerged. There they made a stand, while their pursuers, who were not too flushed with success to be cautious, being still numerically inferior, drew up at a respectful distance and held a council of war.

These snow-ball fights were of tolerably frequent occurrence between the boys who lived in Jack's neighborhood and hordes from other localities, who were apt to be styled muckers by those whose territory they invaded. Once or twice every winter skirmishes such as the one now in progress would develop into battles of some magnitude, enlisting the services, on one side or the other, of all the youth in that part of the city. Contests of this kind had traditions to encourage them. Mr. Warren, of whom you will hear later, who had been the college chum and dear friend of Jack's father and was now his mother's adviser, had often told Jack of how, in the days long before he and Colonel Hall were boys, there had been relentless strife between the Round-pointers and the Nigger-hillers, and the North-enders and the South-enders, and the Charlestown pigs, so called, which last named, in the language of a local bard, —

"Put on their wigs,
And over to Boston came,"

only to be routed and driven back without them.
Jack delighted in the accounts of these old contests, and though the names were now changed he
had no difficulty in seeing in the Anderson-Streeters
and their allies, foes no less terrible than the boys
with whom his forefathers had fought.

But it is time to return to the immediate scene
of action, where both sides were beginning to real-
ize that there had as yet been no real fighting to
speak of, merely a feeling of one another's strength.
Scouts had, apparently, been sent out by the muckers to scour the country, for recruits were coming
in by twos and threes. They were a motley-look-
ing crew, as compared with Jack and his friends,
including some ragged specimens and several
negroes, one of whom, a left-handed lad nicknamed "Custard" on account of the lightness of
his sable, was unerring in his shots. Cardigans,
for the most part, took the place of overcoats
among them, but some wore only tightly buttoned
jackets, and kept warm by kicking their toes against
the curb-stones, and alternately stuffing their hands

into their pockets or blowing on their bare fingers.

From time to time they jeered at and insulted the other army, who, by their pea jackets and rubber boots, suggested the solidity and dignity of grenadiers, an impression which was heightened by the silent disdain with which they received the vituperation showered upon them.

But now the Anderson-Streeters, having accumulated a goodly supply of ammunition, and being twice the numbers of their opponents, show signs of an intention to attack. Their pickets edge up gradually on the sidewalk, more or less sheltered by the trunks of the line of trees which grow there. Snow-balls begin to fly, and Joe Herring at one point and Custard at another move forward simultaneously, which is the signal for a general advance. The grenadiers stand firm without firing a shot. A perfect hail-storm is showered upon them, which they bear unflinchingly. A loud yell spreads along the advancing line, and the flower of all Anderson and Pinckney and Revere streets comes dashing on.

"Now let them have it, fellows!" cries Jack at

last, who, with General Warren's instruction at Bunker Hill, of which he had recently read, fresh in mind, has waited to see the whites of the enemy's eyes before giving the order.

"That's the sort!" shouts Dubsy, as the whole volley delivered at short range goes smashing into the faces of their foes.

It is so deadly a volley that two or three of the muckers clap their hands to their eyes and cry out with pain; others sputter as they receive the big hard balls full against their teeth. Several caps are knocked off and fall into the snow. Jack, with his attention riveted on Joe Herring, sees, to his delight, his first shot take the leader squarely in the forehead, so that Joe shakes his head savagely like an angry bull; yet, putting it down, comes on in butting fashion all the same, and hitting Jack plump in the stomach nearly sends him over. Custard, too, apparently is not struck, or at least, if he is, does not mind it, and though some falter he does not, but with another yell rushes at the grenadiers. These muckers, though checked for an instant, have good stuff in them.

"Give it to them again!" cries Jack, who seems to be recognized as the commanding officer.

This volley is well delivered, too, but the on-comers are too near for it to have full effect. The balls go over the heads of Joe and Custard and the other leaders, and before there is time to say Jack Robinson, the two armies are at close quarters. Joe Herring, with a bound like a wild-cat, gets his arms round the neck of the first of the grenadiers in his path, and over they go together, with Joe on top, and rubbing the snow about his adversary's neck and ears, to accomplish which to the best advantage he squats upon the victim's chest. This is the first feature in a hand-to-hand scrimmage which is waged for several minutes without apparent advantage on either side, for Jack and Dubsy and Bill Dale, who happen to be close together, form quite as formidable a trio as any opposed to them. The muckers fall before them like nine-pins, and scurry out of their way. Jack gets his fingers inside the collar of his original enemy of the morning, and shaking him as a terrier would shake a mouse, dumps him face downward in a pile of snow and slush. This does Jack's heart good. The little wretch blubbers and tries to use the stick in his hand, which Jack snatches away from him, and with

a proper contempt for so unfair a weapon in a snow-
ball fight, sends flying over the wall of a neighboring yard. Sam Willis and George Bird, two more
of Jack's set, do yeoman service also at the other
end of the line, driving their opponents back and
washing the faces of the fallen with energy.

As used to happen in encounters of old, when
knights and other warriors contended together, the
leaders on either side seem at first to fight shy of
one another. They slaughter the weaker at the
outset, making incursions into the enemy's line, so
that often the two armies are hopelessly confused.
Indeed, Joe Herring and Custard are a hundred
yards apart from Jack and his chief allies, and
between them the rank and file are intermingled
higgledy-piggledy. But presently, as fatigue and
lack of pluck begin to tell, the champions find that
the only enemies left worthy of the name are behind them, and by a common instinct turn and eye
one another, while the feebler boys draw off a little
as though waiting for the strife to be settled once
and for all by a battle of the giants.

Jack, at a glance, perceiving that Joe Herring
and Custard and one or two others are between him

and the main body of his friends, and seized by what he feels to be an inspiration of generalship, shouts to Dubsy and Bill, and Sam Willis and George Bird, who are close beside him, "Cut them off! cut them off!"

Whereupon Jack springs forward at the head of this detachment, imbued with the idea, which they all share with him, of raking the enemy's vanguard fore and aft before the chief force of the muckers can come up from behind. Inspirited by the plan, those above, among whom Bill French appears in dry garments, present a bold front, and with a shout charge. Joe and Custard, realizing their peril, hesitate for an instant, while a shower of balls pours in upon them, whether to break through the rallied array of grenadiers or to seek to rejoin their friends; but before they can decide they are forced to defend themselves. There are five of them, just equal in number to their intervening enemies, who, with gritted teeth, bear down upon them. Jack again singles out Joe Herring, who, adopting his old tactics, lowers his head and plunges forward. But Jack does not intend to have his wind knocked out of him a second time. He meets Joe with an upper cut of his hand, which, though covered with a mitten, is full of snow, and, jerking the butcher boy's head up, grapples with him. They wrestle fiercely; meanwhile, three of the other muckers, beset before and behind at the same moment, are rolling on the ground. Only Custard, with Dubsy hanging about his neck and Bill French and another boy on his back, still struggles for freedom, shouting energetically for his friends. They are coming by the score as fast as their legs will carry them, but not soon enough to save their illustrious leader from disaster. Three boys eager to leap upon Joe Herring are prevented only by Jack's decisive "Leave him to me," so stand aloof ready to give succor if it be needed. It is scarcely a fair match. Joe is nearly a head taller and is a year older; his muscles are like steel, and, moreover, he has thrashed everybody in the neighborhood who has ever fought with him. If he can once shake Jack off, he will soon knock the stuffing out of him. But Jack knows this, too, and having got a good hold, means to have no fisticuffs if he can help it. He intends to throw Joe if he can. He hears now, as they pitch from one side to the

other with faces scarcely an inch apart, the yells of
the great body of muckers closing in upon them,
and knows that the fight is being renewed on more
even terms.   Joe knows it, too, and, breathing
hard, makes one grand effort to swing his antagonist
off his feet, so as to be able to bring terror once
more into the general ranks.   Jack, however, is
ready for him, and, resisting stubbornly, waits until
Joe relaxes his muscles a little as the great effort
proves unsuccessful, then adroitly twists his leg
about the champion's and throws him.   Down they
go together, but Jack uppermost, and — long
dreamed-of triumph of his life — able to secure
a seat upon the butcher hero's chest, and to stuff
his mouth with snow.   Joe's eyes are green as they
gaze up at him, and remind Jack of the cat whose
death-throes he once witnessed after the dogs had
left her.   This was the simile employed by Jack
in recounting modestly his victory that evening at
the tea party.

But victory though it was, it was too short for
comfort.   Before Jack has time to rub more than
a handful of slush over his victim's face and ears,
the army of invasion, by dint of numbers, drive back

the grenadiers, disputing every inch of ground, and two big fellows throw themselves upon him and try to drag him off Joe. Harry Dale is on top of them in an instant, and straightway a half dozen on each side precipitate themselves and make a pile, at the bottom of which lies Joe Herring still gripped by Jack. A fearful tussle ensues; the two principals are of course practically powerless to move, and feel that they are well off if able to breathe without difficulty. The legs of both are firmly grasped by a score of arms, which in turn are kept down by boys on top whom others seek to tear away from the pile. As fast as one is pulled off another takes his place; heads, bodies, and limbs are hopelessly intermingled, and neither party seems to have the best of it.

Just as Jack is wondering whether Joe is alive, because he is lying so still, and whether he himself will not stifle, a shrill voice on the outskirts of the fight pipes out, " Cheese it! Cheese it!"

At the words every boy ceases action, those on the pile waiting for confirmation of the news which the alarm has conveyed, and those erect following the gaze of the small mucker who has given it, and who is already preparing to flee down the street.

As their eyes perceive at the street corner the officer in a blue blouse with brass buttons, and armed
with a rattan, advancing upon them at a slightly
quickened gait, a dozen of the urchin's companions
repeat the cry, — "Cheese it! Cheese it!"

In the twinkling of an eye the pile disintegrates
itself; the boys of either faction get up and begin
to scatter, the muckers hastily and fearfully, the
grenadiers more composedly, and yet unequivocally.
Jack and Joe uncovered are free to rise, which they
proceed to do at once without further hostilities.
Jack, with his eye on the policeman, mingles with
the band of his friends who, gathered on the opposite sidewalk to that on which the guardian of the
peace is advancing, are hoping to slip by him without molestation, feeling, perhaps, that inasmuch as
they are on their own territory, and merely defend-
ing themselves against invasion, pardon may not be
withheld from them. They take care to be so far
respectful in behavior as to refrain for the moment
from the insulting allusion to a cheese indulged in
by their late adversaries, which, for some reason or
other, had come to be the recognized phrase of
warning and insult combined, among the youth of

the city, in referring to the constabulary ; its origin
— at least Jack and his friends always supposed so
— being connected with the theft, either real or
imagined, at an earlier date, of one of the commod-
ities in question by a member of the force. They
await his coming, grouped together, with almost an
innocent air. On the other hand Joe, the moment
he is free, glances over his shoulder at the represen-
tative of order, puts two fingers in his mouth preliminary to emitting a piercing whistle, shouts " Cheese
it ! " at the top of his lungs, and scoots down the
street at full speed to the spot where he had deposited his butcher's basket. This regained, he continues his flight at a more leisurely pace until
distance hides him from view. His exodus is the
signal for a general stampede of his followers, who
disappear principally into the cross street by which
they had come, pursued with some swiftness by the
officer, galled, perhaps, by their impertinence, or
encouraged by their pusillanimity. Jack and his
grenadiers, not having hoped in vain that the engine of the law would pass them by unharmed,
survey the retreat in complacent silence until the
policeman is comfortably remote, then at a sig-

nal raise their voices in a prolonged, ungenerous, " Cheese it ! "

The officer turns and looks back at them angrily, and raises his cane in so threatening a manner that some of the fainter-hearted start to run into Jack's alley-way. But the alarm is short-lived; their enemy, after an instant's hesitation, proceeds on his way, reflecting doubtless on the ingratitude of boys. The snow-ball fight is over, and ten minutes later the grenadiers separate to their homes.

CHAPTER III.

A DAY OF RECKONING.

JACK'S first thought on reëntering the house was for his tea-party, so he went into the dining-room, where he found Hannah, to his satisfaction, already setting the table.

"Got the cream cakes?" he asked.

"Yes, sir," answered Hannah. "Sakes alive, Master Jack, where 've you been?"

"Snow-balling. We've had an awful fight with the muckers."

"I guess they gave it to you, then," replied Hannah, whose sympathies in the matter of snow-ball fights were not, perhaps, wholly on the side of her charge, as her home was in the vicinity of Anderson Street. "You're wetted from head to foot; go right up-stairs and get off those things."

"They did n't lick us any more than we licked them. I threw Joe Herring, and they all piled on me, and that's how we were when the 'cheese it' came," said Jack. He went to the mirror and examined his cheek, which was beginning to feel a little swollen where the butcher boy's snow-ball had struck it under the eye.

"I guess it won't be black," he said, under his breath. "Holloa!" he exclaimed, as he seated himself on the edge of one of the leather chairs. "My tails are gone." By way of explanation he held out his Scotch cap, from which both the ribbons which ordinarily fluttered in the breeze had been torn off.

Hannah sighed. "That's the third time this week," she said. "Get up this minute, Master Jack," she continued vehemently; "you're ruining the nice furniture. Your mamma would have a fit if she could see you."

The cause of this outbreak was that Jack, having plumped himself down as described, was trying to remove one of his rubber boots by pressing its heel against the toe of the other. It yielded suddenly, and at the same time a quantity of loose snow was scattered over the carpet.

"Jiminy!" exclaimed Jack.

"Go right up-stairs the back way this minute.

Why, your leg is wet as sop as high as your knee,"
said Hannah.

"The dam was over my boots," he answered.
"We made a bully dam," he continued, hobbling
toward the door on one leg with his bootless foot
drawn up like a stork.

Hannah followed him up to his room, where she
proceeded to pull off the other boot. It was harder
to start than its mate. Accordingly Jack tipped
himself back on the bed so that she could get a
purchase with her foot against the iron frame.

"Golly!" he cried, as a small deluge of water
flowed back over him. The boot stuck like a vise,
and came off at last amid a splutter of slosh.
Hannah was breathless.

"Now take off every stitch of clothes, or you
shan't have a bit of supper this blessed night," she
said with decision, as she turned to go.

Fifteen minutes later Jack sat waiting in the
parlor to receive his friends, looking a pattern of
spruceness. His broad white collar was set off by
a cherry tie; he wore knickerbockers, red stockings,
and pumps, and his hair lay smooth and neatly
parted. Although he appeared ordinarily in trousers,

his mother still made an exception in favor of knickerbockers in the case of his Sunday go-to-meeting
suit. He had walked three times round the dining-
room table, with his hands in his pockets, surveying
the delicacies, so as to make sure that nothing had
been forgotten, before composing himself. But he
had not long to wait; the bell rang loudly three
times in quick succession, and promptly at the hour
set for the feast the three guests and their host
took their seats at table. They all four looked
very smiling, and showed no ill results from the
experiences of the day. Bill French, apparently,
had quite forgiven Jack for his ducking, though he
took a mild revenge by observing — "Your eye 'll
be black to-morrow."

"I threw him, any way," answered Jack, referring, of course, to Joe Herring.

They talked the fight over in detail, and as they
discussed, the good things disappeared with aston-
ishing rapidity. Nothing was wanting; the cream
cakes were fat fellows, and Jack showed strict im-
partiality and skill in dividing the extra two so
that each of the company should get an equal
amount of the inside.

Dubsy had received the wishbone of the chicken, which he carefully picked and held out to Jack to pull with him. " Wish ! " he cried.

" I *am* wishing," said Jack, after a pause.

The others looked on with interest while the two holders pulled energetically to tear the forked bone apart. Not being dry, it resisted their efforts for some moments, but at last broke on Jack's side just below the crotch, so that Dubsy retained the larger piece, thus becoming the winner.

" What did you wish for, Dubsy?" they all asked.

" I wished that it might always be Washington's Birthday," said Dubsy jubilantly.

This seemed to every one an eminently sensible wish, though Harry Dale qualified it by remarking, " I 'd rather have every day Fourth of July."

" That 's so," said Bill French. " Father's promised me a big show of fireworks, this year."

" What was your wish, Jack?" asked Dubsy suddenly.

" That 's telling."

" Of course you ought to tell," said Harry.

" Not if I lost."

"It can't come true, any way," said Bill French.

"How do you know?" retorted Jack sharply.

"What was it, then?" asked Bill.

Jack hesitated a moment. "I wished," he said a trifle bashfully, "that when I grew up there might be a war and I might be a colonel, like my father."

The boys followed Jack's glance at the oil portrait, over the mantelpiece, of the handsome officer gazing down on them, whose face and dark hair were not unlike his son's, and became contemplative.

"*He* was a soldier, too," continued Jack, pointing to a portrait of Israel Hall at the other side of the room. "He was my great-great-grandfather, and was killed at the battle of Brandywine."

"Are all these your relations?" asked Harry, indicating the half-dozen pictures on the walls, among which the strong features of the old Salem sea-captain looked forth stanchly.

"Yes," answered Jack. "The others were merchants."

"That's what I mean to be when I'm a man," said Bill French. "And when I'm rich I mean to have a steam yacht. Father's going to give me a cat-boat, this summer."

By this time they had got to the puff cakes, which proved to be all that Hannah had predicted. After finishing his third help, Dubsy patted his stomach complacently and observed that he was full up to the muzzle, which seemed to be each one's sentiment as regards himself, though to tell the truth there was scarcely anything left to eat on the table.

How to spend the evening was now the problem. For a while a bagatelle board sufficed for their amusement, but growing weary of that, Bill French chanced to draw up the window-shade a little and peep outdoors. It was a fine night, with plenty of stars, but no moon. The other boys joined him, and all four stood with their noses pressed against the pane.

"Golly!" exclaimed Jack suddenly, in a delighted whisper, "I know what we'll do." He put his finger to his lips and proceeded to run upstairs two steps at a time, but noiselessly as a cat, until he reached his room. Without needing to light the gas, for he knew the whereabouts of everything well enough to find it blindfolded, Jack rummaged in his tool-chest for a piece of chalk and a ball of twine. Then he started down-stairs again, stopping in the parlor a moment to obtain a sheet of paper from his mother's desk. With these implements the four boys, having put on their overcoats, slipped out the front way and carefully closed the door behind them.

As soon as they were outside, Jack stooped and with his piece of chalk drew on the bottom door-step the outline of an envelope, which he whitened and whitened within until it stood out so distinctly that any one opening the door would be certain to be misled. Then he rang the bell, after which all four glided across the street to hide in the shadow of the grocer's shop. Hannah, who answered the bell, stared with surprise at first, and then perceiving the envelope, as she supposed, descended the steps to pick it up, but naturally her fingers scratched against the cold granite. A second time she made the same attempt, but with no better result. The chuckle which Harry Dale was just then unable to repress was not necessary, perhaps, to make clear to her that she was the victim of a practical joke; at any rate, she bounced up and slammed the door indignantly behind her.

This trick was repeated once or twice at other houses, varied by a second of a similar character, which consisted in fastening a string to the real piece of paper and jerking it away on to the sidewalk as the street-door opened. The unfortunate maid-servant, supposing that the wind had carried it away, would follow for some little distance the paper flitting along at intervals, until the truth dawned upon her that she had to deal with "them boys."

But the novelty of this mischief wore off after a few experiments, and the culprits arranged themselves on the sill of the grocer's large window, like a row of sparrows, to cogitate as to what they should do next.

"Let 's smash lamp-posts," said Dubsy.

"I 've promised my mother not to any more," answered Jack sadly.

"Well, I haven't," said Bill Dale; whereupon he aimed a snow-ball at the corner gaslight and let drive. A crash of glass followed, and the boys ran like deer until they were safe in Jack's alley-way; from this they cautiously peeped out after a moment or two, and, no policeman or other censor being in sight, leisurely sauntered forth again.

"I know what let's do," said Bill French suddenly in his confidential tone. "Give me the string, Jack." Taking the ball of twine, Bill went noiselessly across the street and up the steps of the house immediately opposite, which was occupied by a gentleman who was known to them all as "Stiffy Bacon." Mr. Bacon, who was regarded by his contemporaries as a very worthy person, had thus far been unable to preserve friendly relations with the boys who congregated at the corner, and who, as a consequence, delighted in making his life miserable. His house and the one adjoining fronted on a narrow terrace, some six or eight feet above the level of the sidewalk, which was approached by a few winding stairs at either end.

Bill fastened the fine twine around the bell-handle, and letting it unwind returned to the alley-way with the ball, having established a taut line across the street at a height which would endanger the hat of any passer. The street was pretty well deserted at this hour, but the boys were content to wait with a patience worthy of a better cause. It must have been five minutes before Jack exclaimed, " I hear some one coming."

They listened, and could plainly distinguish footfalls and the resonance from the ferule of a cane on the opposite side. The person was coming uphill, and soon, to their delight, proved to be a man wearing a silk hat.

" Now 's your time," said Jack to Bill, who had hold of the string.

Bill accordingly pulled the bell and adjusted the line to what seemed the proper height. The mischief-makers were rewarded by perceiving the door open and the gentleman, who was walking rather fast, come abreast of the twine at precisely the same moment, a consummation for which they had fondly hoped. The unwary pedestrian was brought up short; his silk hat flew off and striking upon the bricks with a hollow thud bumped along the street; while the other, who happened by chance to be no one less than Stiffy Bacon himself, encountering only empty space and then hearing the mutterings of surprise and indignation below, stepped forward and peered over the railing. There was a gas lamp a hundred and fifty yards away which enabled Mr. Bacon, as he thought, to distinguish the disaster and to divine the cause.

"What do you mean, sir, by ringing at my bell at this hour in that condition?" he asked angrily.

"What do *you* mean, sir, by obstructing the highway in such an outrageous manner?" retorted the stranger, who, having picked up his hat, was endeavoring to smooth its nap against his coat-sleeve.

"You are intoxicated, sir," replied Stiffy Bacon.

"How dare you insult a gentleman in such a fashion; you are an insolent scoundrel, sir! I will enter a complaint against you in the morning for obstructing the highway and for defamation of character, — yes, sir, for defamation of character."

The unfortunate stranger, who drew himself up to his full height as he delivered this speech, had such an air of injured respectability and spoke with so much assurance that Mr. Bacon, although very angry, peered forward a little further and exclaimed, "I obstructing the highway? Explain yourself."

"What do you call this, I should like to know, but obstructing the highway?" replied the victim, pawing the air in search of the twine which Bill, immediately after the catastrophe, had let drop so that it lay along the sidewalk. "Fastening a rope across the street to cut the throats of honest folk at night is akin to manslaughter. Ah, here it is."

He picked up the string at his feet, and, perceiving that it dangled down from the terrace, shook it indignantly at his insulter. "There, sir, what do you think of that?"

Apprised by the rubbing of the string against his leg that something was wrong, Mr. Bacon glanced around him and in an instant realized the situation.

"My dear sir," Mr. Bacon protested, "you will excuse me. This is none of my doing; it is the work of some bad boys who are a torment to this neighborhood."

"They ought to be arrested; I'd make short work of them if I lived here," said the gentleman, brandishing his cane. "Another time, sir, perhaps you will be more careful as to the aspersions which you cast on respectable people. Good-evening, sir." Whereupon the stranger stalked away at his previous rapid gait.

Meanwhile, the boys had been squatting still as mice in the dark alley, almost afraid to breathe for fear of giving any indication as to their where-abouts. The affair had exceeded in dramatic effect their wildest anticipations, and there had been mo-ments, especially when the stranger had brandished his stick, during which they had felt a common im-pulse to run into the house. But now that they had only Stiffy Bacon to concern themselves about, terrible as he was, a feeling of relief so far took possession of them, that the irrepressible Harry Dale, unable to contain himself longer, chuckled again. Mr. Bacon, who had stooped to examine the arrangement of the device by which he had been victimized, caught the sound, and, turning in their direction, shook his fist and exclaimed, " You young rascals, you ! "

At these strenuous words, which were delivered in what seemed to them a tone of terrible wrath, the young evil-doers turned and fled with precipi-tation up the alley, save Jack, who lingered for an instant to pick up the ball of twine and pull the line as taut as possible with all his might. He could hear the jangling of the bell as he followed the footsteps of his companions, who ran through the back yard into the house again. From the windows of the dining-room the four peeped once more into the street, but all was still. Stiffy Bacon had apparently retired to his lair. After watching a sufficient time to make sure that the enemy was not lying in wait for them, Jack's visitors ventured to take leave of their host, as it was now half-past nine, and in fifteen minutes more Jack himself was sound asleep.

An hour later, Mrs. Hall returned home. Stepping into the laundry, as was her custom every night before going to bed, to make sure that all was safe from fire, she saw Jack's mittens and pea-jacket hanging up to dry, and smiled to herself as she thought of the happy day he must have passed. Hannah, who would sooner have cut off her right hand than have got Jack into trouble, had already reported to her mistress that the tea party had been a great success, and smothered her own resentment at having been made to scratch her finger-nails on the stone step. Before entering her chamber, Mrs. Hall went into Jack's room, and, bending over the little iron bedstead, stood watching for some min-

utes his peaceful, regular breathing.   " Dear boy!"
she murmured, " what should I do without him?"

She stooped and kissed his soft cheek, which **unex-**
pectedly aroused him.

   "Is that you, mother?" he **asked.**

   "Yes, dear; good-night."

"But I'm not asleep; you must n't go." He rubbed his eyes and sat up in bed.

"It's late, dear; lie down again. Have you had a happy holiday?"

"Bully, mother; sit down, I want to tell you about it. You *shall* stay," said Jack, putting his arm about her neck and drawing her cheek against his own.

"You shall tell me all about it in the morning."

"No; now, mother."

"Well, dear?"

Jack was silent a moment. "I smoked to-day," he blurted out.

"Smoked?"

"Yes; it was n't tobacco, it was rattan. Dubsy and Bill French smoked too. Dubsy was sick afterwards; I was n't sick, but I felt queer."

"Why, how came you to do that, Jack? You must have known that it was wrong."

Jack said nothing, but played with his mother's hand.

"Did n't you, dear?"

"Yes," he whispered.

"Who put such an idea into your head?" she asked.

" Bill French.   I guess he smokes lots ; we went
on top of his house, so that no one could see us."

" You forget, my dear, that God saw you," said
his mother.

Jack was pensive a moment.   " And Washington ? " he asked.

" Sh ! "   Mrs. Hall was a little doubtful how to
take this observation.

" Do you suppose," Jack went on after a moment, " that he knows his birthday is a holiday ? "

" I think very likely, dear."

Jack was again silent.   " Mother ? "

" Well ? "

" Bill French says that when you smoke rattan
the blood is sucked out of your lungs ; do you believe it's true ? "

Mrs. Hall started a little, but a moment's reflection enabled her to answer composedly, " No, dear,
certainly not ; such a thing would be impossible."

" He showed us the dried blood in the rattan,
afterwards."

" Nonsense, dear.   Bill French was trying to
make sport of you."

" Charley Buck told him so."

"Charley Buck ought to know better, then. Charley is too old to tell such foolish things to little boys. What he says about the blood isn't true; but it would make me very unhappy to have you smoke, Jack, until you are a man. It's a very bad habit for a boy to get into, no matter what he smokes, rattan or anything else. But I'm very glad you told me, Jack. If you had concealed it from me and I had found it out, I should have been very unhappy."

"I didn't want to go to sleep until I'd told you," answered Jack, drawing her cheek closer to his own.

"You will promise me not to smoke again?"

Jack promised, and then laid himself down again perfectly happy, still clasping his mother's hand, which she did not withdraw until he had returned to the land of dreams.

But while Mrs. Hall was dressing in the morning, Hannah brought word that Jack had waked up covered with a rash, and that he complained of a headache. The doctor was hastily sent for, but on his arrival the fears of anything serious were promptly dispelled by the announcement that Jack had a thorough case of measles. The loss of the

holiday outdoors seemed to be very nearly made up
to the invalid himself by the news that he could not
be able to return to school for a fortnight at least;
and his mother, who sat beside his bed for a while
after the doctor had gone, was on the point of leaving him with a comparatively light heart to his
own devices, when word was brought her that Mr.
Briggs, the grocer, was down-stairs and would like
to see her.

"He has probably come to explain why his last
supply of coffee is so much poorer than I have usually had," said Mrs. Hall to herself.

But Mr. Briggs had come for a very different
purpose. He looked very grave and a little embar-
rassed as she entered the sitting-room into which
he had been shown. He was a tall and rather thin
man, with a worried expression, which became intensified as he proceeded to explain the reason of
his visit. "I 've come, ma'am, to say that something
must be done about that boy of yours. I 've stood
it a good many years, ma'am, and my patience is
pretty much exhausted, I 'm free to confess."

Mrs. Hall colored violently. "Are you speaking
of Jack, Mr. Briggs?"

" Yes, ma'am. If I may be so bold, he's a very troublesome young gentleman, and there's plenty in the neighborhood who think as I do," he said respectfully.

" Sit down, Mr. Briggs; what has he been doing now ? "

" You know it ain't the first time I've had to complain," he remarked apologetically.

Mrs. Hall bowed coldly.

" If it isn't one thing it's another," he continued. " I'm willing to put up with their coming into the shop and purloining beans and dried apples and figs which they don't pay for, knowing as boys is boys; but when it comes to " —

" What! you don't mean to tell me that my son takes things from your store which he does n't pay for ! " interrupted Mrs. Hall, in a horrified tone. " Why, that would be stealing."

" Yes, ma'am, strictly speaking, I suppose it would," replied the grocer, with a judicial air. "But as I was telling you, I'm willing to say nothing about that for the sake of your custom, provided as no more snow is fired into my cellar. The basket into which the baker drops the rolls for my cus-

tomers is so wet every morning that they 're mostly
spoiled, to say nothing of the dents in the door from
the snow-balls and stones which don't go in.   I only
want to be reasonable, or I'd send in a bill for my
wheelbarrow which some of them broke last week
by upsetting it down the area steps.   I 've told you
most of this before, ma'am," he continued, after a
pause, "and you 've promised to speak to your son."

"I have spoken, Mr. Briggs.   I have cautioned
him particularly to let your wheelbarrow alone, and
not to fire snow-balls at your door.   But this stealing is a more serious affair, and shall be put a stop
to at once."

"It is n't the stealing that I care about," replied
Mr. Briggs dryly.   "But if I have to put the matter in the hands of the police, as I 've made up my
mind to do if my cellar ain't let alone, I can't answer for what 'll happen.   I 've put up with their
tricks as long as I can."

"What makes you think that Jack is still concerned in this mischief?" asked Mrs. Hall.   "I
assure you that I have told him repeatedly that he
is not to molest you."

"It does n't seem to make much difference,

ma'am, then, for my clerk see him with his own
eyes shy two snow-balls at the door only yesterday
morning, and one of them went through. Besides,
he's a sort of leader of mischief hereabouts. He
and the Perkins boy and the Honorable Horatio
French's youngest son are up to all sorts of pranks,
and it's hard to say which of them is the worst."

Mrs. Hall sighed and looked sad. She said presently, "I will make a point this time of seeing
that Jack avoids your premises, Mr. Briggs, and if
you will send in a bill covering whatever he has
taken from your store, and the cost of a new wheelbarrow, I will pay it."

"Thank you, ma'am; I should never think of
doing that."

"I insist," said Mrs. Hall decidedly. She felt
fairly ready to cry at Jack's depravity.

"Then I shall consider that from this time forth
there will be a change," said Mr. Briggs, rising.
"It's the last time I shall speak," he added, as he
stood with his hat in both his hands, evidently feeling it his duty to be explicit.

"Very well, Mr. Briggs. Let me say that at
present there will be no occasion for you to trouble

yourself, so far as — as Jack is concerned, for he has the measles."

"I'm sorry to hear it, ma'am; he must have been took sudden."

"This morning."

"Well, I hope he'll get well soon. I bear no malice, ma'am, I hope you'll believe, and if it weren't that I thought him a smart, likely lad, I should have spoken to the police long since. Good morning, ma'am."

"Good morning, Mr. Briggs. Oh, one moment. The last coffee you sent was very poor," she said, unable to forego this opportunity to put the worthy grocer a little in the wrong.

"Very well, ma'am; I will take it back and send you some more."

When she was alone, Mrs. Hall wiped her eyes, which were full of tears. The idea of Jack's taking what did not belong to him! Honesty was honesty, no matter whether it were a question of dried apples or of diamonds, and the boy who got into the habit of thinking trifles of no importance would soon degenerate. Then, too, how often she had warned him not to interfere with Mr. Briggs!

That hole in the area door had been a constant source of trouble ever since Jack had been able to fire a snow-ball. What with catapults and bean blowers in addition, which were the engines of assault when the snow was gone, poor Mr. Briggs had ample cause to complain. It was evident that he had been goaded to a point where he would take desperate measures unless something were done to restrain effectually his tormentors.

This was by no means the first occasion, as Mr. Briggs had seen fit to remind her, that she had been called to account for Jack's mischievous behavior; but somehow or other she had flattered herself from time to time that the grocer was crabbed and prone to fault-finding, and that her son's high spirits would moderate themselves as he learned more clearly to recognize the rights of others. But of late it had seemed to her that instead of improving, Jack was growing steadily worse. Rumors of his ill-doings reached her ears from various sources, and even Hannah had given her to understand that he had been alluded to in neighboring kitchens as little inferior, in capacity for wickedness, to a fiend. His clothes, alternately

soaking wet, stiff with mud, or full of rents, bore
silent but eloquent testimony to the recklessness of
his conduct. She felt that she did not, of course,
mind the mere rough usage, though it entailed perpetually washing and mending; that was to be
expected, perhaps, of an active boy; but his constant return home in a draggled condition made
her anxious as to the character of his amusements.
He was perpetually in the company of Bill French,
whose family, though rich, were new-comers in that
part of the city, and to whose society she would
have liked to see him less devoted. This incident
of rattan-smoking was another piece of testimony
to confirm her opinion that Bill was an undesirable
crony for Jack. Dubsy Perkins and Harry Dale
seemed to her less objectionable, especially Harry,
who was a quieter and more thoughtful-looking
boy than most of the others who made a playground of Mr. Briggs' corner. As for Dubsy, he
imitated Jack in everything, applauding all he did,
and trying his best to keep up with or even sur-
pass him in whatever was proposed.

Little by little, it had come over Mrs. Hall of
late that the best thing for Jack would be to send

him to some school away from home. The growing city seemed no place for a high-spirited boy,
for whatever he did was pretty sure to be mischief
or against the law. Time was when the Common
had been an ample play-ground, but the crews of
children which crowded it now, to the annoyance
and even peril of adult persons, had induced the
municipal authorities to consider whether the population had not become so large as to make it imperative to forbid ball-playing and other healthy
sports to go on there. One strong argument in
favor of the proposed restriction was that the playground was usurped by youths of seventeen and
upwards, large and powerful as men, who kept
away the smaller boys. For a time the vacant lots
on the outskirts of the city had become favorite
resorts, but these were rapidly being occupied by
houses. Only the streets were left, and boys who
tried to play there were involved in an incessant
warfare with the police. To keep Jack indoors
was impossible, and she reasoned that if the natural outlets for youthful energy were obstructed,
others of an unwholesome kind would be found by
him. Nothing disturbed her more than the thought

of Jack becoming old before his time, one of the knowing little gentlemen of fifteen, who sauntered about the streets in standing collars and kid gloves with an eye to the girls. She wished to see Jack remain an unsophisticated manly boy as long as possible, and she feared that another year of city life might bring about a change in him far more to be deplored than any amount of mischievousness.

But the thought of parting with him was unbearable. He was her idol and the delight of her existence. At present he was under her eye, at least for a part of the time, and could not go very far wrong without her perceiving it. Would it be possible to find a school in the country where, in addition to the advantages of a natural boyish development, Jack would find also the watchful care of a home? There were, she knew, academies — some of them large ones — to which certain of her friends had sent their boys, but she had derived the impression that at them excellence in instruction was the chief consideration, and that the masters were not expected to concern themselves with the morals of the pupils — many of whom were day-

scholars who lived in adjoining towns — outside of
the class-room, unless any boy became conspicu-
ously disreputable. She had discussed the matter
somewhat with her adviser, Mr. Warren, who
agreed with her that Jack would be better off away
from the bricks and mortar, and who promised to
make inquiries as to where it was advisable to send
him. He had further made her understand that
the question had only latterly been forced upon the
attention of parents by the growth of our cities.
Hitherto there had been, and there was still in the
smaller places, facilities for children to play naturally and yet to go to school at home. Our system
of free education, which dated from noble John
Winthrop's time, had properly been our boast, and
we had, accordingly, always rather regarded it as
superior to the English system of large public
schools away from the cities, without perceiving
that it might not always suffice for our needs.
Home training was, doubtless, the key to many
virtues, but there was unquestionably a more pre-
ponderating danger to be feared, to the growth of
the muscles, and to the action of the liver, lungs,
and heart, and, most important of all, to the charac-

ter itself, in the cramped, unwholesome life which a boy is in danger of leading who goes to school in a large city.

There was another point of which Mrs. Hall had thought in this connection. She knew that her husband had been very anxious that his son should grow up an American, without false notions of equality, and with pride and faith in his country. It had been his intention to send Jack to the public schools so that he might mix early with all sorts of boys. And yet she could remember hearing him remark shortly before he went to the war, that it might well be a question how far, to insure this, one would be justified in subjecting a child to the companionship of rough or vicious boys. Since then she had discussed the matter with Mr. Warren from this point of view. She was far from wealthy, but she could afford to pay a reasonable sum for Jack's tuition. Would sending him to a school to which the mass of boys were not well enough off to go tend to foster in him undemocratic notions? As her adviser explained to her, it would be folly to assume that because free education was open to all for the sake of the poor, all were obliged to take advantage of it in order not to be regarded as aristocrats. As well say that a man was no lover of republicanism because he lived in a more expensive house than his neighbor.

CHAPTER IV.

JACK GOES TO UTOPIA.

MRS. HALL's reflections concerning Jack were interrupted by the sound of the door-bell. A moment later Hannah ushered in a no less formidable personage than Mr. Bacon. A call at so early an hour was not likely to be merely social Mrs. Hall well knew, and she began to ask herself what Jack had done now, as her visitor made some observations on the weather before proceeding to explain the real object of his coming.

Mr. Bacon was ceremonious in his general deportment, especially toward ladies. Indeed, his erectness, spruceness, and general starched effect, combined with his austerity toward the boys of the neighborhood, had won for him his nickname. Mrs. Hall had a bowing acquaintance with him, but there was none of that familiarity between them which encourages the friendly discussion of a serious affair. Mr. Bacon announced in well chosen

MR. BACON WAS CEREMONIOUS IN HIS GENERAL
DEPORTMENT.

language that his patience (like Mr. Briggs') was exhausted. He had been badgered, so he phrased it, long enough. Only the night before a party of boys, of which, presumably, Master Hall was one, for the reason that they had concealed themselves in Mrs. Hall's alley-way, and had sought shelter in Mrs. Hall's house, had made a barrier across the street with a piece of twine fastened to his door-bell at such a height as to imperil the eyesight, to say nothing of the hats, of the passers. This sort of thing could not go on. He had endured, with forbearance, having his windows smashed by the careless and sometimes deliberate discharge of various missiles, having his doorsteps dirtied by muddy feet, his wife's pet cat tormented, and himself insulted by offensive epithets, hoping that parental authority might interfere. But it seemed to him as if matters were getting worse every day instead of better. To apply to the police to protect him and his household against his neighbors' children was a step from which he shrank, yet something must be done. For some reason or other the boys appeared to pitch invariably on him as a victim on whom to practice their pranks, though he was not conscious of having deserved their hostility. Would not Mrs. Hall remonstrate seriously with her son, whom he had reason to believe to be more or less of a ringleader among them?

Mrs. Hall, who had listened with pain and mortification to this account of Jack's wrong conduct, was too much of a fond mother not to take advantage of Stiffy Bacon's reference to the fact that he had been especially selected to play tricks upon.

"Of course, Mr. Bacon, Jack has behaved very badly, and you must not think for a moment that I wish to justify his actions," she said; "but boys will be boys, and may it not be that if you were a little better disposed toward them they might not be so troublesome? Their annoyance of you is indefensible, I know, still, as you yourself say, they seem to single you out especially to play tricks upon."

Mr. Bacon colored violently. "I don't know what you mean, Mrs. Hall," he answered. "I pride myself that my treatment of the boys who congregate in this street has been most considerate and lenient. The fact is, madam, I am afraid you do not appreciate what nuisances they have become.

If it be true that I have unwittingly incurred your son's ill will, I can scarcely be held responsible for the constant vexation they occasion the worthy tradesman opposite by their mischievous behavior; scarcely a day passes without some cause for complaint on his part."

It was now Mrs. Hall's turn to blush, but she answered, a little warmly, "I think that Mr. Briggs is quite able to fight his own battles, Mr. Bacon. As to Jack, I shall most certainly forbid him to go upon your premises in future. There will be no chance of it at present," she added, rising, "as he has the measles."

"Oh," said Mr. Bacon. "Very sorry to hear it, I'm sure. It is not a serious disease, I believe."

"I believe not," she answered coldly, and so they parted. But there was further mortification in store for Mrs. Hall.

Ten minutes later Hannah, in an awe-struck tone, informed her that there was a policeman in the front entry. It occurred to her at once that Mr. Briggs had repented of his leniency and sought protection from the law without waiting for another breach of it. The sight of the tall officer in the

blue coat and brass buttons, with a number shining
on his breast, filled her with dismay. At least he
would have to wait until Jack was well before he
carried him off to court.

"The captain has sent me to say, ma'am, that
this breaking of lamps must come to an end.
There's been sixteen smashed at the corner here
in the last month," he began.

"Do you mean that he suspects my boy of being
concerned in it?" asked Mrs. Hall, as he seemed to
be waiting for an answer.

"Boys did it, ma'am; or rather snow-balls fired
by boys, and I guess what your son don't know
about it ain't worth knowing," replied the officer
confidently.

"I feel sure that Jack has not broken any for —
eh — a week," she faltered. "At least he promised
me faithfully that he would not, and I never knew
him not to keep his word."

"Can't pretend to say who did it," he said. "If
I'd seen it done while I was on the beat, there'd
been an end to it mighty quick; they take precious
good care to wait until I'm not round. All I'm
saying is, some one did it, and that some one is

boys; and, what's more, there's got to be an end
of it, or there'll be trouble. I've tried to be easy
with them, but it's no use; the more I overlook
the saucier they get, and it's about time to cry
halt. My instructions, ma'am, are, to make arrests,
if another lamp is broken."

"But you can't arrest a boy if he is innocent,"
exclaimed Mrs. Hall, who was becoming alarmed.

"I guess there ain't much danger of my making
any serious mistakes," said the officer, with a grin.
"I've been on this beat for the last four years, and
I know pretty well by this time who's innocent and
who's not."

"The boys all appreciate how lenient you have
been with them," she said, hoping, perhaps, to
mollify him by flattery. "They quite look upon
you as a friend."

"Maybe it would have been better if I'd been
strict with them from the first. There's no trust-
ing them; the moment my back's turned they're
making faces at me or shouting after me," he said,
somewhat bitterly, evidently reflecting on his experience of the previous afternoon. "There ain't
much gratitude in boys if you come to reflect upon

it; leastways, I ain't found much so far. Well, ma'am, I bid you good morning," he added. "A warning's a warning, and that's all there is about it."

"If there are any lamps broken during the next fortnight," Mrs. Hall hastened to say, as the officer turned to go, "it won't be Jack's fault, for he has the measles."

"Sho! Has he though? Want to know!" he said slowly, by way of comment, pausing between the phrases. "Well, 'tain't as bad as scarlet fever. I hate to see boys sick, though. *Good* day, madam."

That afternoon Mrs. Hall put on her bonnet and went down town to call on Mr. Warren, whom she always consulted when she wished advice. She told the lawyer briefly, in rather a despairing tone, all that had come to her ears during the morning, and ended by saying that if a good school could be found outside the city, Jack must be sent to it, even if her heart were broken as a consequence. Her heart was certain to be broken if he remained at home.

Mr. Warren listened to her patiently, and when

she had finished took a letter from his desk which
he handed to her.

" You see I have been making inquiries," he observed, as he watched her read. " Schools of this
sort are cropping up all over the country. You
have no idea how many there are until you begin to
investigate. But I am told that this is one of the
best."

" Utopia School. What a curious name ! " said
Mrs. Hall, musingly.

" It suggests progress and hope."

" Decidedly. But I don't care to have any experiments tried on Jack."

" Not even if he turns out a fine manly fellow as
a result of them ? " asked her friend, with a laugh.
" But you need have no fear that there is anything
unduly visionary in the curriculum of Dr. Meredith,
my dear Mrs. Hall. Those who know him best say
that his aim is merely to turn out his pupils, at the
end of their course, gentlemen and scholars."

" John Meredith. That is an attractive name ;
how old is he ? "

" A young man, but then remember we have faith
in young men in this country. Between thirty-five

and forty, I should say. By the way, he is neither
a clergyman nor a doctor; his Dr. means simply
that he has taken the University degree of Ph. D."

" The school was founded eight years ago, I see,"
she said, referring to a prospectus inclosed in the
letter.

" Yes," he answered; "it started with twenty-five
pupils and has now about two hundred, who rep-
resent nearly every State in the Union. It was
founded by individual enterprise and generosity;
half a dozen wealthy men, who, very likely, were as
puzzled what to do with their sons as you are with
Jack, put their heads together at the suggestion of
this young Meredith, who felt that he had ideas on
the subject, and subscribed the money to build a
tasteful schoolhouse, with dormitories for the boys,
and a wing for the master's own use, all under a
single roof. And now, not ten years later," — Mr.
Warren reached out his hand for the prospectus,
which he perused an instant to refresh his memory,
— " yes, here it is, now there are three new dormitories, each adapted to house sixty boys, a schoolhouse where the lessons are recited, which includes
a fine library as well, a chapel, and a gymnasium,

all forming a large quadrangle. Within the quadrangle is a foot-ball ground and a base-ball ground, and around the foot-ball ground is a running track. Outside there appear to be lawn-tennis courts, and not more than a quarter of a mile away, a lake a mile and a half long and a quarter of a mile wide, on the banks of which is a boat-house. Add to this picturesque country surroundings, good food, and the personal supervision of the masters over the morals and health of each boy, — you will notice that point insisted upon, — and it seems to me that you have a paradise."

" I could go and see him occasionally ? "

" As often as you please, I imagine. Five or six hours in the train would bring you to him or him to you at any time." .

" But I shall miss him so much, Mr. Warren. In England it is a matter of course to send boys away from home, and the parents don't seem to mind it; but we are more like the French, we cannot bear to be separated from our children."

" I remember," replied Mr. Warren reflectively, " being told by a young man who had been a pupil at one of the large English public schools, — Eton, or Harrow, or Rugby, I forget which, — that whereas his parents, who were then living in London, came to see him a number of times in the course of the year, it was unusual for the rest of the boys to receive a visit from a relation from one end of a term to another. English fathers and mothers like to affect not to have feelings, on the theory that the display of emotion and affection tends to make boys unmanly. They would consider one who wept on parting with his mother rather a milksop, I imagine; and on the same principle they consider it better discipline to keep away during term time. But we have no such theory as yet, Mrs. Hall."

" I should hope not," she replied. "I should feel very badly if Jack did n't shed a few tears on parting with me. As for myself, I can't say what I might not do in my despair. I suppose that I must bring myself to it, Mr. Warren," she added. "You feel sure that Jack will be well looked after? He needs personal influence; all the floggings and punishment in the world would n't do him any good. What he requires is to have his mind awakened to the fact that there are more important matters in life than snow-balling and coasting and base-ball, and to recognize that he owes something to others. At present he seems to think that if the whim seizes him he is justified in playing the most disagreeable tricks on people, even to the extent of ignoring the rights of property, if Mr. Briggs is to be believed. While remaining the manly, earnest boy that he is in many ways, I wish to see him become more thoughtful and considerate. Do you think Utopia School will produce those results?"

"So I am assured. We have no very old schools of the sort in this country, therefore the testimony must needs be imperfect as to their value. But, as that letter informs you, Dr. Meredith's first aim is that his pupils should be, at graduation, high-minded youths."

"I suppose I must consent to it," murmured Mrs. Hall presently, and so her resolution was taken.

Correspondence was at once opened with Dr. Meredith, who suggested that Jack should come to him after the Easter recess, as there happened to be a vacancy in the school. Before this time Jack had recovered from his illness, though he looked somewhat pale and thin. His mother did not inform him of her intention to send him away from home until about a fortnight before he was to go. Jack manifested, on hearing the news, unmitigated satisfaction, but as the day drew near which was to separate him from his mother, he became very quiet and unlike his usual self. He sat beside her in the evenings, his shock of dark hair nestled upon her breast, while she gave him counsel as to what he must be sure to do and not to do when he no longer had her to watch over him. She made him promise to study well and to obey his new master, and he would listen in thoughtful silence to her instructions as to keeping his clothes neat, and not forgetting to say his prayers morning and night, and sometimes to read his little Bible, her gift on his tenth birthday. "And whatever you do, Jack, remember, always speak the truth and never do anything mean."

"Yes, mother."

"Your father had a horror of falsehood above everything else; he used to say that he had no patience with a lie. Ah, how I shall miss you, my dear little man! You will not forget me, will you, Jack?"

Forget her! Then was the moment for him to fling his arms about his mother's neck, and kissing her again and again, vow that he would be miserable away from her, and that he would far rather stay at home, — which whole-souled protestations sounded sweet in the poor widow's ears, and helped to ease the pang of parting.

Both she and Hannah were kept very busy in getting his wardrobe ready. There were new sets of shirts and stockings to be bought and marked, and the old things had to be darned and generally put in order. He was pleased beyond measure by the purchase of a leather trunk, stamped with his initials, to carry his belongings, which were numerous, and would have filled two or three trunks had he been permitted to carry them all. It was difficult for Jack to decide what to leave behind; everything was dear to him, from his discarded rocking-horse with its moth-eaten hide to his latest treasure, a small engine, which was operated by steam, and which he had bought by saving up his pocket-money. His room was full of toys: there were tin soldiers and forts in the defense of which to employ them, a splendid tool-chest, a theatre, a magic-lantern, and an assortment of marbles, shuttlecocks, bats, and balls, the accumulations of his childhood. He persuaded his mother to let him take the engine, but he was compelled to see most of the other things, which Hannah stigmatized as truck, put away to await his return. An exception was made in favor of his favorite base-ball bat, which he was to carry in his hand, a few tools, the shuttlecocks, and his bag of marbles, all of which would take up but little room, and which would be useful to him at Utopia.

Outside the house, the news of his proposed departure had aroused great interest among his companions, who one and all expressed their envy of what they considered his great good-fortune. Dubsy Perkins was inconsolable, and Bill French announced an intention of persuading his father to let him follow Jack in the autumn. Even Mr. Briggs, when Jack for the fourth time in three days went into the grocer's store to be weighed, remarked, with a commendable degree of warmth, considering their relations toward one another, " I hear we 're to lose you soon, Master Hall."

" Yes, I 'm going to boarding-school, where there

are two hundred boys, next week," replied Jack proudly.

" I want to know," responded the grocer, and he added a moment later, by way of expressing his interest or gratitude, — let us believe it was the former, — " Have some dried apples ? "

The invitation was meant to include the group of half a dozen boys in the store at the time, who accepted it. gladly, but with some wonderment. Since the visit of Mr. Briggs to Mrs. Hall and several of the other parents, the behavior of his tormentors had shown marked improvement; though they still meandered about and through his premises on the smallest pretext, the pilfering had mostly ceased, and the snow-balls found in his bread-basket were less numerous. As, owing to his mother's strenuous exhortation, Jack had restrained his fingers ever since from the barrel containing the beans and dried apples, and the box of figs, the permit dazed him for a moment ; but when he realized that " Old Briggs " was actually " standing treat," his heart felt warm toward his old enemy, and some shame for his own cruel treatment of him was mingled with his reflections.

Indeed, Jack had also the satisfaction of parting with Stiffy Bacon under peculiarly pleasant circumstances. That gentleman's irate threats, as repeated by Jack to the other fellows, had produced such a feeling of alarm that none of them had dared to venture on his premises ever since. On one of the few balmy days which come early in April to herald the approach of spring, the boys, who had assembled at the corner to enjoy the first game of scrub of the season, were astonished to see Stiffy Bacon come down the steps of his house with two new cricket bats and a set of wickets in his hands, with which he advanced toward them. The boys stopped their game and gazed at him in bewilderment, scarcely believing their eyes and half inclined to run. The sight of a Greek bearing gifts is not apt to be assuring, but in this case there was no cause for alarm. Mr. Bacon stopped a foot or two away, and addressing them all, but more especially Jack, said :

" Young gentlemen, I am very much obliged to you for being so quiet and behaving so well during my wife's illness, and I ask you to accept this cricket set as a token of my good will." Whereupon he held out the bats and wickets to Jack, who received them mechanically, so utterly at a loss was he in common with all the others to understand what Mr. Bacon was driving at. The fact was, that Mrs. Bacon had presented her husband with a fine baby a few weeks before; but this interesting circumstance was quite unknown to the boys, who, accordingly, were feeling very shame-faced at the praise bestowed upon them, knowing that they had been quiet for quite another reason.

The donor further heaped coals of fire upon their heads by producing a cricket ball and the bails for the wickets from his pocket, in response to which there came a feeble murmur of " Thank you, sir," from the group, who stood like gawks, half frightened and yet very much pleased withal. Jack, who, as the one to whom Mr. Bacon had principally addressed his speech, felt that it was incumbent on him to make an appropriate acknowledgment of the gift, stood uneasily shifting his feet and trying to think what to say. As in the case of Mr. Briggs, such unexpectedly friendly conduct had produced a revulsion of feeling toward his former enemy. Just as Mr. Bacon, after an awkward pause on both sides, was turning away, Jack, seized by an inspiration, exclaimed, "Now, fellows, three cheers for Stif — *Mr.* Bacon !"

They were given with a will and a tiger, and at the sound of them the gentleman in question looked back evidently much gratified and lifted his hat, for he could not help being extremely polite even when he was most gracious.

"Thank you, very much, sir," several boys cried now that the ice was broken, and Bill French was hypocrite enough to add, "I hope Mrs. Bacon is quite well again," which nearly caused a titter. Jack, congratulating himself that the word "Stiffy" had been repressed in time, struck up the song, "For he's a jolly good fellow," which was continued by all hands until Mr. Bacon was in-doors again. First and last the affair was a most auspicious one, and let it be hoped that henceforward a perpetual truce was observed between the boys and the Bacon family.

On that point Jack was never fully informed, for he left home a week later for Utopia. When the day actually arrived he was much too elated to feel any severe pangs at leaving the dear old street where he had done so much mischief during the past four or five years, and even his partings with his friends were so jolly that nothing but the delightful prospect before him could have excused such light-heartedness.

Mrs. Hall, like the brave woman she was, had shed her tears in secret or was saving them up until she should be left alone, for her face was wreathed in smiles as she clasped her darling to her bosom for one last hug after the driver announced that there was no time to lose if he wished to catch the train. Jack was in an exuberant state of mind, for in addition to the proud consciousness that he was to travel alone for the first time in his life, he had been allowed a full cup of coffee for breakfast, which was a great treat to him. Beside Hannah, who threw her apron over her head every minute or two to hide her eyes, there were Dubsy Perkins and Bill French and Harry Dale in the hall to see him off, and each had brought a parting gift. Bill French's was a knife with eight blades including a gimlet, a cork-screw, and other useful devices, which, as Bill explained with pride, cost ten dollars. Beside it Dubsy's present looked very insignificant, but a tip-cat made by Dubsy was regarded in the neighborhood as a work of art entitling its possessor to the congratulations of his friends. "I made it on purpose for you, Jack," said the manufacturer, with a look of genuine affection on his honest but not over-clean face. Harry Dale had brought a book entitled " Every Boy his own Carpenter," which gave directions how to make everything under the sun.

Jack's new trunk had been strapped on behind, and all was ready. After that last hug he ran down the steps crying " Good-by, everybody," and got into the carriage. The boys thrust their hands through the open window for a final shake, and just as the driver had said " Clk ! " to the horses, Hannah came rushing out with some cold chicken and a turnover done up in a napkin, which had almost been left behind.

But at last he is really off, with his head out so as to wave one more " good-by " to his mother, and after he has drawn it in out it flies again on the other side, for in turning the corner he perceives old Briggs in his white apron standing on the threshold of his store grinning like a Cheshire cat.

"Good-by, Mr. Briggs, good-by!" he shouts, while Hannah murmurs, "God bless his heart; there isn't a soul in the street who won't miss him," a remark in which the worthy henchwoman might have found herself, it is to be feared, in a minority, if the vote had been taken.

Meantime, Bill and Dubsy and Harry, who being each armed with a catapult have let fly simultaneously some tolerably large shot at the little window in the rear of the carriage as it rolls off, one of which just misses the driver's ear, run to the corner and watch until the carriage reaches the foot of the street and turns again, being rewarded by a final wave of Jack's arm as he catches a glimpse of them, to which they reply with a prolonged "Ehu—ehu—ehu." Wafted on his way by which familiar war-whoop of his childhood, Jack Hall takes his first step forward in the battle of life.

CHAPTER V.

DR. MEREDITH.

UTOPIA SCHOOL takes its name from the small town adjoining, to reach which Jack had to change cars and run twenty odd miles on a country branch after traveling several hours on the main line. But time passed all too quickly for our hero, who never wearied of looking out of the windows at the landscape flying away behind, in the intervals of exhausting the resources of the train peddler, a boy of about his own age, in whose stock in trade Jack took a keen and very soon a substantial interest. He let the books tossed on the seat beside him be gathered up again without remonstrance, though he cast sheep's-eyes at a small treatise on base-ball with an illuminated cover representing a player in the act of striking. A banana and a small drum of figs were temptations, however, to which he succumbed, and just as he was finishing the last of a roll of lozenges which had won him

over after these were gone, the crowning attraction
of the day appeared in the form of prize packages
labeled to contain any number of useful articles
in the way of stationery and jewelry, and costing
only a quarter. But their more potent charm lay
in the further inscription, well adapted to dazzle
youthful eyes, — "One package in every hundred
issued contains a hundred-dollar bill. This is guar-
anteed by the company. Try your luck."

Jack's reasoning was, that the quire of paper,
pens, pencil, sealing-wax, and "three separate articles of jewelry," which every one of them was
warranted to include, must be worth far more than
the price demanded. So in any event his money
would not be squandered, and there was no telling
— for he was pretty lucky as a rule, having on one
occasion picked up a cameo pin in the street, and
on another a silver coin — that he might not happen on a package which had a hundred-dollar bill
in it. The one which the boy had left on the seat
looked plump and satisfactory. Jack squeezed it
and held it up for a moment to the light, but there
was nothing gained by that. When the boy came
back he examined the dozen others in the basket
critically.

" Did you ever see any one get a prize ? " Jack asked, when he had completed the inspection.

" You bet your life," responded the peddler. " I see a young feller aboard the train just your size find one of them hundred-dollar bills only last week."

" Swanny ! " said Jack; " I wish I knew which one to choose."

" You pays your money and you takes your choice," answered the lad impartially.

" Well, I 'll take this one, I guess," said Jack, with a sigh, at last.

The one chosen was down at the bottom of the pile, and looked a trifle bulkier than the others, though they were all very much alike. The peddler had evidently little curiosity as to the result of the selection, for he continued on his way the moment after pocketing the quarter, rather to the surprise of the purchaser. Jack proceeded to open the envelope with eager anticipation. The first thing he noticed was a number of sheets of very common ruled note-paper, beside which lay a lank pencil, a penholder of a kind which can be duplicated for a cent, three pens, a half-dozen colored wafers, a miserable bit of red wax, a few envelopes, a ring set with a small green glass stone, a bangle of thin platinum, and a brass watch-chain. These were the entire contents. Jack peeped between the sheets of paper, but no bank-bill had been skillfully concealed there. Ruefully he began to examine the collection of trash which he had acquired for twenty-five cents, and was wondering whether the green stone could possibly be an emerald, and what he should do with his purchases, when the train stopped and the conductor called out that passengers for Utopia and certain other places must change cars. Jack stuffed the contents of the prize package into his pockets and obeyed orders.

Five minutes before Jack's train reached the station, a train from the opposite direction had arrived with passengers from the West, one of whom, a bright-looking lad, was already seated in the car on the branch line which Jack entered, and it so happened that when the conductor cried "All aboard" the two boys found themselves the sole occupiers of it. The new-comer was neatly dressed, was a bit taller than Jack, slim and wiry, with a wide-awake expression.

The boys exchanged shy glances, and Jack experienced a thrill of sympathy in observing the torn envelope of another prize package lying at the stranger's feet. Presently, with the restlessness common to youth, the latter got up and, putting a hand on the arm of the seat on either side of him, started to propel himself along the aisle in the manner of an athlete on parallel bars, with the result that, after a spasmodic jump or two, he fell in a heap on the floor, whereupon he arose, and, brushing the knees of his trousers, looked at Jack and laughed. Then he proceeded on his way, like an ordinary mortal, to the end of the car, which, being the last in the train, commanded an absorbing view of the road-bed over which they were spinning at ever so many miles an hour. Here he was soon joined by Jack, and the pair stood side by side looking at the long line of track, until the other boy said suddenly, after a more than common oscillation of the swaying car, which nearly upset them both, — "That's nothing. You ought to see how fast they go on the New York Central." Then he added, "Going to Utopia School?"

" Yes," said Jack. " Are you? "

The boy nodded. " My name 's Frank Haseltine," he said. " I live in Cincinnati. My father 's
in Congress, and President of the Haseltine Iron
and Steel Works. I hate school, but father says
I'm to go to Utopia for six years, and then to
college. I 'd rather be a professional, would n't
you? "

" A professional? I don't know what you mean,"
said Jack doubtfully.

" A base-ball player, of course. I 'd like to be
on one of the champion nines. Foxy Ricketts,
who 's only five years older than I, is to be change
pitcher for the Red Stockings this season. He
used to be captain of the Rising Suns. That 's the
club I belong to. I 'm only third base in the second
nine, but I guess I 'd have played catcher next year
if I 'd stayed. What club do you belong to? "

" The Massasoits," said Jack.

" Never heard of them," answered Haseltine decidedly. " What 's your name? " he inquired.

" John Hall. Most people call me Jack, though."

" Where were you raised? "

Jack looked puzzled. " Do you mean where do

I come from? Boston." As he felt that his answer seemed scant in view of Haseltine's details, he added, "My father was a colonel, and was killed in the war."

"Is that so? I've an uncle who's a general. He was wounded in the war but got well again. If I can't be a professional when I grow up, I'd rather be a soldier than anything. What did you play on the Massasoits?"

"Short stop."

"That's a first-rate position," responded Haseltine, patronizingly.

After these remarks, the boys sat down side by side and were soon deep in a cordial conversation, very early in which they emptied their pockets for the benefit of one another. Jack's new knife, all the blades of which he opened admiringly, the tipcat, and two splendid agate marbles were matched by Haseltine with a fascinating little compass in a shiny, round metal case, a silver-mounted whistle in the shape of a dog's head, and, most exciting of all to Jack, a tiny live snake in a wooden box, which crawled and wriggled about its owner's hand in a most approved fashion.

"He's real tame," observed Haseltine. "I've had it six months. He lives on flies, and I would n't lose him for anything; would I, Bill?" he added, caressing the small reptile.

Jack was silent a moment. Then he asked, "What 'll you take for the snake?"

"What 'll you give?"

"I 'll swap one of my agates for him."

"Not much. Will you give me the knife?"

"I guess *not*. That knife cost a lot of money."

"It 's mighty difficult to get a snake tame as Bill."

"Will you take both the agates?" asked Jack presently.

"Let 's see them," said Haseltine. He examined the marbles critically. "What else 'll you give?"

"I 'll throw in a blood alley."

"Let 's see the blood alley." After inspection he inquired, "What else you got?"

"Is n't that enough? I 'm willing to let you have this, too," Jack said at last, indicating the watch-chain. They had already compared experiences on the subject of prize packages. Needless to say, Haseltine had been no more fortunate in finding a hundred-dollar bill in his, but though they had come to the conclusion that the jewelry was not quite up to the mark, there was sufficient uncertainty regarding its value to make the ownership of it seem not wholly undesirable.

Haseltine weighed the chain pensively. "See here," he said, " if you 'll give me the two agates, the blood alley, the chain, and the ring, you may have Bill. Is it a go?"

Jack hesitated ; he felt that he was asked to pay a high price, but a glance at Bill, who in response to his master's effort to show him off was wriggling delightfully, settled the question in his mind. "Give me the snake," he said, handing over the specified articles in exchange. Jack returned the little creature to his box and deposited it in one of his trousers' pockets with the air of a proprietor.

Just then the train stopped at a station, and the boys, owing to the great uproar which was going on outside, popped out their heads. The platform of the station was crowded with young fellows of all ages and sizes, some of them nearly grown up. About half of them were in uniform, part of whom wore drab flannel shirts trimmed with blue and embroidered in the middle of the breast with a large blue **U**, drab knickerbockers, and blue stockings; the others, armless white shirts adorned with a flaming constellation, red belts, and nondescript trousers, which showed clearly to the boys that they were in the presence of two rival base-ball clubs and their respective constituents.

"I wonder which licked," said Haseltine excitedly, and under a common impulse he and Jack started for the rear door.

But here their progress is blocked, for the boys with the **U** on their breasts and their friends are by this time clambering up the steps and beginning to swarm into the car. There is a great hubbub and shouting and shaking of hands between the rival factions, which is followed by a sudden hush, for the captain of the home nine — a strapping-looking country lad who reminds Jack of Joe Herring — has got his men in a bunch together and now cries, " Three cheers for the Utopias, boys! Now, one —

" Hurrah ! "

" Two " —

"Hurrah!"

"Three" —

"Hurrah!" And then at the close came a delicious "tiger-r-r," in which the entire juvenile population of the town joined.

"The Utopias must have won," whispers Haseltine.

"Why?" asks Jack, who is really beside himself with excitement.

"Because the others cheered first."

As the reverberation of the tiger dies away a handsome, bronzed, athletic-appearing boy, with a little down on his upper lip, and who seems to Jack a man, steps to the edge of the platform, and swinging his cap above his head, exclaims in a dignified tone, but with great enthusiasm, "Now, fellows, nine rousing cheers for the Foxbridge Stars, — and any time they will come to Utopia we will give them their revenge."

"'Rah, rah, rah, rah, rah, rah, rah, rah, rah! — Utopia-a-a-a!" rings out on the air in short, sharp response.

"Time's up, gentlemen," cries the genial conductor, who stands watch in hand. "All aboard!"

He waves his hand to the engineer, the engine gives a snort and a whistle, and amid a great shouting and waving of hats and bats and handkerchiefs the train moves slowly away from the station, the Stars and their satellites following it on its way for two hundred yards or so, leaping like greyhounds, until fairly distanced.

Jack, who has had the satisfaction of interpreting to Haseltine the cheers of the victorious nine as an imitation of the Harvard University method, watches eagerly the body of Utopia boys as they pour into the car and take possession of the seats. They are in tearing spirits over their success, and for some time talk of nothing but the details of the game, recollecting with enthusiasm the fine points of play, — Bedlow's pitching, Goldthwaite's one-handed catch at second base, and, most glorious of all, Ramsay's home run, which won the game when the score was tied. Ramsay is captain, the manly-looking fellow who proposed the cheers for the Stars, and Jack feels, as he watches him leaning back against the seat, with his hands resting on the handle of his bat, and accepting modestly but with a smile of permissible pride the congratulations showered upon him, that he would give anything to be in his shoes.

The boys are of all sizes, for at least fifty, big and little, have come down from the school to back up the nine, and even to the smallest they are decked with blue ribbons, stamped "Utopia" in silver letters. No one pays attention to Jack and Haseltine, who are sitting side by side at the end of the car with their ears open.

"Won't the Doctor be pleased!" exclaimed one of the players, breaking a momentary pause in the rejoicing.

"What a pity he did n't come!" said another.

To this there was a general assent, after which some one cried, "Give us a song, Jumbo."

"A song! A song!" repeated several jubilantly, and then as the boy called upon did not immediately respond, there was a universal call, "Jumbo, Jumbo! Hit her up, Jumbo!"

Jack and Haseltine, following the direction of all eyes, perceived an especially fat boy in the middle of the car, who was just beginning the words of a taking song, which was very spirited. After each verse there came a ringing chorus, in which all joined ecstatically: —

"Stop that knocking; let me in;
Stop that knocking; let me in;
Oh, I tell you stop that knocking at my door."

This was always repeated, and every time they sang it the swell of the voices grew louder and the enthusiasm greater, until, what with the hammering on the floor with bats to express the knocking, together with the increasing tendency to sacrifice harmony to sound, it seemed as though the roof of the car would come off. It was a thorough pandemonium; and Jack thought the occasional transposition of the first phrase of the chorus into "knock that stopping" one of the funniest things he had ever listened to.

When Jumbo finished, Goldthwaite the second base, who had made the one-handed catch, sang in a rich tenor voice, "Aunt Dinah's Quilting Party," which had a sentimental refrain about seeing Nelly home by starlight, and made Jack feel pensive, though he preferred the humorous song. Everybody sang the chorus with a great deal of sentiment, especially Ramsay, who sighed perceptibly when Goldthwaite pictured Nelly's hand as resting on her lover's arm " light as oc an's fcam."

Presently there were cries for " Jack Spratt and his Wife," presumably a ditty, but who turned out to be two inseparable friends thus nicknamed because one was very stout and the other unusually slim. The pair contributed an amusing double-part song, which set everybody into peals of laughter, and restored the spirit of hubbub subdued by passing thoughts of Nelly. Just as the last verse came to an end, the train began to slow up, and amid shouts of " Here we are," every one started to his feet and made for the door.

" Utopia!" cried the conductor vociferously.

" As if we did n't know that, Henry," responded the foremost as they rushed out.

Jack and Haseltine brought up the rear, and found themselves on alighting face to face with a ponderous, hearty, red-faced man carrying a whip, whose face was one broad grin as he listened to the joyful tidings of the victory from a dozen lips at the same moment.

" And won't the Doctor be tickled to death!" Jack heard him exclaim with a chuckle. " Mr. Percy's yonder," he continued, indicating with his thumb a barge drawn by two horses, into which the majority of the boys were already precipitating themselves. "He could n't wait to hear who 'd won. And so you beat 'em, did you? Well, well ! "

At the mention of Mr. Percy's name there had been a further diversion to the barge, and only three or four still remained, pouring a few last details into the ears of the man with the whip, who now asked, "Has any one of you laid eyes on the two new boys I 've come to fetch ? "

" Your kids are all serene, Horace; I saw them aboard the train," said a boy in answer.

" Master Hall, — Master Haseltine ? " inquired Horace, stepping forward as he caught sight of Jack and his friend.

" All right," said Jack; " I 'm Hall."

" And I 'm Haseltine."

" Checks, please," said Horace. Then pointing to a vehicle half-wagon, half-carryall, a few yards beyond, he told the two boys to get in while he looked after their baggage.

Before they had well seated themselves, the barge, filled almost to overflowing with its noisy freight, started off at a goodly pace to the accompaniment of fish-horns and fiendish cat-calls. As it swept by the smaller conveyance a shower of beans fell rattling about the ears of the new-comers, which caused Jack instinctively to clap his hand on the side-pocket of his jacket in search of his catapult; but before he could get at it the grinning faces of his assailants were out of range.

"By gum!" Jack muttered belligerently.

"It's no use, any way," said Haseltine. "If you had hit them, it would have been all the worse for both of us afterwards. I expect to be half killed as it is."

"What do you mean?" asked Jack.

"They'll haze us, of course. I know a fellow who was made to jump into the river on a Christmas eve, and who, as the result of it, had pneumonia and nearly died."

"At Utopia?"

"No, it wasn't at this school; but they're all alike. They make you stand on a table and recite poetry, and do all sorts of monkey-tricks."

"I wouldn't."

"You couldn't help yourself; they'd stick pins into you if you refused, or burn you with a red-hot iron."

"They should kill me before I'd do a thing," said Jack stoutly, but, nevertheless, he continued contemplative until their conductor arrived with the trunks. A moment later they were off.

"That's great," Horace observed with gusto, after a period of reflective silence.

"What is?" inquired Haseltine.

"The ball game. Them Stars has been all-fired cocky since way back, and boasting as how they could n't be beat. But they're done for this time, sure. Fourteen to thirteen — tidy score, too; that home-run was what done it. Great boy, that Harry Ramsay."

"He's captain, is n't he?" asked Jack.

"Yes, captain of the nine, and cute all round. I tell you, the Doctor's proud of him, and 'll be mighty sorry when he goes to Harvard next year. He is smart at his books, too."

"Tell us about some of the other players," said Haseltine.

"Well, they're all pretty stout. Bedlow's a rattling good pitcher, and when he's in shape it takes an A 1 player to get base hits off him, I can tell you. Goldthwaite's good, too, at second base, and

Bobby Crosby at left field, though he goes in more for foot-ball. He'll be captain of the eleven, fast enough, when Burbank goes. He's a great hand at kicking goals. There ain't a better nor a smarter set of boys in the country than the boys of Utopia School, take 'em all together," continued Horace, giving a flick with his whip to ·emphasize his words; "and as for the Doctor, there ain't his equal anywhere that ever I see. He's a gentleman, if there is one, and a scholar too, for the matter of that. What he don't know ain't worth knowing, I guess."

"What's *your* name?" asked Haseltine boldly.

"Horace Hosmer. The boys, leastwise those who've been here any time, call me Horace. I've done the driving for the school since it was first started, and that's a matter of close on ten years, now."

"Much hazing?" inquired Jack presently, in what he intended to be an indifferent tone.

Horace glanced sideways at his questioner before replying. "Fair to middling," he said gravely. "Two boys died from it last term; Doctor called it chicken-pox; but I know better," he added, with an ominous nod. "I see them after they were laid out, and they were a mass of bruises from the crown of the head to the soles of the feet."

Haseltine nudged Jack, who, it must be confessed, felt uncomfortable, and who exclaimed, after a moment, "I should. n't think Dr. Meredith would allow it."

"Well, he does try to stop it, but some of them fourth-class boys are dreadful hard to manage. There's Jack Spratt and his Wife, for instance, —

I tell you they 'd as soon break every bone in a new boy's body as not," continued Horace confidentially.

" They were the two who sang last," observed Jack, gloomily, to Haseltine.

" There 's nothing really vicious about 'em, — they 're just playful," Horace went on to say. " But singing or no singing, if I were a new boy I-should n't want to have 'em down on me. It 's hard to say which - is the worst, Spratt or his Wife."

" What are their real names ? " Jack inquired.

" Tobey and Donaldson; but no one ever calls 'em anything but Jack Spratt and Wifey; that 's because they 're so thick together. Most of the boys have nicknames of some sort, though there ain't much sense in 'em if you come to think it over. There 's the Spider and the Lamb, and the Titmouse and the Shark, and ever so many more. But you 'll know all about it soon, for here we are," said their mentor, as the pair of horses turned sharply.

They were borne swiftly through a gateway and along a smooth, graveled avenue, under a vista of fine trees which had evidently once formed the approach to a private residence. On either side an expanse of level field stretched away, which was dotted with boys busy at play, of whom Jack got a few glimpses as Horace, nodding to right and left, exclaimed, "Lawn-tennis courts, — base-ball practice ground;" though a bell pealing from beyond had mostly caused a cessation of the games, and the boys in the field on the right-hand side had begun to throng into the avenue, or to cross it into the other field.

"It's supper-time," Horace vouchsafes to inform his charges, who are craning their necks in absorbed inspection of the score of young fellows in white flannels, with tennis rackets in their hands, advancing at an easy jog in detachments of two and three, in response to the reverberating summons. It is shorter for those who have been practicing scrub in the left-hand field to keep straight on, for the avenue winds to the left along the top of that field, until it reaches another arched gateway situated midway between two spacious dormitories which form one side of a large quadrangle. There is a solid stream of boys passing through this gateway on the way to their rooms to tidy up for supper,

which will be ready in fifteen minutes in the old
schoolhouse, — the original structure built by the
founders, — which faces Jack as he is driven into
the quadrangle and finds himself squarely within
school bounds.

On his right stands the tasteful chapel, from the
tower of which the ten-minute bell is still ringing,
and just beyond it the gymnasium. Facing these,
at the other end of the broad campus, is the building devoted to schoolrooms, and still another dormitory, all exactly as the prospectus, which Jack
had read many times, described. Both the exten-
sive playgrounds, the one laid out for base-ball and
the other for foot-ball, lie deserted; for every one
within the quadrangle has hastened to welcome the
victorious nine on the arrival of the barge, about
which a cheering throng is now collected in front
of the old schoolhouse.

"There's the Doctor on the steps shaking hands
with 'em," exclaimed Horace. "I tell you he's
proud to-night. Look at that now; it's Ramsay
they've got."

A cheer that does one's heart good had preceded
Horace's last words, occasioned evidently by some

compliment which Dr. Meredith had paid the modest captain, and thereupon a score of hands have
seized Ramsay and lifted him on to a phalanx of
shoulders. "'Rah, rah, rah, rah, rah, rah, rah, rah,
rah! — Utopia-a-a-a!"

Off they go tearing like mad, bearing their laughing, struggling burden, who is plainly protesting
against so extravagant a tribute to his prowess,
to the ball ground and round the bases in fine
style, closely followed by another throng doing similar honors to Bedlow and Goldthwaite, picked up
together and transported side by side, each with an
arm round the other's neck.

Horace has reined in his horses in order to give
a satisfactory view of the ovation, which is so de-
monstrative and engrossing that the ten minutes'
grace before supper would more than have slipped
away had not Dr. Meredith and two or three of the
masters interfered in time to send every one off to
his room just before the second bell rings.

It is pealing with a will when Jack and Haseltine
alight and stand hesitating on the steps of Granger
Hall, — which is the name of the old schoolhouse,
— uncertain for a moment what to do. The en-

trance, in front of which Horace has drawn up his horses, is on the hither side of that where the Doctor was congratulating the nine a few minutes ago, and leads into the domain of Betty Martin, as the housekeeper is called, who has charge of the domestic management of the whole institution, with headquarters at Granger. This is her wing, flanked by the great dining-hall where the whole school breakfasts and dines and sups together. The other wing is devoted to the Doctor's private apartments. A few boys still live in the old schoolhouse, — which not so very long ago was dormitory, refectory, and class-room combined in one, — but the mass have been relegated to the three new, roomy dormitories, known, respectively, as Rogers, Fullham, and Dudley, after the benefactors who gave the money to build them.

It is Mrs. Betty Martin herself who appears, smiling, on the threshold to relieve the uncertainty of the two boys. She is portly and motherly in appearance, and wins Jack's heart at once by suggesting supper in the housekeeper's room, and a postponement of an introduction to the Doctor until later. They feel a little weary with their long journey and relish the fresh milk, the honest bread and butter, and the slice of cold beef to which they sit down, immediately after they have dipped their faces in a basin of water under her maternal supervision. Meanwhile the whole school has passed into the main hall, and after a short silence, — which Jack learns by and by marks the blessing asked on the meal by the Doctor, who always eats with the school, — there begins a distant clattering and chattering which is pleasant music in the ears of the two new boys as they sip the hot chocolate which Mrs. Betty has made to warm them. This goes on for nearly half an hour; then follows a momentary creaking and scraping of chairs and shuffling of boots that makes one think a menagerie has got loose, after which there is a rush for the door, which is midway between the Doctor's and Mrs. Betty's entrance, and the school comes trooping out again.

" Scrub one "

" Two "

" Three "

" Four "

" Five "

"Six "

" Seven "

Twice that number of applicants are disporting themselves in the direction of the ball ground, which, though reserved at other hours for the work of one of the regular nines, is free after supper to the first comers. There is room on its ample surface for several games of scrub, and as the tide of would-be players increases, the adjacent foot-ball ground is usurped by some who prefer knock up, two or three big fellows sending up sky scrapers for the benefit of the many scattered over the field. A few pass ball, and, though it is not the season for foot-ball, there are always boys so fond of it as to like to keep their hands, or more properly their feet, in at all times of the year. A half dozen of these practice kicking goals over the two bars which mark either end of the foot-ball field. Although so soon after supper, a couple of boys, who look as if they were cut out for runners, appear in tights and start around the running track on time. On the terraces in front of the various halls, a number more leisurely inclined indulge in ring-taw and various other games of marbles, which

make Jack think of his agates and wonder if Haseltine has not, in their possession, the best of the
bargain.

All this is visible from Mrs. Betty's threshold,
where the two boys establish themselves after supper while waiting for the Doctor to send for them.
Now and then small urchins — favorites of Mrs.
Betty — slip past them in search of a cooky, or a
taste of jam, relying on the good-nature of the
buxom housekeeper, which is not altogether to be
counted on, however, for if for any reason the pe-
titioner does not happen to suit her he gets sent
about his business in a most summary manner and
has to slink out again empty-handed. It is a lovely
evening with a promise of summer in the atmos-
phere, so enticing that the Doctor's wife is giving
her baby an airing prior to putting him in his
crib, while her other child, a pretty girl of five, is
skipping about before their door like a young
gazelle. Close at hand stands the Doctor, watching
contentedly the sports which nightfall must soon
bring to a close, smoking his cigar, and chatting
to some of the masters and boys. When a more
than usually good bit of play on the ball field

takes his eye, he claps vigorously and cries, "Played, Longworth," "Well played indeed, Henshaw," with genuine enthusiasm; and once when the ball is knocked so vigorously that it runs out of bounds and along the terrace up to the Doctor's very feet, he picks it up and sends it back again in a style that reveals abundance of muscle and a physique second to none which any one of those whose master, guide, and friend he is can boast.

It seems to Jack, whose ideas of masters are not rosy, so to speak, wonderful that the boys and Dr. Meredith are on such evidently familiar terms, suggesting an absence of awe on one side and the existence of an almost fatherly interest on the other. To joke with the teacher of one's Latin lessons would have struck him an hour ago as akin to merriment in church, or at a funeral; and yet right before his eyes is a state of things which startles his preconceived notions most effectually and makes him rub his eyes, especially when the head of the school so far abates his dignity as to pass ball with a wren of a boy no bigger than Jack himself. Albeit a great weight is removed from his heart, he looks on puzzled and bewildered, half expecting to hear at any moment the thundering tone of authority assert itself and prove what he sees to be only a deceitful lull in the conventional relations between masters and pupils.

But the only voice of authority which makes itself heard, scattering masters and pupils alike, is the bell in the chapel tower, that breaks in presently on the scene, but scarcely too soon, for the twilight is at hand. It is time to go to the schoolrooms for an hour before the day's work is over. Thither the boys flock, and a few moments later Jack and Haseltine are informed that the Doctor is ready to see them in his study.

Jack's heart is sinking as he walks along the corridor, but he keeps before his mind's eye the picture which he has just seen, in refutation of his fears. He knocks timidly, and in response to a cheery " Come in " enters. It is a spacious yet cosy room, a veritable study with books lining the walls and scattered over the centre table, but bright too with photographs on the mantelpiece, below which a wood fire is sputtering and snapping gaily on the hearth, and pictures, busts, and bric-à-brac betokening that a woman's taste has helped to decorate it.

"This must be Hall; am I right? How d'y do, Hall? How d'y do, Haseltine? Glad to see you both." So exclaims the Doctor, rising to greet the two timid youths, speaking so pleasantly, and giving them each so hearty a grip of the hand, that they are kindled in spite of themselves and lift their gaze to his.

How shall I describe the head master of Utopia School? A man in the prime of life, not quite forty, tall, stalwart, and commanding, with a sunny smile but firm mouth, piercing eyes before which a sneak or liar might well quail, yet in which the sincere, manly boy, the forlorn or puzzled boy, or even the mischievous, disobedient boy who owns his fault, might find the sympathy, encouragement, or mercy which he needs. One sees at a glance, which requires no discrimination, that there is nothing small or petty about him, nothing of the pedant, the martinet, or the ceremonious prig. It is, perhaps, beyond the imagination of boys so full of misgivings as Jack and Haseltine, to appreciate all this at once, but their awe gives way to surprise and their tongues are gradually loosened under the influence of his reassuring words of inquiry in re-

gard to their journey, their families, and their past
lives, in the course of which his wife comes in and
perfects the welcome by her sweet voice. Haseltine is the first to thaw, amusing them all by his
quaint frankness, which includes a confession of
Jack's and his experiences in the line of prize
packages, at the mention of which the Doctor looks
a trifle grave, but forbears for the present to utter
a deprecating word, deeming, without doubt, that
to check the boy in his first confidences might work
far worse results than could possibly follow from
the failure on his own part to point a moral. Haseltine goes on to tell of their barter and exhibits
triumphantly the two agates, with the exclamation, " Which of us, do you think, got the best of
the swap, Dr. Meredith ? "

This frankness amuses them all ; and the Doctor
asks Jack to let them see the snake, which he pro-
duces shyly. The little reptile vindicates — at least
in his owner's eyes — the wisdom of the trade
by a fine display of his wriggling powers ; after
which (the Doctor having chosen to abstain from
any expression of opinion as to whether he would
rather be in Jack's shoes or Haseltine's) the con-

versation goes on easily for a few minutes. The Doctor's wife, who regards Jack very kindly, perhaps because he seems less at ease than his more forward companion, questions him about his home and his mother, and makes him promise that if he feels lonely he will come to her and let her know; all of which is so contrary to what Jack had expected that he could almost cry with pleasure. As for Haseltine, his relief is so great that he prattles on like a mill-stream, to the evident entertainment of his listeners, relating naively his impressions of his long journey from the West, and his views of life in general, including his intention to adopt base-ball as a profession when he grows up; an announcement which causes Mrs. Meredith to put her handkerchief to her mouth to avoid laughing outright. But it is no laughing matter to Haseltine, who believes every word he is saying, and who proceeds to describe with enthusiasm the exploits of the Rising Suns, and the standing of the various players composing that formidable nine.

"Base-ball is a fine game, and I don't wish to speak a word against it," says the Doctor, when he sees a fair chance to get in a word. "I dare say

IN THE DOCTOR'S STUDY.

that you will be a great acquisition to our nine,
in course of time, Haseltine, and you too, Hall,
though you tell me that your specialty is foot-
ball. That's a fine game, too. You boys will have
plenty of chance to consider the matter during
the next six years, but I rather think that you
will come to the conclusion, before you leave us,
Haseltine, that you would prefer to be in Congress, or the manager of a railroad, or a merchant,
or a lawyer, than a professional base-ball player."

There was a pleasant twinkle in the Doctor's eye
as he paused, but though Jack felt that his master's prophecy might, perhaps, come true, Haseltine shook his head doubtfully.

"Both you little fellows are tired with so much
travel, I know," the Doctor went on, a shade more
seriously, "and I am going to send you off to bed
without much good advice. I shall take it for
granted that both of you are good boys, and anxious to obey the rules. You'll be told what they
are to-morrow, when I decide upon the classes you
are to belong to. And now, before you go, I desire
to say just two things: the first of which is, that I
wish to impress upon you at the start to avoid

falsehood and deceit. There are times when most
boys are tempted to lie; when those times come,
be brave and speak the truth, for, believe me, there
is no vice more cowardly and degrading to the character than any form of falsehood. It is mean,
contemptible, and unworthy of men. The principle of this school is self-government; my desire
is, as far as possible, to let the scholars govern themselves; I trust to their honor largely, and I look to
see that trust respected."

Jack is listening with all his ears; the room
seems very still, and the Doctor's wife is looking
gravely at the carpet.

" The other is this," — the Doctor glanced especially at Haseltine, though what he is about to
say is every whit as applicable to Jack's needs, if
he did but know it, — "I believe enthusiastically
in all manly sports, and do my best to encourage a
taste for them in the school; but let me remind you
that what you have been sent here for is not to become good cricketers, oarsmen, foot-ball kickers, or
even " — here he smiled kindly — " base-ball players. To desire to be proficient in any or all of these
games is a laudable ambition, but I pity heartily

the boy who, during his stay here, thinks of nothing else ; and I grieve to say there are a few who do. Sport is an incident, not an aim of life, even of a boy's life. You have been sent here to learn to become high-minded, upright gentlemen, with lofty aims and sterling good sense in the first place ; in the second, — and without this the first can never be completely realized, — to acquire a good education by means of faithful study. Intelligent scholarship is the promoter of many virtues and the key to success in after-life. Do you understand me, boys ? " he asks, at the conclusion of these impressively spoken words.

" Yes, sir," the two lads murmur, in faint succession.

" Then I will hand you over to Mrs. Martin, who will show you to your dormitories," he says, touching the bell. " Hall and Haseltine, I hope you will each regard me as one of your warmest friends, and never hesitate to ask my advice or assistance, if at any time you are in need of either." ·

" Nor mine," adds his wife, drawing Jack to her and kissing him on the cheek, which cheers him mightily.

"You must be good friends together, too," continues the Doctor, looking from one to the other. "Far East and far West! Remember we are all one nation, and that no part of it can get on without another."

While, as a consequence of this recommendation, the two boys are exchanging smiles, which, though somewhat sheepish, express cordial good-will, Mrs. Betty arrives, under whose guidance they take their departure, after Mrs. Meredith has impartially bestowed a kiss on Haseltine also, and the Doctor has shaken them both by the hand in his hearty fashion. They pass out of the old schoolhouse across the quadrangle to Fullham Hall, where Mrs. Betty tells them they are to be lodged. A short climb upstairs and a turn or two through a corridor brings them to a spacious apartment running half the length of the building, with rows on either side from one end to the other of what seem to Jack, at first glance, like stalls in a stable. The partitions dividing these stalls — which a second glance proves to be sleeping-rooms large enough to contain a bed, a bureau, and a row of nails for clothing — rise but ten or a dozen feet. The ceiling is far above; two lines of windows let in abundance of light, and one has only to breathe the cool air to feel sure that care has been taken to make the ventilation all it should be. At the end which they enter is the comfortable-looking study of one of the masters, into which they get a peep as the housekeeper calls him to his door to introduce her charges to him. They are to be quartered nearly opposite to one another on different sides of the dormitory. Their trunks have already been brought up and placed at the foot of their beds, which have a neat and comfortable appearance. There would be just room inside to swing a cat, if one should so feel inclined, and it is easy to see that there can be no difficulty in producing the effect of great cosiness by an artistic arrangement of photographs and knick-knacks. Jack looks into several of the little rooms and is charmed at the taste and cleverness displayed in this respect.

It is not quite bedtime, but a few of the little boys, tired out doubtless by the excitement of the match, are already tucked up for the night, or, partly undressed, are flitting between the dormitory and the wash-room, into which Jack and Has-

eltine are next ushered to be shown the excellent
bathing arrangements.   Each pupil has his separate set-bowl and soap and towels, and there is a
liberal number of bath-rooms, in some of which a
fine splashing is going on.   At the doors of two of
these, Mr. Sawyer, the dormitory master, who has,
perhaps, made the arrival of the new-comers an excuse for an unlooked-for tour of inspection, knocks
sharply, exclaiming, "Time's up, Rogers. Been in
that tub long enough, Dickson;" in response to
which, two watery faces peep out in respectful ex-
postulation.

But now the chapel bell rings again, this time
for prayers, to be followed by a dismissal of all
but the oldest boys to slumber. Mr. Sawyer has
to go, but Mrs. Betty remains to see Jack and
Haseltine snugly established in bed, where Jack is
very happy to be, partly because he is very tired,
and partly because the hints on the subject of Jack
Spratt and his Wife, thrown out by Horace Hosmer, have filled his mind with grim forebodings.
He reflects that if he can conceal himself from
public view, he may yet be spared from torture
for another twenty-four hours, and makes haste
accordingly.

Mrs. Betty has taken her departure only just before the boys who share this dormitory come trooping in, making a din which puts sleep, for the moment, quite out of Jack's head. It seems that fifteen minutes are allowed to undress, after which the lights are put out, all talking is forbidden, and any one caught in another's room is liable to punishment. The master at one end, and one of the prefects — who are certain of the older boys clothed with a share of authority — at the other, keep a lookout for whispering or unlawful expeditions. By degrees the tumult dies away, but before it has wholly come to an end both Jack and Haseltine have ceased to notice it. The assurance, in answer to an inquiry hazarded by Haseltine at the last moment of Mrs. Betty, who must have wondered at the question, that Jack Spratt and his Wife sleep in another dormitory, has done much to tranquilize them. Though each listens intently in trepidation for some minutes, weariness gets the better alike of fear and curiosity so soon, that Mr. Sawyer, who draws aside their curtains to see that they are all right before the watchman on his rounds puts out the light, is satisfied that they are fast asleep. And so they are.

CHAPTER VI.

FIRST IMPRESSIONS.

How many of the fathers of the boys who are reading this story look back on their school days with any great degree of satisfaction as concerns the time spent in the schoolroom? Not a large number, it is safe to assert, if the truth were known. You young fellows do not appreciate your advantages, or, at least, you have small comprehension of what lessons and masters were like twenty and thirty years ago. Not that we were badly treated, in one sense. Even then floggings were in tolerable disrepute; the birch was practically discarded, and if the ferule was employed with some frequency in extreme cases, its popularity as an educator was on the wane. Our teachers, though rarely genial, intended to be just, and though strict were not harsh. Stiffness and constraint were still deemed essential to secure decorum, but the czar-like despotism which made the pedagogues of former generations terrible had passed away.

On the other hand, we were one and all mere machines for the acquisition of so much Latin, Greek, and mathematics; machines, of which some ran faster than others and with a certain show of brilliancy, but the best of which did their work in the mechanical, unintelligent way that machines invariably do. Most education then was a grand system of memorizing, of getting by rote whole pages of Latin grammar, and other subjects, so as to be able to spin them off as fast as the tongue could move without hesitation or mistake. If you made either, and were ambitious, it meant disaster, for there was always some slick-haired, pale-faced lad on the watch to pick you up anywhere and put you down a peg in the class as a consequence. What feats of marvelous mechanism in this line were daily performed with the dry bones of " Andrews & Stoddard's " and " Baird's Classical Manual " ! Ask your father, any one of you, if he can repeat that memory-confounding list of adjectives which have no superlatives. There are twenty-eight of them, beginning with "*adolescens adolescentior* young, *agrestis agrestior* rustic." If he cannot, there was a time when he could, and when — at

least if he were what was called in those days a
good scholar — he could rattle off, besides, the
twenty-six prepositions governing the accusative
and the nouns of the third declension with either
e or *i* in the ablative, not forgetting at the same
time that "*occiput* has only *i, rus* has either *e* or *i,*
but *rure* commonly signifies 'from the country'
and *ruri* 'in the country'; *mel* has rarely *i.*"

We were expected to divine, apparently, for few
hints were given us of the beauties of Cæsar and
Virgil and Ovid, of the Anabasis and the Iliad, of
the manners, thoughts, and customs of the Greeks
and Romans, and the relations of the classic tongues
to ours. But every one of us was expected, when
the master gave out from that gloomy little com-
pilation on ancient geography, "Baird's Classical
Manual," *Sybaris* for instance, to be able, if called
upon, to answer like a flash: "Proverbial for the
luxury of its inhabitants;" and then to continue in
sequence: "*Thurii* founded by the Athenians B.
C. 443, with whom were Herodotus and Lysias the
orator. In the west also, on the coast *Elĕa, Helĭa,*
or *Velĭa,* the birthplace of Zeno and Parmenides,
the founders of the Eleatic School of Philosophy;"

and so on until bidden to stop. It is no exaggeration to state that there were boys who, if started at any point in its sixty closely printed pages, could recite to the end without slip or falter, and yet who had no further knowledge concerning the places or individuals enumerated than was contained in the brief paragraphs of which those just cited are prolix examples.

It may have been noticed by the parents, if not by the boys who have followed Jack's experiences up to this point, that very little has been said on the subject of his lessons, and that consideration has been mainly given to his sports, his snow-ball fights, his mischief-making, and what he did in general outside the schoolroom.

Let us look the matter squarely in the face and acknowledge that the least said regarding his schooling before he went to Utopia the better. But in justice to the masters who had to undergo the discouragement of seeing their efforts to make him learn prove of no avail, it should be stated that the fault lay neither in them nor seriously in their system of teaching. Already the theory of cultivating the memory alone at the expense of the

other faculties had fallen into disrepute in the public schools of his native city, and was being sup-
planted by methods calculated to make boys and
girls think for themselves instead of developing
into mere machines. But it is to be feared that up
to this time the advantages of living in an enlight-
ened age had been lost upon our hero, if the interest he took in his daily tasks be regarded as evidence. To tell the truth, he had been incorrigibly
idle; his thoughts rarely kept themselves fixed for
five minutes at a time on any branch of knowledge
disassociated with the Frog Pond, Ma'am Horn,
Joe Herring, or some one or other of the interesting localities or personages whose acquaintance we
have already made. It had always been a moment
of supreme happiness to him when the bell sounded,
announcing that he was at liberty to pitch his
dog's-eared, pencil-marked books into his desk and
to depart for the day, and the hours preceding that
welcome summons were too apt to drag heavily
unless relieved by oases of mischief. It is no easy
task, be the master ever so conscientious, to engage
the interest of those boys in a large class who count
the school hours in much the same spirit that a

prisoner counts the weeks which must elapse before he is free. To one fond of his calling and ambitious to have his pupils shine, the good scholars must inevitably commend themselves, and he is only too likely to let the rag, tag, and bobtail shift for themselves, feeling, doubtless, that time and energy spent in endeavoring to make them fond of their books cannot fail to be wasted. It was to the rag, tag, and bobtail emphatically that Jack had belonged. With three or four other boys, among whom was the ever faithful Dubsy, he had disputed the doubtful distinction of being at the foot of his class, and the monthly reports which he had brought home to his mother were monotonous in their uniform lack of excellence.

It will, therefore, be seen that the good advice, regarding the purpose for which he had been sent to Utopia, delivered by Dr. Meredith on that first evening, was peculiarly adapted to Jack's needs, and should have sunk deep into his heart. But just as one swallow will not make a summer, a single homily will rarely suffice to change an idle boy into an industrious one. If the truth must be told, there is reason to doubt whether Jack gave

that part of the Doctor's lecture — although it impressed him greatly for a moment, I dare say, and
made him inwardly resolve to be very diligent for
the future — a second thought after he went away
under the wing of Mrs. Betty.   And if he neglected
to consider the matter further that night, he certainly did not think much about it in the morning,
when, having escaped molestation from Jack Spratt
and his wife, he awoke and found himself face to
face with, and fairly entranced by, the great school
world.   No wonder that the master who examined
the pair after breakfast, with a view to discovering
their acquirements, held up his hands in horror
upon making his report to Dr. Meredith, and observed, pathetically, that he was at a loss to decide
which of the two had made the worse showing.

"They both seemed bright boys when I saw
them last night," answered the Doctor.

"Oh, they're bright enough," said Mr. Percy.
"I judge, however, that neither of them has ever
been made to study."

"Then we shall have to begin at first principles,"
was the reply.

Accordingly Jack and Haseltine were enrolled

in the lowest of the six classes into which the school was divided, but in the first of the two divisions composing the class. As they were not to take their places until the following morning, they were free for the rest of the day to look about them. They were left pretty much to their own devices during the forenoon, for until half an hour before dinner time the whole school was busy with recitations and study. So they improved their opportunities, to begin with, by wandering around the large quadrangle, peering up at the buildings, stepping for a moment into the chapel, where they admired, with bated breath, the carving and the stained-glass windows, and bringing up finally at the gymnasium. Here they spent some time in the inspection of the bars, weights, rowing-machines, and other apparatus, the use of which was explained very kindly by the superintendent, Dr. Bolles, who introduced himself to them, and who, at the close of his instructions, invited them into his private office that he might take their measurements. After they had stripped themselves to the skin, Dr. Bolles — having entered their names, age, and birthplace in a large ledger, a separate page

of which was devoted to every boy in the school —
proceeded to tap their bodies and to listen to their
lungs and hearts, in a very attentive manner.
Then he weighed them, ascertained their height,
and the number of inches they measured round the
chest, forearm, biceps, hips, and calves.

Haseltine, who was the first to go through the
ordeal, looked a bit lanky, stripped, and somewhat
flat-chested. There was not much flesh on his
bones, as was apparent from the manner in which
his ribs stuck out.

"You must learn to hold yourself up straight,
and not to stoop, Haseltine," said the superintendent, scrutinizing him critically. "You'll become
round-shouldered if you don't have a care. You
should use the upright bars every day. Appetite
good?"

"First rate," answered Haseltine, looking rather
crestfallen at this depreciation of his physique.

"Food runs to muscle, then. No spare flesh
here," he observed, passing his hand over the little
fellow's frame. "Pretty wiry. Sound as a trivet;
but those chest-muscles need strengthening; we
must build you out. Good arm, very good," he

added, as Haseltine doubled up his biceps with a smile of conscious pride. " Base-ball, I suppose; yes, out of all proportion to the left; I thought so. Ever been examined before?" Haseltine shook his head. "I suppose not. You've come here just in time. We'll make a man of you yet. Now Hall."

Jack was all of a tremble. In the first place, the stethoscope business was rather alarming and suggested all sorts of possibilities in the way of broken wind and heart-disease, and then he did not relish at all being picked to pieces before Haseltine. He wondered whether he looked equally scraggy, and derived his first ray of consolation from the complimentary expression of Dr. Bolles' eye, as the superintendent (after taking several measurements in silence) stood off and surveyed him with evident complacency.

"Ah, Carlisle, good morning," Dr. Bolles exclaimed to a delicate appearing boy who had just entered the office. " There's a good all round fellow for you to model yourself on. No dyspepsia in him. He does n't know what nerves mean. If you don't grow up into a healthy, well-formed man," he continued to Jack, "it 'll be your own fault. You 've got a good start; you can't be a Hercules, there 's not enough of you for that, but you 're cut out for health if you take care of yourself. You 've been looked after at home, evidently. That 's all."

Jack put on his clothes again, feeling proud as a peacock, and entirely reconciled to the fact that Haseltine's biceps was bigger than his own. The boy addressed as Carlisle, who was sauntering about in the office quite at his ease, gave Jack and Haseltine a critical glance from his handsome dark eyes, and then examined for a few moments the doctor's entries in the ledger regarding them. He was a striking-looking lad, with an intelligent and at the same time attractive expression, and though he was slight and evidently far from robust, there was nothing effeminate either in his appearance or manner.

"How are you, to-day?" Dr. Bolles inquired of him.

"Oh, I 'm better; I feel like a fighting-cock," was the reply.

"You look better. But now, my dear boy, pray

give yourself a chance. You can't do everything,
— be a ball-player, good oar, crack sprinter, and
the head of your class, all at the same time, with
your present physique, and keep well. Hall and
Haseltine," the superintendent added, " let me
make you acquainted with Louis Carlisle, our
champion short-distance runner, and poet laureate.
He has been in the infirmary for the past fortnight
because he wouldn't take care of himself. I dare
say that if you two boys are so inclined, he will
stroll with you up to the lake to show you the
boat-houses and enlighten you a little as to how
we live at Utopia."

" I shall be very glad, I'm sure," answered Carlisle politely. " The walk will do me good."

He was half a head taller than either Jack or
Haseltine, and evidently two years their senior.
In a tone not unduly patronizing he proceeded to
make a running commentary on what they saw, as
they accompanied him a few minutes later on the
projected tour of investigation.

" What dormitory are you in?" he inquired at
the start.

" Fullham," said Jack.

"That's mine, too. I'm to go back in a day or two. It's dreadfully lonely in the infirmary when no one else is sick. I caught cold after winning the hundred-yard dash, and Dr. Bolles says I was threatened with typhoid. There's the infirmary," he added, pointing to a good-sized cottage in the field behind Granger Hall. "You can just see it. Every one who is sick is sent there. A year ago there were eighteen cases of measles at the same time. Can either of you leg it any?" he inquired, eying them each in turn with a scientific air.

"I used to run pretty fast at prisoner's base," said Jack.

"I've practiced stealing second a good deal," replied Haseltine.

"There's the track," continued Carlisle, indicating the flagged half-mile course which surrounded the foot-ball field. "Like to see it near to?"

The boys assented and followed their guide over the terrace for a few yards, until they came to a kind of stand not unlike a witness-box, to which they ascended. "Here's where the judges sit and where we finish," he said. "We have athletic sports, that is, running and jumping, and all that sort of thing, twice a year, once in the spring and once in the autumn. The spring meeting comes off in about a month. The hundred-yard dash, which I won, was an extra match got up by the backers of Coleman, Junior. His brother, Coleman, Senior, who went to Harvard last year, was champion of the school for three years, and he is trying to follow in his brother's footsteps."

" Were' you ever licked?" asked Jack, looking up in the crack runner's face with respectful admiration.

"Oh yes, often. Coleman, Senior, licked me right along until the last time, when I beat the school record. I dare say Jessup 'll make it warm for me before long. He 's only in the fifth, but I 'd almost back him to-day against Coleman, Junior. Are you both in the sixth?"

The boys nodded.

" I 'm in the third; quite a patriarch, you see. There 's no reason why both of you should n't make good sprinters if you give your minds to it."

This prophecy sounded agreeable to Jack and Haseltine as they trotted along, one on either side of him, on their way to the lake, passing out of the quadrangle through the same arched portal by which they had entered it the night before, and so over the base-ball practice field to the main road, from which Carlisle presently diverged to take a cut across the meadows. He explained to them, among other things, that every one had to be inside the quadrangle at the close of the curfew, as the supper-bell at half-past six was called, on pain of an interview with Dr. Meredith.

" Are you on the nine ? " inquired Haseltine, who had been burning to ask the question.

" Not on the school nine. I was on the dormitory nine, but I 've decided not to play this year. I 'm trying not to spread my butter too thin, as Dr. Bolles calls it. He thinks I do too many things," he added by way of explanation. " You know each of the dormitories has its separate nine and football team, and there 's great rivalry between them. Fullham beat Dudley the first match of the season last Saturday, and plays Rogers this afternoon."

This announcement was very interesting. Before they reached the lake, Carlisle had also informed them that there was a cricket eleven, a weekly newspaper called " The Utopian," of which he was one of the editors, a glee club, and four eight-oared crews, — the Atalantas, Orions, Nimrods, and Mohicans. " There are, besides, ten single-scull shells and several pair oars," he said, leading the way into one of the two tastefully built boat-houses, perched side by side on the bank of the broad lake, each with a covered piazza in front.

The main space in the centre, as they entered, was filled by the eight-oared racing-boats, the sight of which lying side by side delighted and almost awed Jack, who had never examined anything of the sort, and who straightway made the resolution that, no matter what else he did or did not do at Utopia, he would go in for rowing. He had often heard his mother tell that his father had been a famous oar in his day, and he himself was entirely at home in a dory, and able, in his own opinion, already to scull nearly if not quite as well as the fishermen at Nahant and Swampscott, whose companion he was wont to be in the summer time on their expeditions after cod and haddock. He had often wished to look at a paper shell near to, and now his ambition was gratified. There were rests on each side of the building, reaching nearly to the ceiling, along which the small boats were arranged in tiers, and in one corner was a snug little room hung with flags, and photographs of winning crews and crack oarsmen, and furnished with a round table and chairs, where, Carlisle said, the meetings of the club were held. In the adjoining boat-house were more boats, including an eight-oared barge, of which, as Carlisle told them, Mrs. Meredith was the coxswain whenever she was willing to go out on the lake.

"It's great fun here a little later in the season," observed their guide as they sat down to rest on the piazza after everything had been inspected. "On a pleasant, still afternoon there are sometimes more than twenty boats out, of one kind and another."

"Who's the fastest rower?" asked Jack.

"The Doctor is the crack single sculler."

"The Doctor? Does he row?"

"Oh, yes, indeed. He came pretty near being beaten, though, last year. Whitehead crawled up on him so that there was n't more than half a length between them at the finish. You never saw such excitement."

"Was n't he mad?" inquired Jack, to whom

the idea of a master being beaten by one of his scholars seemed most extraordinary.

"Who, the Doctor? Not a bit of it; he's a true sport," said Carlisle. "There was no one more pleased than he at being forced to pull for all he was worth."

Further inquiry revealed that the Atalantas were for the time being the champion of the eight-oared crews; and after a score more questions, which Carlisle answered most good-naturedly, the boys retraced their footsteps so as to get back in time for dinner. Seeing that their mentor was so well disposed, Jack took occasion on the way to impart a little of what Horace Hosmer had dropped regarding Jack Spratt and his Wife, which Carlisle listened to at first with no other comment than an occasional sidelong glance, which struck them as far from reassuring. Once Carlisle started to speak, but some impediment in his throat checking him, he seemed to change his mind, until Haseltine's remark that they were fortunate in being in a different dormitory from the formidable pair drew out the laconic observation, "That won't help you much."

"Why?" asked Jack.

"Those fellows are all over the lot," was the answer. "They 'd think nothing of snaking a new boy out of bed in the small hours of the morning, no matter where he was."

"But I wonder the Doctor allows it," said Haseltine, hoping for a more satisfactory response to this exclamation than it had elicited from Horace.

"Who 's to tell him?" cried Carlisle sternly, looking straight at the offender. "You boys may count on one thing, and that is that tale-bearing does n't go down at Utopia. Any fellow who told tales here would be hustled out of the school, and the Doctor 'd be the first to avoid him."

The decision with which these words were spoken caused Jack and Haseltine to hang their heads guiltily, and presumably to reflect that the couplet—

> " Tell-tale tit,
>   Your tongue shall be slit,
>   And all the dogs in the town
>   Shall have a little bit,"

formed a no less important part of the code of youth than of childhood.

" It 's hard on new boys, I admit," continued
Carlisle, after a moment, in a contemplative tone,
"and if those fellows keep on in their cruel ways
they 'll kill somebody next."

" Horace Hosmer told us they did kill two boys
last term," said Jack, in a stage whisper.

"Yes," exclaimed Haseltine; "it was reported
to be chicken-pox, but he says he helped to lay
them out·after they were dead, and they were a
mass of bruises from the crown of the head to the
soles of the feet."

Carlisle looked very grave and nodded his head
with an ominous air. "I did n't suppose Horace
knew about it," he said; " it was kept very dark."

" Then you knew of it?" asked Jack.

" Bless you, yes. It ought to have taught Tobey
and Donaldson a lesson," Carlisle added gloomily,
" but it did n't. They 're just as bad as ever, this
term."

" What is the best thing to do if — if they should
ever happen to fix on us?" asked Jack presently,
with a slight gulp.

Carlisle whistled reflectively. "I 'll be doggoned
if I know," he replied at last. "I 'd keep a stiff

upper lip, if I were you, and be as sandy as you can. They 'll let you off easily, perhaps, if they see you 've got grit; but if you funk, I would n't give much for your chances of getting through with a whole skin. I 'll say a good word for you in advance. It may save you a broken leg or arm."

After the delivery of this speech, Carlisle indulged in a short, hysterical laugh, which seemed to his listeners quite out of keeping with their own feelings. But it was evidently a mere spasmodic expression of sympathy, for his countenance immediately regained the expression of deep gloom which it had worn ever since the subject of Spratt and his Wife had been introduced.

"Thank you very much indeed," answered each of the boys in turn.

"Not at all — not at all. I fear that my words cannot avail you much," he responded.

They were now within school bounds again, and there was only just time to go to their rooms before dinner. Carlisle, in keeping with his previous kindness, announced that as it might be advisable to say what he had to say to Tobey and Donaldson at once, he would take his dinner with the school.

Accordingly, assuring the boys that he felt well enough for this exertion, he started off at a lively jog for the infirmary so as to be on hand.

Jack and Haseltine had been given provisional seats at breakfast, but Mrs. Betty, who presided over the younger boys, now assigned them to places not far from one another at her own table. It was an impressive moment, and one could have heard a pin drop while the Doctor asked a blessing in his clear, manly tones on the repast spread for his two hundred hungry pupils, who stood behind their chairs in long lines up and down the big hall waiting for the signal to fall to, which they did with a vengeance you may be sure, when they got it. Dr. Meredith and his wife, the married masters, and a few of the prefects occupied a table on a platform at one end of the room at right angles with the others and overlooking them all. There was a master at the end of each, who did the carving and kept good order.

The dinner was simple but extremely good. A clear, honest soup well flavored with vegetables; ribs of roast beef carefully basted and neither done to death nor so distressingly blue as some cooks are capable of sending it up from the kitchen; potatoes, tomatoes, macaroni, light bread, sweet butter, and for dessert a cup of baked custard invitingly served. Everything was clean and neat, thanks to the vigilant eye of Mrs. Betty and her assistants, and thanks, first of all, to the founders of Utopia, who laid it down as one of the principles of the school that so everything must be. No extravagance, no rich dishes, no wine or beer, but plenty of blood-making, sinew-strengthening, bone-building food, fresh, appetizing, and unspoiled.

I have seen school tables, and between you and me private tables also, at which such a dinner as that just described was made thoroughly unpalatable by the manner in which it was prepared; where the soup was a thin, unseasoned, straw-colored fluid, the beef ruined by one of the extremes of cooking already referred to, the vegetables greasy, the bread clammy, the butter rancid, and the cup of custard pale and watery. There are persons who do not think such matters worth considering, who believe that any time devoted to making our daily repasts savory is misspent, and that young people, boys in particular, should eat what is set before them without asking questions, thankful that there is anything to eat at all.

It is easy to perceive that such doctrines are thoroughly pernicious and unsound, if you reflect that our capabilities as men and women are chiefly dependent on what our bodies permit us to be, and that the component parts of these bodies are determined in the main by the food we eat, the air we breathe, the clothing we wear, and the sleep we get. There is no greater mistake in the world than to disregard the laws of health under the plea that they are not worthy of notice; and if they are thus important for those of us who are grown up to bear in mind as essential to human wellbeing, how much more vital is it that the young should be given every opportunity to fit themselves physically for the battle of life. Bear this in mind, boys, and when you are served with slovenly, unwholesome cookery, protest with all your might. Do not be ashamed to know and recognize good things to eat. The temperate enjoyment of the pleasures of the table is a legitimate and important element of happiness.

Meanwhile our young friend, Jack Hall, has

been enjoying his dinner mightily, though it is no
better, in truth, than what he has been accustomed to at home, which is not surprising if we
recall the double devotion of his mother and the
faithful Hannah, whose hearts are doubtless pretty
sore at this time. When his hunger is somewhat
appeased he ventures to gaze about him a little,
exchanging a few shy words with the boys near
him, all of whom seem friendly and willing to receive him as a companion. He makes the acquaintance of Buck on one side of him, Horton on the
other, and Travers, Bailey, and Cunningham across
the table. Horton, who is a plump, talkative little
chap of his own size, points out to him the various
school celebrities, including Ramsay, Bedloe, and
Goldthwaite of the nine ; Burbank, the stalwart,
bearded captain of the fifteen ; and little, active-
looking Bobby Crosby, who, as Jack knows, is
expected to take Burbank's place next year ; Hazelhurst, the stroke of the Atalantas and champion
oar of the school (always excepting the invincible
Doctor) now that Whitehead has graduated ; and
Carlisle, who nods across the room in a friendly
manner from his seat with the big second-class

boys, so that Horton asks with interest, " Do you know him ? "

" I was introduced to him this morning at the gymnasium," replies Jack. " He showed Haseltine and me to the boat-houses."

" He 's the smartest boy at Utopia, — first rate at games, head of his class, and champion sprinter. There 's Coleman, Junior, sitting with the third next to Jumbo, — his real name 's Blair, but every one calls him Jumbo because he 's so fat, — he can run pretty fast, and it 's neck and neck between him and Jessup, that boy on the right of Mr. Sawyer, but neither of them can catch Carlisle. You ought to hear Jumbo sing; he 's the best tenor we 've got."

Most of this information is not new to Jack, but he is glad to hear the heroes catalogued again at a time when he can take a good peep at them. He feels proud of his acquaintance with Carlisle, and glances from time to time in that direction, for he has not forgotten his senior's promise to speak a good word for him.

" I wonder what 's up at the second form table," says Horton presently. " Some one or other keeps turning round and laughing. There must be a gag on you," he adds, turning to Jack, who has already noticed this tendency on the part of the boys in the vicinity of his benefactor. "Have you done anything fresh?"

"Not that I know of," answers poor Jack, who is feeling far from comfortable.

The dessert is finished, and in another minute dinner will be over. All of a sudden Carlisle gets up, and after saying a word to the master at the head of the table, crosses to one of those occupied by the fourth class, and stoops to speak to two boys sitting side by side, whom Jack recognizes instantly as Tobey and Donaldson, the redoubtable Spratt and Wife. He has not perceived them before, though he has been on the lookout for them, and now that he takes a glance at them they do not strike him as very terrible in appearance. They are good-natured looking enough, but appearances are deceitful in this world, as Jack very well knows, and he quails as he observes the gaze of the trio rest on him and Haseltine alternately. Carlisle's eyes sparkle as he talks, and he keeps his hand to his mouth so that Jack cannot judge much by its expression. Spratt and Wifey listen for a moment or two in judicial silence, then a broad, convulsive smile, which suggests, at least to Jack, the hilarity of a hyena, overspreads the features of each, only to be succeeded by a look of glowing fierceness, which seems to the unhappy lads — for Haseltine is no less conscious of it than Jack — to argue ill for the future. While they are still beneath its spell the school rises from table, and the two boys are swept along to the terrace, where Carlisle presently joins them, but only to draw them aside and whisper the ominous tidings, "I've done my best for you, but they think you look too cocky," an announcement which makes them both feel very miserable.

Just then a big boy, bat in hand, and wearing a large F embroidered on the bosom of his shirt, accosted their mentor with the eager inquiry, — "Won't you help us out, Carlisle? Dobson has a game knee and can't possibly play."

"Wish I could, Chalmers, but I've promised Dr. Bolles to let up on base-ball for the rest of the term. I'm only just out of the infirmary."

"Yes, I know; but it's mighty tough lines on

us to have so many of our best men knocked up. Potts had word this morning that his mother is sick and started for home before dinner, and Plummer bust his finger against the Stars yesterday."

"What's the matter with Cochrane?"

"Oh, Cochrane's no good.   He'll fan himself out every time, cock sure, on Bedloe's pitching. We're hard up for third base, and Cochrane's useless except in the field.   They've got their strongest team," said Chalmers impatiently.

"What is it?" whispered Haseltine to Carlisle.

"Fullham against Rogers."

"I can play third base," continued Haseltine, to Jack's infinite astonishment.

Carlisle laughed gayly.   "Here's your chance, Chalmers," he said.   "This new Fullhamite says he's an artist."

"What's your name?" asked **Chalmers**, scanning Haseltine from top to toe.

"Frank Haseltine."

"Have you played much?"

"I've played third base on the St. Louis Rising Suns for two years."

"Are you in practice?"

"First rate."

There was an assurance about the applicant that evidently impressed Chalmers. " Would you try him ?" he asked Carlisle.

" He talks well."

" Talk is cheap," growled Chalmers. " Well, be on hand, then," he said to Haseltine. " Get into your togs as soon as you can. The game 'll be called in fifteen minutes."

Haseltine looked radiant with delight as the large boy strode away. " Do you think he 'll let me play?" he inquired beseechingly of Carlisle.

"I guess so; he 's captain of the Fullham nine. It 's a big chance for you, youngster, to show what you 're made of. Now run along and get ready."

Jack felt rather envious, but not so much so as not to be thoroughly glad of his friend's good fortune. Indeed, as he sat by while Haseltine got into his flannels, he was very well pleased to think that he was not going to play himself. It was pretty evident from the way Haseltine had spoken of the Rising Suns the day before, that they were a much superior nine to the Massasoits, of which club Jack knew that he had by no means been the strongest player, a conviction which helped to reconcile him to being left out.

CHAPTER VII.

HASELTINE MAKES HIS DÉBUT.

IT has been, and still is, the fashion in certain circles to decry base-ball, and to hold up to the youth of the country the superiority of cricket, as a pastime. The arguments, such as they are, — chief among which is the plea that cricket is a more gentlemanly game, for the reason that one can play it with exceeding comfort after ·leaving school· and college as well or nearly as well as before, — need not be reiterated, inasmuch as there is no longer room for argument. The case is closed. The boys have heard what was to be said on either side, and have come to a final conclusion in regard to the matter. Base-ball is undeniably the national sport from one end of the land to the other, and no amount of chafing on the part of those who think the decision unwise can make the long cherished cricket of our English cousins widely popular on this side of the water. And after all, if we ex-

amine the reasons, the boys are not far out. Be it
said with bated breath and yet clearly and unequivocally, that it requires more skill, far more skill to
excel at base-ball, as it is played to-day, than at
any other sport. Talk of muscle, nerve, wind,
quickness and correctness of eye, fleetness of foot,
temper, bottom, and grit, — what one of these
qualities is not put in training when two closely
matched nines meet to play ball? Try it, gentlemen of England, for yourselves and see. You will
have to come to the conclusion — take my Yankee
word for it — that there is more in our game than
you think; and what is more, you will know in
your hearts, though you will never acknowledge it,
that an all-day cricket match under the trees, relieved by respites for beef and beer and dawdled
the whole time, — for you take things pretty leisurely after every " over," — is a tame affair, though
a very gentlemanly and delightful one, compared
with what we are able to show you under the head
of ball-playing. Don't mistake us, gentlemen of
England: we know that cricket is a grand old
game, we have watched it often (though it is a
trifle dull to watch), played it, too, and we continue

to play it at times, but when you come to talk
about muscle and nerve and temper and bottom
and grit, and all that, as we have said already, we
are ready to back our national game against the
world.

Chalmers and Hackett, the captains of the rival
dormitory teams, are tossing up to see which nine
shall go in first, as the two new boys arrive on the
scene. Fullham wins and sends its opponents to
the bat. "Game called!" cries the umpire, and
Haseltine has just time to throw off his jacket and
get into position at third base before Rainsford,
who is to pitch for the Fullhamites, enters the box.
Rainsford is known as "the kid" because of his
slight appearance. He is only in the fourth, but
his drop balls have proved successful teasers ere
this.

See how every player on the fielding nine has
his nerves taut as Billy Douglas steps to the home
plate to lead off, and poises his bat! They are
boys, of course, — they have not the experience
and sinew of professional or college teams, — but
they are sturdy fellows for all that. They mean
business: so does Billy; there is blood in his eye;
he hopes to start off with a three bagger.

"One ball!" cries the umpire.

"Two balls!"

That won't do, Rainsford; you can't afford to let him get his base on balls. Carefully now.

"One strike!"

Ah, that's better; the kid is settling down to his work. Now another! A hit, a palpable hit! Away scuds Douglas with all the vim of his Scotch forefathers, to get to first before the ball. No use, Billy; Goldthwaite has it at second easy enough and pops it to Maitland, who, as every one knows, is pretty sure to hold on to anything that comes within his reach. A shout goes up from the Full-hamites, who to the number of a score or more, including Jack, are grouped together on one side of the catcher, which is answered by a bracing cheer from a similar posse from the rival dormitory at the other side.

Pousland, the next striker, makes a base hit, but not to much purpose, since Hackett knocks up an easy fly for the kid to absorb without difficulty, and Johnson succumbs on a foul tip to Chalmers catching under the bat in his iron mask and padded gloves with an eye to second which Pousland is hoping to steal. But the third out settles that question, and down goes a goose-egg for Rogers.

The formidable Bedloe is a brawny lad to look at, and he has to back him Bobby Crosby at left field and Harry Ramsay at first, making three of the school nine against only Chalmers and Goldthwaite on the side of Fullham. Chalmers goes to the bat to give his team courage, and sends a sky scraper to centre field which is captured cleverly. The kid falls a prey to an easy grounder to short stop, and it looks as though the innings would pan out poorly for the Fullhamites. But one can count on nothing at base-ball until the last man is out; in testimony to which Hamlen, who comes next in order, is given his base on called balls, steals second by a judicious slide, and is sent to third on a fumble of a hot liner, — a corker, — which Jackson hits to second, getting his base thereby. Then Goldthwaite comes to the bat amid great applause, and some one cries out, " Now for a grass-mower, Goldy ! "

Goldthwaite proves worthy of the confidence reposed in him. Two strikes are called on him while he waits for a ball just in the right place. He gets

it at last, when Bedloe, hoping that the umpire
will call another strike (for until this year you
know three strikes was the limit), eases up and
throws in a slow one. Goldthwaite swipes with all
his might and sends the ball between left and centre field, but clean out of reach of Crosby and
Plympton. A home run ! No, not quite, only a
three bagger. Goldthwaite holds his third, but
Hamlen and Jackson have scored. Two runs to a
goose-egg ; not bad to start with. But there is
Ogden out on a foul and the innings over with
Goldthwaite still on third.

Three innings more on either side do not vary the
lead, for while Rogers gets a run in the third, Fullham caps it with a single in the fourth, and the score
is three to one. No chance now for a complete
whitewash, which some of the enthusiasts among
the lookers-on, encouraged by the start, have hoped
for. On the contrary, the shrewder mind knows
that it will be all Fullham can do to hold her lead.
Rogers has been settling down to work. Bedloe is
in fine form, and is being backed up bravely. They
are getting on to the kid, too, and pound him for a
run and two base hits in the fifth, being prevented

from tying the score only by a magnificent double play of Goldthwaite and Maitland. Then they put the Fullhamites out in one, two, three order.

Haseltine has been doing fairly well, though as yet he has had but two chances in the field, the first of which, a fly, went up a moderate distance and fell so plump into his hands that he did not have to budge. The other, a gently ambling grounder, shot between his legs just as he thought he had it; an error which elicited from Horton, who was sitting beside Jack, the unflattering exclamation, " Beastly butter-fingers ! " However, there is a style and general air of knowingness about him which has attracted attention, and Chalmers has so far continued his own confidence in him as to fling twice to third in order to frighten men who were off their bases, on each of which occasions Haseltine got on to the ball, and once came very near putting the too daring adversary out. He is evidently no green hand, as he has further shown by the way he handles the bat. Though apparently too small to be a very formidable willow-wielder, his first whack sent the ball far to right field, where it was taken into camp very prettily, it must be owned. The second time he got his base on balls, but was put out trying to steal second, in spite of a most admirable slide on his stomach for several feet. The decision of the umpire displeased the crowd of Fullhamites, who manifested their resentment by crying " Not out, not out ! " vociferously, and applauded Haseltine as he came in from the base crestfallen and covered with dust. It had been in the next innings that he muffed the grounder, and he was now feeling very much dissatisfied with himself and eager to wipe out these spots on his record by some brilliant stroke.

The sixth innings adds another goose-egg to each score, in spite of hard hitting on both sides, and the seventh begins amid a hush of suspense. Jack can scarcely sit still, he is so nervous with excitement, and he is hoarse with spelling out at the top of his lungs, after every favorable play, "F-U-L-L-H-A-M ! Fullham ! " which is the dormitory yell. It is anybody's game, as Rainsford, the kid, well knows, and he plants his feet in the box with the air of one aware that the least let-up or carelessness will be fatal. Pousland is at the bat again, and whacks at the first ball. It flies whizzing in Hasel-

tine's direction, but out of reach, and a shout from
the Rogers crowd rends the air. But it is short-
lived, for the umpire, who is watching carefully,
cries, " Foul ball ! " Whereupon Pousland, who is
halfway to first, has to retrace his steps in a mel-
ancholy fashion. Had it but struck just the other
side of the line, it would have been good for two
bags. He poises his bat again viciously.

" One strike," calls Prendergast, the umpire, who
is captain of Dudley.

There is a roar from Fullham, and the striker,
glancing round at the umpire sulkily, strikes the
tip of his bat against the ground and grits his teeth
as he makes ready for another ball.

" Foul, — out ! "

The tick is plainly audible, and Chalmers' gloves
have closed firmly on the ball. Pousland drops his
bat and walks away in disgust. His place is taken
by Hackett, who strikes at the first two balls without hitting either, but sends the third over second
base skimming to centre, where Ogden jumps a little and holds it above his head, — a pretty but not
very difficult catch, whereat the welkin rings.

" Here come Dr. and Mrs. Meredith," says Horton to Jack, as the uproar gradually subsides.

Sure enough, they are close at hand, having come down expressly to see the end of the match, and are given good seats on one of the few benches supplied for such celebrities. Several of the masters have been watching the contest since the beginning, but the presence of the head of the school is evidently a new incentive to every player to good work, if any were still needed.

Johnson is the third man at the bat. Prendergast calls one ball on the kid, and Johnson swipes the next. It somehow or other gets past Goldthwaite, and before Hamlen can field it to Maitland the striker is safe at first. It is now the turn for Rogers to howl, which it does with a vengeance, — " R-O-G-E-R S ! Roger-r-rs ! "

Ferguson is to strike now. He is third base and one of Rogers' heaviest sluggers. Hackett goes down behind first to coach Johnson and tell him when to try to steal second.

" One strike ! "

" One ball ! "

" Two balls ! "

Johnson, meanwhile, is bobbing up and down hesitating whether to run or not. The kid, just as he looks ready to pitch the fourth, turns and makes the gesture of hurling to first.

"Look out!" bawls Hackett, and Johnson rushes back to the base and plumps one foot on it.

There is no need for so much exertion, as it happens, for Rainsford's throw is make-believe. He has only pretended to fling the ball. Whereupon he turns and pitches rapidly.

"Go!" holloas Hackett, excitedly. "Go-o!"

"Three balls!" cries the umpire.

Johnson is scooting for second at the top of his speed. Although the pitch was a trifle wild, the padded gloves are in the right place, and Chalmers slams it to Goldthwaite, who claps it on to Johnson, and holds up his hand claiming an out. But Prendergast, who has run forward nearly to the pitcher's box in order to see distinctly, shakes his head and waves Johnson to hold his base, amid deafening cheers from the Rogerines, and groans from the Fullhamites.

Let me say right here, boys, that the trick of "downing" umpires is cowardly, and smacks of the blackguard. Be careful, to begin with, whom you select to act; but when your choice is made,

be men enough to keep your temper and accept his
decisions without kicking. It has come to be the
fashion among the great crowds that attend base-
ball matches over the country, to abuse umpires in
language worthy only of Billingsgate, and even to
threaten them with personal violence. It is a mean
and contemptible method of bullying a man in a
position where he is powerless to defend himself,
and at a time when he needs to have all his faculties bent on the game, and no gentleman will take
part in it.

Johnson holds his base, and the kid prepares to
pitch again.

" Four balls ! "

Rainsford must be getting nervous.

" Five balls ! "

This will never do.

" Two strikes ! "

Ah, there ! Now or never !

" Six balls ! Take your base."

Ferguson trots leisurely to first, and his place at
the diamond is filled by Plympton, the centre field,
who hits the first ball for a clean single between
short and second, letting in Johnson, and advanc-

ing Ferguson a base. The score is tied, and the hubbub is very disheartening to the backers of Fullham.

"Looks sort of sick for our side," Jack hears some one say to Carlisle, who is squatting not far from him.

"Game's young yet," is the cheery answer.

It is Bedloe's turn now. He advances confidently, and in imitation of Plympton's example lifts the first ball and drives it to left field, where Jackson gets under it, and — sad to chronicle — drops it. Ferguson comes in, of course, and Plympton too, although he should have been out; but Chalmers fails to hold Goldthwaite's swift throw from second. Five runs to three! Those muffs were very costly.

Bobby Crosby hits an easy grounder to Haseltine, which the little fellow picks up neatly and throws to first. Maitland holds it, and the Rogerines are out at last.

Jackson is at the bat first. He hits hard, anxious, doubtless, to atone for his error; but Hackett is on deck at second and fields beautifully to Ramsay. There is a flutter of anticipation as "Goldy" steps to the front. Like several of his opponents he swipes at the first ball pitched. "Hurrah! Look — look — is it a home run?" Everybody is on his feet following the ball to left field. Bobby Crosby, there's your chance. Gently now, or it will be over your head. It is going faster than it seems. Oh, well caught, well caught, youngster, and well judged, too, which is more than half the battle! Right over your left shoulder and on the full run, too! O-U-T! Everybody is cheering, for even Fullham can afford to applaud a play like that, and the Doctor, shouting as loud as any one, waves his hat and cries, "Well caught, Crosby!" Hard luck, Goldthwaite. It was a good crack, but not quite elastic enough. Who's the next victim?

It is Ogden, who pops up a fly which falls into Bedloe's hand, snug as a bug, and the side is out.

"Confound it!" says Horton, a sentiment which Jack echoes at heart.

Ramsay begins the eighth with a single to right field. Pousland goes out on a foul tip once more. Hackett takes a base on balls. Johnson hits to Jackson at left, who does not muff this time. Ferguson, the slugger, swipes hard and misses.

"One strike!"

"Two strikes!"

Ramsay is on third and Hackett on second, so that if Ferguson can make a safe hit there is a good chance for two more runs.

"F-E-R-G-U-S-O-N! Ferguson-n-n!"

The kid examines the ball and puts down his head to pitch. The slugger does not move.

"Three strikes!" cries the umpire. "Out!"

This is better, and revives somewhat the drooping courage of Fullham. Carlisle proposes three cheers for the kid, which are given with great enthusiasm.

"Now, Maitland," says Chalmers.

Charley Maitland waits for two called balls and one strike before he gets the one he is hoping for. Then he hits with all his might a driver to the inner centre field, where there is no one to catch it, and takes his first. The kid, who receives another round of applause as he steps to the plate, knocks one to Johnson at short, who lets it by him this time.

There are two on bases, Merriman. A good deal depends on you. Pshaw! straight into Ram-

say's hands. Run, Rainsford ; run, if you do not
wish to be cut off at second. Safe ! but only just in
time. If Ramsay had not waited so long you were
a sure out. The Rogerines are taking a turn at
muffing. Next striker.

It is our friend Haseltine. He glances across at
Jack as he goes in.

" One strike ! " calls Prendergast, though Haseltine has not. moved.

" Don't get flustered ; take your time, youngster," says Chalmers kindly.

" One ball ! "

This gives the ex-Rising Sun hero courage.
Charley Maitland and the kid are edging off their
bases ready to proceed the instant the ball leaves
the bat.

All of a sudden there is a terrific roar, and every
one starts up again, craning forward to see the
third base line.

" Run ! " bellows Chalmers to Haseltine, who
cuts away for first. But before he reaches it, the
umpire, who has shaded his eyes with his hand so
as to make no mistake, cries " Fair ball ! " and on
Haseltine dashes to second and again to third.

Here Chalmers stops him with an emphatic " Hold
your base!" Meanwhile, Maitland and the kid
have come home. The score is tied again, and the
uproar is prodigious. Panting but thoroughly
happy, Haseltine waits at third, and Captain Chalmers takes his turn at the bat.

We are viewing the game through Jack's eyes,
to whom every safe hit and every good bit of fielding seems marvelous; but though the standard of
play may be higher among some of you older boys,
there can be no denying the absorbing interest inspired at Utopia by these yearly contests for supremacy between the respective dormitories, second
only to the occasional contests with nines from
other schools. The thrill felt by Jack as Chalmers
takes his position to strike is shared by every one
of the two hundred boys and their masters present. For by this time there is scarcely a soul in
the school who is not a spectator. Even Horace
Hosmer is squatting at the further end of the field
beyond the possible reach of the ball, and Jack can
see him clap his big hands in honor of Haseltine's
three bagger.

But Chalmers is at the bat.

" One ball ! "

Haseltine evidently has it in mind to try to steal home, for if Chalmers does not get his first the side will be out; but " Goldy," who has taken the captain's place as coach, cautions him with " Steady now," and " Bide your time, youngster," not to stray too far from the base.

" One strike ! "

Pousland, the catcher, hurls to third to intimidate Haseltine, who dodges back in time to get his foot on the bag before Ferguson can touch him.

" Two balls ! "

Well done, Chalmers! Another shout, this time louder and more star-striking than any yet evoked, bursts forth from the Fullhamite ranks. There is ample reason for it, too. Both Bobby Crosby and Plympton are in full career after the ball, which is bounding beyond them at a fearful pace. They make superhuman efforts to overtake it, and Bobby returns it magnificently, but to no purpose, for Chalmers has made a clean round of the bases and is safely home. As for Haseltine, he has trotted in comfortably and is sharing with the captain handshaking and back-slapping from a score of palms.

He knows that the score is now seven to five, and that he has wiped out his early errors. His happiness, already complete, is made ecstatic by the congratulations of the Doctor, who comes up to him just as he is on the point of going over to Jack and says, "You're beginning bravely, Haseltine; if you go on at this rate you will be in training for the school nine before long."

"The school nine!" Could there be a more enviable compliment to a new boy on his first day at Utopia? He sees Mrs. Meredith smile at him from her seat and clap her hands. He touches his cap in sheepish fashion, and with cheeks aflame is glad to get down beside Jack and, riding his bat, watch Hamlen strike.

"Ah!"

This time the cry of triumph is premature. The ball goes afield grandly, but Billy Douglas is under it before it falls, and Hamlen makes the third out.

The Rogerines are rather quiet. They have only this inning in which to win the game. But the nine is not going to give in without making a hard fight for it, you may be certain. Two runs will tie

and three put them ahead.   Not so very many to
get, if fortune favors them and they can work in a
batting streak.

Plympton is the first on the list of strikers.   He
is a determined-looking fellow, with a bull-dog sort
of jaw.

"One strike!" cries the umpire.

The Fullhamites shout, but the batsman, whatever his feelings, never winks an eye.   He is dan-
gerously cool.

Whack!   One can hear the sound all over the
field.   The bat is split as completely as ever oak
was riven by the lightning.   But now Rogers has
a right to shout.   Another home run just in the
same place as Chalmers', and just as perfect.   The
din is deafening, and the prospects for a tenth
inning look very favorable.

"One more in the same spot will tie them," exclaims Hackett, as Bedloe nods at the kid to show
he is ready.

"One ball."

"Two balls."

"One strike."

"Three balls."

" Four balls."

" Five balls."

" Six balls ; take your base."

Rogers howls once more. Bedloe has a level head, and knows enough to play a waiting game. Perhaps he has reasoned that the kid is young, and may lose his head in a tight place. It looks a little like it, now ; if he does, there are sluggers enough on the nine to knock him out of the box.

It is Crosby's turn next to have a hack at him.

" One ball."

He hits the second. It is a scorcher to short stop, which strikes one of Merriman's feet and bounds into the air. Merriman looks in one direction and the ball comes down in the other. Before he can collect himself Bedloe is safe at second and Crosby at first.

Now, Harry Ramsay, captain of the school nine, is your chance. A rattler from you like that you struck yesterday, ought to win the game. One could hear a pin drop, it is so still. The excitement is almost painful.

" One ball," calls Prendergast.

" One strike."

" Ah-h-h ! "

That cry is because Bedloe has stolen third and Crosby second. Chalmers, a little bewildered it may be, has hesitated until too late which to throw to.

Ramsay has hit the third ball. What a paste! Where is it? Where has it gone? He is tearing to first. Great heavens! what is the matter? Is the game over? Everybody on the Fullham side is dancing and screaming and waving like mad. The crowd is mixing with the players, and Crosby and Bedloe and Harry Ramsay are coming in from the bases with a shamefaced air.

" What is it? I don't understand," asks Jack of Horton, who is shouting loud enough to burst a blood-vessel. Jack knows that Haseltine has stopped the ball and done something big, but it was all so quick, he cannot quite make out what.

" A triple play — all three out," Horton answers.

" H-A-S-E-L-T-I-N-E — Haselti-n-n-n-e ! "

A moment later Jack understands it all. The ball from Ramsay's bat had gone straight into Haseltine's hands, and though it had almost knocked the little fellow over, he had managed to hold it, to step on to third before Bedloe, who had started for home, realized the situation, and then, keeping his wits still about him, put it in to Goldthwaite, at second, with all his might, just in time to cut off Bobby Crosby, who was between the bases. Three out — side out at one fell swoop. Bull luck, as the Rogerines said, in speaking of the game afterwards.

It was luck, of course, that the ball went just where it did, making such a combination possible; but many an opportunity in life, no less favorable than Haseltine's, is lost every day by the inability of man or boy to avail himself of it. The ex-third base of the Rising Suns was equal to his emergency when it came; though, between ourselves, it was always a wonder to him that the ball had stuck in his hands. He had caught it before he knew it.

So the dormitory match was over, and Fullham champion for another year, by the close score of seven to six. It was a proud moment for Haseltine when Harry Ramsay, the great school captain, went out of his way to shake him by the hand and tell him that he was sure to make a strong player in a year or two. He received quite an ovation, and made the acquaintance on the spot of most of his own dormitory, and many from Rogers and Dudley. Jack stood by thoroughly satisfied with his friend's success and proud to be the bearer of his jacket. Really, to rejoice at another's triumphs is quite as sterling a trait of character as to bear modestly one's own.

As the two boys were returning to their dormitory in company with several others, they were overtaken by Carlisle, who, after a few words of congratulation on Haseltine's play, brought a host of fears, which the excitement of the afternoon had banished, back to the minds of both of them by observing in a low tone, —

"I'm sorry to say Jack Spratt and his Wife will be all the more down on you after this. They are Rogerines, and it's the cockiest thing a new boy has done for a dog's age."

This was very depressing, and took the edge decidedly off the happy frame of mind in which they would fain have remained. The game had consumed most of the afternoon. There was an hour and a half of recitation remaining before supper, the practice at Utopia being to have recitations from nine until half-past twelve, and from half-past four until six, during all but the last two months of the school year, in order to let the boys have the best hours of sunshine on the playground. In another week the rule was to change, and study would follow dinner, as the afternoons were growing long and favorable for sport.

When supper was done there was singing twice a week, and this was one of the evenings. All the school gathered informally in the big schoolroom, where, sitting round anyhow and anywhere, masters and boys mingled together, chatted, and listened to songs supervised by the singing-master, Mr. French, but entirely spontaneous. After the singing was over, there was a short lee-way before bedtime, and every one was left to his own devices. Most of the boys went back to their dormitories, but the sixth class had the run of Mrs. Meredith's parlor during half an hour, where there were quiet games and puzzles of various kinds to amuse them.

In returning to Fullham from this last-named entertainment, it was necessary, of course, to traverse the quadrangle. When Jack and Haseltine were about fifty yards from Granger, proceeding without suspicions, they became suddenly aware of several figures in masks and long cloaks, looming up ahead. At the same moment their feet were tripped up from behind, a rope quickly and strenuously twisted around their bodies, and a large hand compressed upon each of their mouths. They had no time to cry out. After a few frantic, futile efforts to get free, Jack ceased to struggle, and permitted himself to be bound by his captors, whom he assumed with a sinking heart to be no other than the notorious Spratt and Wife. A bandage had been fastened over his eyes almost immediately, and, helpless as a dead man, he was borne along in silence for a considerable distance, as it seemed to him, at a slow jog trot. Presently the procession stopped, confronted by some obstacle, and Jack was able to distinguish the voice of Carlisle remonstrating with his persecutors. He heard him say distinctly, " They are good fellows, both of them, I assure you ; let them off this time."

" They 're too beastly cocky," was the reply, in a shrill, hyena-like tone.

" That 's so," broke in another with a no less bloodthirsty modulation, whom Jack judged to be

Wifey. "I vote we smash every bone in their bodies."

"On to the torture chamber," continued the first speaker, a sentiment which was received with an approving Ah-h-h! by the others present.

"I've done all I could to save them," observed Carlisle, with a gloomy sigh of resignation.

Jack, who had been laid upon the ground during this interlude, now felt himself being carried up a flight of winding stairs and along a corridor, to an apartment where, after some whispering on the part of those about him, he perceived that he was being lowered into a narrow box. This, it suddenly occurred to him, was a coffin. A fear which brought the perspiration out in cold patches seized him. At its height the cover was pressed down, and he was left to his own gloomy reflections, which included the expectation of stifling. But though the space was contracted and the air hot, he experienced no real difficulty in drawing breath.

Here he lay for what seemed an eternity, listening to the preparations which were evidently going on around him. He could hear the hum of conversation and occasionally a smothered laugh, but the voices had all the shrill, fiendish pitch of those which had replied to Carlisle's protestations. What were they going to do with him? Was he dead already, and was this his funeral? He stirred one of his legs a little and pinched himself to make sure that he was alive. Yes, he was still in the flesh. The torture, then, was yet to come. Well, whatever happened, he would die bravely. Not a groan, not a cry for mercy, would he utter. He would be game to the last, and his tormentors should not have the satisfaction of seeing him funk while they were breaking his bones. A tear did come to his eye as he thought of his mother, and how she would miss him; but he braced his nerves as he felt it trickling, unwilling to be guilty of weakness, even under the shelter of the coffin-lid.

At this moment he was lifted, box and all, and placed on what might be a table. Immediately the cover was raised, and in spite of his bandage the fact that the room was lighted became apparent to him, while a low chorus of groans suggestive of animals eager to slake their thirst in human blood vibrated on his imaginative and frenzied hearing. Then there was a hush preliminary to the dreadful remark which proceeded from the foot of the coffin, "Are the irons red-hot?"

"They are, your Mightiness."

"Let the neophyte's arm be bared."

Jack, though ignorant as to the meaning of the word neophyte, did not doubt for an instant that he was referred to. He was seized straightway on either side and raised to a sitting posture. The rope was unbound from his right arm and those in charge of him were about to roll up the sleeve of his jacket, when the voice of his Mightiness enjoined, —

"Let the left be seared instead of the right, for in case the neophyte chance to survive the operation he will thus not be disabled in his base-ball arm. It is fitting that mercy should temper justice."

This piece of executive clemency was scarcely reassuring to poor Jack, for the reason that there was evidently occasion to believe that he would not outlive the torture about to be inflicted on him. He gritted his teeth to avoid trembling, and tried to show no signs of fear, while the assistants bared his forearm well up to the elbow. Just when they had completed their task there came a loud knock at the door, and whoever went to answer it announced, after a moment's delay, with a chuckle of exultation, " The other neophyte is dead."

A savage yell of pleasure followed this announcement, which was a dagger, as it were, in the bosom of our hero. Haseltine dead! He had been tortured, doubtless, in another chamber and had not been able to endure the agony.

But there was no time for reflection. A powerful wrist had grasped his arm and was holding it out at full length. Then something which felt like a glowing coal was pressed down on it with force and imbedded in his flesh. Jack knew that it was the red-hot iron. The pain was terrible and he was tempted to cry out, but by biting his lips he managed to restrain himself. Somehow or other the suffering did not increase after the first few moments, and as he was wondering at the circumstance he was astounded to hear, " Let me go! let me go!" uttered in a voice of agony close at hand. The conviction that it was Haseltine's voice eclipsed the consciousness of pain, and in another instant his arm was let go, the bandage snatched from his eyes, and Jack found himself in a blaze of

light, surrounded by a host of laughing counte-
nances which greeted him with a roar of laughter.

At first he was completely dazed and unable to
credit his senses ; then, as he gradually took in the
situation, he perceived that he was sitting upright
in an old shoe box lined with a shawl and supported
by a table. Not more than a yard away sat Haseltine in a similar predicament, with his left sleeve
rolled up, and looking extremely sheepish. On a
throne — an arm-chair surmounting a pile, the
component parts of which were concealed by a
table-cloth — was perched Jack Spratt, wearing a
paper crown, bearing a cricket bat as a sceptre,
and sharing royalty with Wifey at his side in female attire, intended to simulate a queen, but suggesting to practiced eyes a gown borrowed for this
occasion only from Mrs. Betty Martin. A row of
Apollinaris bottles, in each of which was a lighted
candle, blazed along the edge of the dais, at either
wing of which stood a score of schoolboys shaking
with merriment at the appearance of the two un-
fortunates.

Jack's first reflection was one of self-congratula-
tion that he had not cried out. Then it occurred to

him to glance at his arm, a proceeding which was
the cause of another burst of laughter. To his surprise, there was no mark of any sort beyond a
slight redness which was scarcely noticeable. But
his skin looked somewhat wet, as though water had
been brought in contact with it.

After a moment, his Mightiness, having induced
silence by a wave of his sceptre, exclaimed with
great seriousness, " The chief executioner will read
the indictment against the neophytes."

Whereupon, to Jack's intense surprise, that func-
tionary stepped forward in the person of Louis Carlisle, fantastically attired in a black Oxford gown
and carrying a meat chopper as the symbol of his
office. Having bowed to their majesties, he gravely
drew forth a manuscript and addressed the two
bewildered lads as follows : —

" Know all men by these presents, that you, John
Hall, of Boston, Massachusetts, and you, Frank Haseltine, of St. Louis, Missouri, are greener than the
grass when it flourisheth in the early days of summer, fresher than paint just after it is spread on
the door of a mansion, more guileless than the kid
which gambols in the pasture beside its female

parent. You have been sent here with your mouths wide open and ready to swallow anything that is stuffed into them. Such innocence is praiseworthy in the extremely youthful, but a time comes in the experience of us all when it is meet to be undeceived even at the expense of dire mortification.

" Learn of me and be wise. Firstly and foremostly, you have been made sport of — victimized — fooled, or, to speak more succinctly, sold. You have been made egregious asses of, and led to believe that you were to be the victims of physical violence, to have your bones broken, your heads punched, and what not. You expected to be hazed and we did not like to disappoint you ; hence the midnight seizure, the rope, the bandage, the coffin, the red-hot iron, the branding. You have been taught to tremble at the blood-curdling names of Jack Spratt and Wifey. Behold them in the flesh and bow before them ! You came here stuffed with old women's yarns, and Horace Hosmer has loaded you up to the muzzle with a fresh supply. Poor little lambkins ! "

As Carlisle paused in his sarcastic peroration the audience broke into another shout of laughter, which caused Jack to blush vividly. He appreciated now for the first moment that he had been the victim of a huge practical joke.

"Secondly," continued the orator, with a wave of his hand, " let whoever will search the universe from one end to the other, and I defy him to produce two more thoroughly mild and amiable specimens of the genus *homo* than Tobey and Donaldson, who have been made to figure as monsters of cruelty for your edification. In justice to them, neophytes, I bid you approach them. Exhume yourselves, so to speak, and go up to examine them. You will perceive that they are perfectly harmless, and even unusually good-natured fellows. You may touch them without fear that one of your bones will be dislocated. Approach, neophytes, they are prepared to embrace you."

Again everybody laughed, while Jack and Haseltine looked at one another, at a loss, not unnaturally, to know whether the order to leave their coffins was to be taken seriously. But this uncertainty was solved when his Mightiness reiterated, at the same time removing his crown and assuming an exaggerated expression of meekness, "Approach, neophytes, we are prepared to embrace you."

In a shamefaced manner, but doing their best to enjoy the laugh against themselves, which now made the room ring, the two boys clambered down from their boxes and walked toward the throne. Its grinning occupants sat for a moment enjoying the confusion evinced by the poor lads before them, then Jack Spratt put out his hand and said, —

"Shake, neophytes. My bark is worse than my bite."

"Me, too," piped Donaldson, in semblance to a female falsetto, which elicited a roar.

"Thirdly and lastly," exclaimed Carlisle, after Jack and Haseltine had finished this hand-shaking and been relegated to their coffins, on the edge of which they were permitted to sit, — "thirdly and lastly," he repeated, "there is a moral to all this, without which our efforts in your behalf might be misunderstood, and that is, don't be too English. You boys — for I address you no longer as neophytes, but as Utopia boys — must get out of your heads that an American school is just like an English one, for it isn't. You've come with the idea that we have fagging and hazing and all that sort of thing, but it's a mistake. There isn't a fag at

Utopia, and if a big boy wants anything done he has to do it himself. Every tub stands on its own bottom here, and a sixth-class boy is just as good as a first. No running errands — no cleaning out studies — no cuffing! That may be English; but it isn't American, is it, fellows?"

"Not much," answered several voices.

"We're all equals here. There may be a bully or two, — I don't say there is, — but there may be in any school. There's no system of bullying, though, and no boy thinks he has the right to order others round. If he tried it on he'd soon find out his mistake."

"That's so."

"And now, fellows," continued Carlisle, whose satirical tone had changed to a pleasant seriousness, "I tell Hall and Haseltine, in all our names, that we're glad to have them at Utopia; and some day they'll bring credit on the school, for they are both plucky boys. Hall didn't whimper once to-night; he was game from the word 'go'; and we Fullhamites haven't forgotten that triple play of Haseltine's, and we shan't for a good while to come."

Whereupon the chief executioner, having divested himself of his robe of office, emphasized the plaudits of the roomful of boys by coming forward in easy, smiling fashion to grasp the two victims of his oratory by the hand, in which example he was being followed by every one, when a knock at the door introduced Mr. Sawyer, the dormitory master, who had come to ascertain the cause of the merriment. He stood on the threshold looking round the small study — it was Carlisle's own — packed with boys, quite unable, it was evident, to explain the signification of the boxes, blacking-bottles, and various paraphernalia of royalty which met his sight. Some of the participants seemed rather disconcerted by his appearance, but there was a general disposition to laugh, and one boy exclaimed, —

" You ought to have heard Carlisle, Mr. Sawyer; he was really as good as Dr. Meredith."

This necessitated an unfolding of the whole affair, which was listened to somewhat dubiously until it appeared to the master's satisfaction that no real harm had been done, and that the moral deduced to justify the high jinks was not without its value. Mr. Sawyer was fain to laugh himself at the villainous traits ascribed to Spratt and his Wife, and took occasion to clinch the lesson imparted by saying, as he patted Jack on the head by way of sympathy for his discomfiture, —

"So you expected to be a fag, did you, my little man? We have nothing of that sort here, you may take my word for it. Come," he added, "it is time for prayers and bed."

While they were undressing, half an hour later, Haseltine whispered to Homer, "What was it they put on my arm which stung so?"

"A lump of ice, you loony."

CHAPTER VIII.

SETTLING DOWN.

THE remaining weeks of the school year passed very rapidly with Jack. Indeed, before he had become accustomed to his new life they were gone. After Carlisle's peroration the two new-comers were allowed to drop into the obscurity which befits small boys, and to find their natural level among their associates. They made friends easily, and Jack in his letters home described Utopia in glowing terms. The lack of a wherry of his own seemed to be the only drawback to his happiness. So picturesquely did he lay this want before his mother that she wrote back that if he made a fair showing in the way of scholarship by the end of the term he should have one, with the consent of Dr. Meredith. Poor Jack little knew his own propensities in imagining that he would find slight difficulty in fulfilling this condition.

But as there were several wherries belonging to

the school, he was able within a very short time to gratify his ambition to handle the sculls. He and Horton went down to the lake before breakfast one morning, especially to engage two crack boats for the afternoon, as there was a great demand for them at this time of the year. Jack started off confidently, hoping to dazzle the occupants of the float by the knowingness of his style, but at the third stroke caught a crab which nearly upset him and made him extremely cautious henceforward. After paddling about a little he managed to get the knack of keeping his balance in the cranky concern, but he had to own to himself that he knew very little about rowing, and must begin to learn all over again.

This was rather a come-down for Jack, but he was not alone in his discomfiture. In spite of Haseltine's brilliant performance against Rogers, his place on the Fullham nine was filled by convalescent players, and he had to endure the mortification of becoming one of the herd who practiced scrub. It galled his pride to be unattached. That the ex-third base of the Rising Suns should be shunted off to find equals among the mass on the practice-field wounded him to the quick. However, he went in hammer and tongs to improve his game, with a determination to be satisfied with nothing short of the captaincy of the school-team at last. It did not take him long to convince the younger boys that he was an authority on base-ball matters. He knew the standing of every team, and the record of every player in the country, and once a week he received from home a newspaper devoted to the interests of the national game, every item in which he could repeat by rote.

There is a certain number of people who argue that it makes very little difference after all whether a boy studies at school or not, provided he is turned out at the end of the curriculum an upright, honorable gentleman, with a clean mind, a manly tone, and generous instincts. While, as between the alternatives of inferior training in the way of books and neglect of the moral character, one could scarcely hesitate which to avoid, the parent content to have his or her son graduate merely a good-natured, well-mannered, easy-going athlete has sadly misconceived the proper relation between master and pupil. Indeed, it may be said that

nothing can be more deplorable than a system of
education which does not stimulate excellence in
scholarship, unless it be one that promotes it at
the expense of high principle. We often hear it
said that the chief benefit of school or college is
the effect on character. Very good; but surely it
is no error to maintain that the character of the
boy untrained to use his mind intelligently is not
highly to be extolled. This idea, boys, of becoming easy-going and nothing else is a very unfortunate one to entertain, especially in our country,
where every man is expected to contribute in some
way toward making the world more civilized, and
a sweeter, happier place to live in. We need to-
day the services of keen, disciplined minds in active life, and in its quiet walks those who love
learning for her own sake, and are ready to devote
patient days to the pursuit of ripe scholarship.

Fortunately for Jack — though he was slow to
think it fortunate — Dr. Meredith was determined
to have as few dunces as possible at Utopia. He
was a fine scholar himself, and had to help him a
corps of enthusiastic instructors, most of them men
fresh from some university. Experience had al-

ready taught him that chronic idleness and dislike for study cannot be cured in a fortnight. Hence he and his assistants were content to peg away at incorrigible pupils without expecting to work wonders all at once, but never yielding an inch nor losing ground once gained.

This studying business was the only part of the school programme which Jack did not thoroughly enjoy. He started off in his old way by merely glancing at his lessons and floundering through them as best he could, never doubting that after a lecture or two on the subject of idleness, he would be permitted to lag along at the foot of the class without remark. He was used to being brought up with a round turn once a month or so, and after the scolding was over knew that he was safe to relapse until the next time. But he could count on that comfortable condition of affairs no longer. The continual pegging away referred to, of which he was now the victim, was inexpressibly irritating. His masters — he had a different one in almost every study — excited both his resentment and his wonder by patiently trying to make him take an interest in his tasks. Instead of being ordered in

a peremptory tone to "sit down," after an egregious mistake, he was kept upon his feet and not
only told the answer (generally from the lips of
some other boy), but asked to repeat it, and to
remember it too at the next recitation. This was
harassing, especially so when he found himself
obliged to spend part of the afternoon in the schoolroom instead of on the playground, because he
persisted in considering his lessons of no account.
His little soul was fairly in a ferment of indignation. What was the use of study, he would ask
himself. As for books, he would be glad for his
part never to see another, unless, of course, one of
adventures on the sea or in the far West. Would
Latin or arithmetic make him a better oar or a
surer short-stop? Not a bit of it, he was certain
of that; and so, masters or no masters, he was disposed to let his lessons slide.

Accordingly, Mrs. Hall was made to feel badly
by receiving, soon after Jack went home for vacation, a report of his progress as a scholar very far
from satisfactory, accompanied by a few lines from
Dr. Meredith, calling attention to the fact that her
son was inclined to be lazy, and urging her to use

her influence to correct this failing. She did, and
so persuasively, that Jack promised with sobs — and
he was thoroughly penitent — to turn over a new
leaf when he went back. He got his wherry, too,
in spite of not deserving it, for his mother had not
the heart to disappoint him, which gives one the
opportunity to suggest that perhaps Jack had been
a little spoiled ever since he was a baby. However, if our mothers did not make light of and
forgive our shortcomings, who would? Nevertheless, I think he had been sent to Utopia School
none too soon for his welfare.

There were changes, of course, when he returned
in the autumn. Harry Ramsay, Bedloe, and
Goldthwaite of the nine, Burbank captain of the fifteen, and Hazelhurst the champion oar, were gone
and their places as leaders filled by others. Bobby
Crosby was, on the whole, cock of the school, being
captain of the foot-ball team and a rousing fellow
generally. The kid, who was only in the second,
had been promoted to pitch for the school nine,
and Chalmers the old captain of Fullham had succeeded Harry Ramsay, which left two vacancies on
the dormitory nine, for one of which — right field

— Haseltine was selected, an unusual honor for so young a player.

Both he and Jack felt quite like old boys in coming back as members of the fifth class, and entered upon the new year in the best of spirits. Foot-ball was the school game just now, at which neither of them was slow in acquiring some proficiency. Early in November the autumn athletic meeting was to take place, and there was much training among the competitors for the various events. The school interest which had been much exercised over the two-hundred yard dash waned greatly, however, when it became known that Louis Carlisle had withdrawn, thereby giving a walk-over (according to the general opinion) to Coleman, Junior. Rumor was loud in some quarters in describing Carlisle's action as a "squawk," and Jack found difficulty in understanding the reasons which the champion gave for his refusal to run.

It is not easy to explain the origin of friendships, but ever since the evening when Jack had acted so pluckily in not crying out when he felt what he believed to be the branding-iron on his arm, Carlisle had shown an interest in him. If this were not the cause that had attracted the older to the new boy, it may have been the lack of jealousy which our hero had showed at Haseltine's success against the Rogerines. At any rate, for some reason or other Carlisle had taken to him from the very first, evincing a liking by superintending Jack's rowing on the lake; asking him to walk on Sunday afternoons; and, now that as a member of the second class he had a study to himself, by inviting his young crony to share its comforts whenever he might see fit to do so. The good will thus shown was duly appreciated, and the intimacy between them became marked and firmly established.

At first Jack was chiefly absorbed by and grateful for the instruction in the way of handling the oars, and of making progress in the various sports in which he was interested, which he received from his new friend, so that he thought of very little else; but he found it pleasant, nevertheless, to establish himself from time to time in Carlisle's cosy apartment and listen to his mentor prattle on about whatever happened to be in his mind at the moment. Carlisle had a way of ignoring the youngster's presence and of talking as though he were all alone, merely appealing to Jack in much the same way as one will appeal to an imaginary second self, not expecting an answer. Indeed, Jack was quite incapable of answering the conundrums proposed to him in this manner, and much of what he listened to was very perplexing to him. He enjoyed it, however, though he found it very difficult to understand how anybody could spend so much time over books and study as Carlisle did. His amazement found voice when, early in the term, Carlisle announced his intention not to try for the school nine, and to knock off from exercise of every sort except a daily row on the lake to keep himself in condition.

"What, not go in training for any of the running races?" asked Jack.

"No."

"Why not? You 're sure to win."

"I think I am," Carlisle answered, with a smile. "There's no one that I know of who's come up since last year."

"There's Coleman, Junior," said Jack doubtfully. He did not suspect his friend of funking, but the remark popped out in spite of himself.

"Yes, I know. Some of the fellows will say I'm scared. Well, let them. I don't care. As I've told you before, Jessup will beat Coleman, if nothing happens. I can't afford to waste my time merely to please a few fellows."

Jack could not understand speaking of winning the championship of Utopia on the running track as a waste of time.

"Shan't you kick foot-ball either?" he went on.

"No; I've had my fill of games for the present," Carlisle answered, in his soliloquizing way. "I've made up my mind that it pays to do a few things well, and to stick to them instead of straying all over the lot. I've kept going at full pitch in sixty different directions' ever since I was your age, and it's time to quit. I can't stand it, that's the long and short of it. 'Je plie et ne romps pas,' is a motto that can be run into the ground."

"What does that mean?" asked Jack. "I suppose it's French."

"Tough on my accent," responded Carlisle, with a grin. "Yes, it's French, and means 'I bend and do not break.' But bending is about as uncomfortable as breaking, in the long run, youngster."

"What *are* you going to do then?" continued his interrogator, for Jack like most American boys was not to be deterred from obtaining information for lack of persistence in asking questions.

"I 'm going to study, chiefly."

"Study?" Jack stared aghast. "I should n't think there 'd be much fun in that," he added, after a pause.

"Because you don't know anything about it."

"I hate study," observed Jack dogmatically.

"Oh, no, you don't."

"I tell you I do. I detest it!"

"Oh, no, you don't, for you have no conception what it is," replied Carlisle, laughing. "I don't believe you ever did an hour's real study in your life."

This view of the case had not occurred to Jack, and he was not prepared to gainsay the statement. Something prompted him to glance around the room at the rows of books nearly covering two walls of the den, and the three or four poetically conceived pictures in tasteful frames to which he had never given a second thought before. On the table were writing-materials and other paraphernalia suggestive of a student. "You see," continued Carlisle quietly, "I 'm fond of study. I really enjoy Latin and Greek and history. We 're just beginning Homer, and there are parts of it that are delightful. I don't care much for algebra, but they say it strengthens the mind. I shan't go in for anything very desperately, though, this year," he added. "I 've been thinking over Dr. Bolles's numerous lectures to me on the subject, and have decided to limit myself to three things, — study, the school paper, and rowing, — and not to overtax myself at any one of them. If I don't, Dr. Bolles says there is no reason why I should n't grow rugged. It 'll be pleasant to feel at the end of each day that I have n't used up every spark of vitality I possess."

To Jack, whose ideas of responsibility were at this time excessively vague, this sort of talk must have sounded almost unintelligible. However, it soaked in with everything else that was part and parcel of his daily experience; and whatever he may have thought of the views expressed, he lived to see Carlisle's prediction regarding Coleman verified by Jessup's comparatively easy victory in the two hundred yard dash at the athletic meeting in November.

These half-yearly meetings were great occasions at Utopia. In addition to the foot-races, which included both long and short distances, there was rope-climbing, fence-vaulting, standing and running high jumps, sparring and wrestling in three classes, — feather, middle, and heavy weight, — and a tug of war between teams from the several dormitories to end up with. Altogether the scene was decidedly Olympian. There were so many events that almost every boy felt that he had a chance in one direction or another. Jack entered for the feather-weight wrestling, but only to be thrown, after a savage tussle, flat on his back, and to have his shoulders pinned to the ground by Carpenter, who, though a year older, was just about his size. It was a very even contest, though, everybody admitted. He also was one of the field of seven who contested with Jessup the two-hundred yard race, having been advised by Carlisle to go in just to show what he was made of, and he was rather proud at coming in fifth, being beaten by Hopedale, of the next higher class, only by a shave. Haseltine, who also entered, was sixth, which was a considerable comfort to Jack.

But the contests with the gloves were what took
his fancy more than anything else, and he was fired
at once with the desire to learn boxing. This was
easy to do, for Dr. Meredith was decidedly of the
opinion that boys should understand the art of self-
defense, which was accordingly taught at the gymnasium by Dr. Bolles and his assistant, to all who
desired to receive instruction. There were a good
many competitors for distinction in this line, and
the rivalry resulted in some hitting and receiving
of tolerably hard knocks, which now and then bore
fruit in the shape of a bloody nose or black eye in
spite of well-padded gloves. And yet, notwithstanding all this emulation, it was very rarely, if ever, as
Jack soon realized, that the combatants had occasion to make practical use of the knowledge thus
acquired, so long as they were at Utopia. Indeed,
it may almost be stated as a general truth that the
American boy does not go in for the deliberate slug-
ging contests one reads about as common among
the youth of the Mother Country. Unless from a
spirit of sheer imitation, it is unusual, I believe,
for you young fellows to settle bad blood by a cut-
and-dried fight after the manner of " Tom Brown

and 'Slugger' Williams," with whose thrilling set-to you should all be familiar. Plenty of you get mad and in the heat of the moment slap a fellow's face, or slang him until he cuffs you; and then there is give and take for a few moments, in the course of which science may get in an upper cut or some such telling stroke; but your friends are almost certain to drag you apart before much damage is done, and hold you back until you have cooled down. The idea of forming a "ring" with backers and sponges "to fight it out" does n't seem to occur to either of you, or, if it does, public opinion — and by that I mean school opinion — is against you. I rather think that any boy, whether a Utopian or otherwise, can count on the fingers of a single hand the number of regular out - and - out fights in the course of his school-days he has either participated in or been present at.

There must be some reason for this, and you do not need to be told that American boys are neither effeminate nor afraid to use their fists when occasion requires. Lack of pluck is not a national failing. We stood up at Bunker Hill against bullets long enough to convince our enemies that there was mettle in us, and there are graveyards within walking distance of every lad under the stars and stripes who may read this story, in which can be noted the tribute of posterity to those who died in defense of their country. There is no sort of doubt that our boys can hit straight from the shoulder whenever it is worth their while to do so.

I have an idea — it may be a mistaken one, though I am fatuous enough to have faith in it — that the world in growing older has grown wiser, and less cruel and brutish. We elders proscribed duels long ago on the score that they were unmanly and inconsistent with the requisites of Christian character; and dreadful as are the preparations which even to-day are going on in so many countries of the globe with an eye to deadly strife, there can be no doubt that civilized nations are much less ready to plunge into war than they used to be, and much more inclined to submit their differences to arbitration. There are cynics — at least they seem such to me — who maintain that there must always be wars until the end of time, if for no other reason than to dispose of the surplus population, and that national reluctance to engage in them proceeds from economic rather than humanitarian scruples. But those of us who still believe that mankind is surely, even if slowly, making progress toward a higher state of civilization, cannot but be of the opinion that wholesale resorts to force to settle disputes must inevitably become less and less frequent, from the growing conviction among human beings that they are a relic of barbarism. Already has this conviction made such headway that the most autocratic governments would hesitate at the present day to declare war without first invoking the aid of referees, if the matter at issue were capable of peaceable solution.

In like manner it is fair to believe that the doctrine of forbearance is so much in the air that you boys have become inoculated with its spirit, and have learned to abstain from blows until every other remedy has failed. There is no cowardice in such a policy. Mere fighting for the sake of fighting savors of the brute, not of the gentleman. But this is to be borne in mind notwithstanding, though I have no doubt that you do not need the prompting : when you *are* struck, hit back with all your might. Be slow to strike the first blow, or to pro-

voke assault, but beware of letting forbearance outrun its usefulness as a virtue. Sunday-school teachers may argue as they will, but the world will never
learn to applaud or to respect the man or boy who
allows his rights to be trampled on without stubborn
resistance.

December brought with it ice and snow, coasting
and skating, which for the time being overruled all
other sports and interests for Jack. For a good four
months the school was face to face with winter,
which means in this country something worthy of
the name, — genuine stinging cold, which makes
boys' cheeks glow if they move briskly, but numbs
their fingers if they sit still; and a roaring fire in
the great schoolroom in the evening, around which
it is the fashion to group and sing. At this last-
named trysting - place serviceable friendships are
formed, and, in the case of Jack, an old one is
renewed. December brought with it Bill French,
the same Bill as of yore, and yet developed, as it
were, in that he is no longer the street urchin of a
year ago, indifferent as to his clothes and hair. Bill
has spruced himself eminently, and is quite the little gentleman now in his cut and manner. He does

not take much part in sports himself, but he knows
all about them, and is eager to back this sprinter or
that oarsman for anything from a nickle up to five
dollars, which is a fabulous sum at Utopia, as you
may well imagine. He has at the very outset created
a profound sensation by managing to retain green-
backs to the amount of five times that sum about
his person, in spite of the school rule that all
money, save a very small stipend for the pocket, is
to go into the Doctor's strong-box for safe-keeping.

"How did you manage to hold on to it?" whispered Jack, whose admiration for Bill's cunning
ways is still deep.

"Did n't give it to him, that's all."

"Did n't he ask you for it?"

"What if he did? It's my money, not his.
Father gave it to me, and I mean to spend it as I
choose."

This deliberate springing in the teeth of authority was something new at Utopia, and, like most
novelties, gave its originator notoriety at once.
Jack felt proud at being on such terms with the
new school favorite, who before long took upon
himself the airs of a leader among the younger

boys, with revolt as a motto. The Doctor was all very well, but he, Bill French, was not going to bend the knee to any Doctor, no matter how wise and good. He had come there to have a good time, and he meant to have it.

It took Bill some months, naturally, to raise his standard. His methods, as you know, were for the most part underground like the mole. He did not believe in being found out, and he had no intention of getting into open trouble with the powers that were, if he could help it. His fad was for managing and directing, and he was content to suggest, and to let others work out his theories without asking for more than a tithe of the glory. Great schemes must move slowly to insure success.

So Bill to the ordinary eye appeared rather a desirable addition than otherwise to the make-up of the school. He had always been rather quick at his books, and found no difficulty now in taking a respectable place in Jack's class, where he kept his head above water easily, thus hoodwinking one of the eyes of Argus. Where Bill really showed himself in his true kidney was about the aforesaid fire on cold winter nights, when he had an opportunity to fascinate the circle snuggled around him by hints as to what might be done if one only dared. Many listened, and Jack most eagerly of all. Were they not Americans? Bill argued. And when did a true-born patriot, whether man or boy, put up with being hedged about with laws which he despised? As a proof of what might be accomplished in the way of resistance without difficulty, the arch-conspirator excited the envy of all whom he took into the secret by exhibiting on his return to school at the beginning of the fourth-class year a pair of white mice in the corner of one of his bureau-drawers. Nor was Bill stupid enough to let them remain there long enough to fall under the eagle eye of Mrs. Betty, who was liable to come prowling round at any time with power paramount to overhaul to her heart's content. When the little creatures, a month later, presided over a family, — another triumph for their proprietor, — it was in the pocket of a pair of trousers hanging harmlessly from a peg.

The influence of genius such as this was hard to resist, and had it stopped here, authority might justifiably have been disposed to regard it without concern; but Bill was not always so happy in his infringements of the law. He was wont to exhibit with pride a small silver case in which reposed real cigarettes, — no blood-sucking rattan subterfuges, but the genuine aristocratic article, which he was in the habit of smoking when he could safely do so with the air of a thorough-going sport, as any one at Utopia who witnessed the performance would agree. At such times Bill was a decidedly agreeable companion. In the first place he could talk knowingly by the hour on dogs and horses, a subject which was imperfectly understood at Utopia prior to his arrival. All the cant phrases of the stable were at his command, and he replenished them by the perusal of a weekly sporting paper to which he subscribed, and which put Haseltine's base-ball sheet completely in the shade. In his opinion, life at the school was tame, and stood in need of thorough reorganization.

Much as Jack admired Bill, he was not really surprised to hear Carlisle observe, some weeks after the first appearance of that wily youth, "I don't care much for your new friend, youngster."

"Why not, Louis?"

" I guess he 's sneaky, is n't he? Looks it, any way."

" He 's mighty smart," answered Jack evasively.

" I dare say."

" You ought to like him," pursued Jack, " for he 's a first-rate scholar. He could stand a good deal higher if he chose to study."

Carlisle laughed. " I set store by study I know," he said, " but it is n't a free pass to my favor, as you appear to think. Strange as it may seem, I prefer you, idle as you are, to your industrious friend. And by the way, Jack, you have been worse than ever, lately. You must brace up or you will have the Doctor down on you."

Both were silent for a moment. It was something new for Carlisle to lecture, as he would have called it. He had always shrunk from preaching to his friend deliberately, intimate as were their relations, preferring to indicate by chaff and indirect suggestions what might be in his mind regarding Jack's needs. But these few words were spoken so seriously that the culprit looked at him astonished.

There was a reason for them. Dr. Meredith,

having great faith in the influence for good which
the larger boys at a school like Utopia can exert
upon their juniors, lost no occasion to impress upon
his favorites their duty in this respect. Only the
day before he had chanced upon Carlisle strolling
down toward the river alone, and had joined him.

"You're looking better, Louis, I'm glad to see.
Your more sober life agrees with you."

Somehow or other the Doctor knew the imperfect joint in the armor of every one of his pupils,
and he was no less prompt to seize an opportunity
to speak a word of encouragement, than he was
courageous in probing a weakness to the core.

"I'm in first-rate condition, sir. Gained five
pounds this term."

"I wish, now that your hand is in, you'd see
what you could do with Hall," the Doctor had continued. "I am disturbed at the way the boy is
going on. He seems a manly, spirited fellow, and
I like him, but he won't study. In fact, he's getting more of a shirk every day."

"Yes, sir, he doesn't study much, that's a fact,"
observed Carlisle.

"A word from you, Louis, might do an immense

amount of good. He'd listen to you when he would n't to me."

Carlisle had hung his head and remained silent. He knew very well what Doctor Meredith meant, for had he not observed Jack's idleness with increasing regret, and yet been content to pass it off with an occasional jest? All his talk during their intercourse had been about himself, concerning which he could discourse glibly enough; but such speculation as he was wont to indulge in, however suggestive to an intelligent listener, was scarcely the sort of pabulum by which to convert a hobble-de-hoy offender like Jack. He had been conscious for some time of what with his disposition to call things by their right names he considered his own selfishness and self-absorption, and this solicitation of the Doctor's thrust them forward into the light.

" I know what you would say," his master had continued. " You have a horror of sermonizing. You don't wish to spoil your relations with him, as you think, by being serious. You are right, Louis, in that. But I don't believe, if you look at the matter squarely, that you would drive Hall into his

shell by letting him see that you don't approve of
his present way of going on."

" He knows I approve of study."

" Yes, for yourself," had answered the sagacious
Doctor. " Let him understand thoroughly that it
is just as imperative for him."

" I'll try, sir," the older boy had answered, after
a pause.

" I shall be infinitely obliged to you; and while
we are on the subject, what sort of a boy is this
William French? I understand that he and Hall
are old cronies. Don't answer if you'd rather not,"
had added the Doctor, who sympathized with the
code of honor which prompts a schoolboy to abstain
from speaking ill of one of his companions.

" He doesn't seem to me very straightforward,"
had blurted out Carlisle, instigated perhaps by a
desire to protect Jack from the evil machinations
of the new-comer.

" Indeed! That is not a pleasant trait. Thank
you, Louis. Such boys as you can do a great deal
to help me, if you only will, without in any way
impairing your obligations as ' good fellows.' "

The first result of this conversation has been indicated. Carlisle's words, limited as they were, came at a moment when Jack was sorely in need of them. Although he made no comment at the time, other than to look grave, and though he sought to brush the remembrance of them away as speedily as possible, he was nevertheless face to face with the consciousness — a consciousness of which he had caught occasional glimpses before of late — of dissatisfaction with himself. What was more, it enthralled him like a net, and the more he struggled held him the tighter. Vague lack of content with one's own career is not synonymous with an intention to reform, but it is a step in the right direction. Jack would never be able to feel again, except through utter callousness of soul, that satisfaction in wrong-doing which exists before the sense of responsibility is awakened.

There is little further to chronicle regarding the second year of Jack's school-life, which sped along from week to week without revealing much outward change in his daily routine of duties and pleasures; the former endured with unwillingness and neglected so far as was possible, the latter participated in with untiring enthusiasm. In the class-room he was the same mischief-making, idle urchin as ever, distinguished for his dog's-eared, caricature-lined books of study, and an utter ignorance of their contents. On the playground every faculty seemed alert, and all his energy centred in excelling at whatever pastime he was for the moment fascinated by.

CHAPTER IX.

THE BIG FOUR.

As a fourth-class boy Jack fairly felt his oats, and with justice, if one considers what a satisfactory status was-meant by that term at Utopia. A fourth-classer had nothing to learn, so to speak. He knew all the ropes. He had at his fingers' ends every thing connected with the ways of the school, and was entitled to regard himself as untainted by greenness of any description. Pride and some bumptiousness were the result, but more particularly a rattling way of doing things as though those engaged in whatever was in hand had unlimited confidence in themselves, as indeed they had. To be a fourth-classer, if one were a prominent fellow, was the same as being one of the cocks of the lower school, and a person to be deferred to whenever any matter was mooted concerning the more juvenile half of the body politic.

Taking the list by and large, there were no more

prominent fourth-classers in their year than the quartette who trained together under the pseudonym of "The Big Four." These were Jack, Haseltine, Bill French, and Horton. In justice to Bill, his name should have been written first, for it was he who had conceived the idea of welding into one compact body the best material in the class, with a view to coöperation in various directions. To his brain was due the origin of the mysterious secret society, of which he and his three pals were the units. At Utopia, where there had never been a secret society up to this time, whoever referred to "The Big Four" spoke with bated breath, as of an organization very little understood, and in awe of which it was incumbent to stand.

Bill came back after vacation full of the scheme, and found little difficulty in making its merits apparent to Jack. After some cogitation the number was swelled by the election of Haseltine and Horton. The constitution was a sort of cross between the Declaration of Rights and such an instrument as a community of bandits might have drawn for mutual protection. It began as follows: —

" This society is organized to secure to free-born American citizens the enjoyment of their natural liberties."

A sentiment distinctly praiseworthy, at least on the surface, and broad in its scope. After this general definition of usefulness and certain provisions as to name, membership, and grip, appeared a few by-laws, embodying a most salient code of behavior, among which was the third, to wit : —

" No member shall, on pain of expulsion, kiss any female except his mother."

To cap and clinch the whole, thus heading off treachery at the start, it was laid down, —

" Whoever shall at any period of his existence divulge, or in any manner make known, the secrets of this society, or shall with or without malice-aforethought break its laws or abandon its principles, shall suffer death with torture, to be inflicted by the members for the time being, except as otherwise herein provided."

This joint production, for each of the four had a hand in its composition, was solemnly signed and sworn to at midnight in the lavatory where the whole society assembled by concerted action. To make the oath more binding, the pen was dipped in the blood of the successive signers, at Haseltine's prompting, who fully believed at the time that whoever should violate it could not escape a lingering death. He even went so far as to suggest that a burning-glass focused upon the abdomen would probably produce as exquisite suffering as any of the appliances known to inquisitorial or savage torturers. To Jack belonged the credit of devising the already quoted clause relating to women, the reception of which was unequivocally enthusiastic, and seemed to them to stamp the organization at once as a manly body, proof against Delilahs, or all feminine influence except that prescribed by early piety.

"I hate girls; they're silly little things," continued the originator of the by-law in question.

"I'd like to see one of them try to kiss me!" said Haseltine.

The latter idea did not seem so repulsive to Bill and Horton, though they acquiesced in the provision as smacking of wisdom, on the whole. Indeed, almost from the start, there was a difference of opinion, scarcely perceptible at first, but constantly growing wider, as to the real functions of " The Big Four."

To Jack and Haseltine it stood for freedom, and defiance of authority in any form, and especially defiance against the Doctor, to be evidenced by disobedience, as the spirit might move, whether in the way of marauding expeditions or midnight feasts. Caution, more than was absolutely necessary, was disregarded by them, and concealment was a policy which they despised. They were indifferent, not only as to what authority might think, but even as to whether authority was aware of what they were up to. War to the knife, without mercy or compromise on either side, was what they craved, proudly confident of their ability to trample authority in the dust.

But the other two were wiser in their generation, with the wisdom of the serpent. They believed distinctly in lying low, and in masking the countenance both metaphorically and literally. " Do *wrong* by stealth and blush to find it fame," would have seemed to them an admirable epitome of their views. And just as their methods savored of craft

and underhandedness, so their favorite acts of
defiance — for in throwing off authority all were
united — were apt to be such as would not bear
the light of day.   Vice is a parasite that flourishes
best in the shade.   There Bill French's whisper
sounded most seductively, and his "I say, fellows,
I know what let's do," was least easy to resist.

. Such was the attraction of this new interest that
Jack thought of but little else.   Not only did he
begin to neglect Carlisle, but he ceased to feel his
old ambition to excel at games.   At the spring
athletic meeting of the year before he had followed
Carlisle's advice to hold off for another six months,
but when the time came the following autumn he
failed to make as good a record as when he had first
appeared on the track.   He was only seventh this
time in a field of eight, being almost distanced by
Hopedale, whom he had pressed so close on the previous occasion.   Such were his disgust and mortification that he thereupon had his name scratched
from both the feather-weight wrestling and the
feather-weight sparring, in each of which events he
had intended to be a competitor.   He felt thoroughly angry, and the secret cause of his anger was

the consciousness that it was all his own fault. He had not taken the trouble to train, so certain was he in his self-conceit of sweeping all before him. Now, like Achilles in his tent, he preferred to sulk. He would cut sports altogether. The game was not worth the candle. But in his heart was a sore spot. He had meant to win that race. He could see Carlisle's eyes fixed on him gravely as he slunk away panting — and fairly blown — at the finish, and recalled his friend's subsequent reproof.

" The trouble with you is that you want the earth, Jack. You can't expect to win without buckling down to it beforehand."

" I 'm in first-rate condition," Jack had growled.

" Over-trained, then, perhaps," had been the sarcastic answer.

Even in rowing — his pet hobby — he could not boast of having made any marked progress. Although in the two upper classes there was no aquatic luminary at the moment, a very clever oarsman was developing in the person of Tom Bonsall of the third, a clean-cut, well-shaped fellow, some ten pounds more beefy than Jack, and at once his secret admiration and despair. To watch Tom row, fairly goaded him into fury. He was only a year ahead of Jack, and yet he was in the Mohicans, and, what is more, was able to boast, after the autumn races, that he belonged to the champion crew. The long victorious Atalantas, weakened by the loss of Hazelhurst, were a poor second. Then and there Jack vowed, when he realized what had taken place, that he would from this moment have but one object in life : to transfer the laurel from his rival's brow to his own.

A very pretty sentiment, and quite at variance with the cynical communings of a fortnight earlier, when he had resolved to renounce sport utterly. But it is one thing to make vows, another to carry them out. Jack had not overestimated, even in his inner consciousness, his lack of condition, both physical and moral. When one is distinctly flabby in body and soul alike, a good resolution is too apt to resemble one of these rockets that flare up grandly and gaudily for a moment, only to leave the night the darker through their inability to last. To feel virtuous and heroic during a transcendent hour is not much to boast of, unless one has the grit to stand firm when face to face once more with the commonplace and the every-day, those disarming begetters of temptation.

But one must not be too hard upon poor Jack because his vows proved no more stable than do those of all of us at some time or other. For at the worst he was not a very hopeless case. Even when sitting up in the lavatory into the small hours of the morning, sipping beer and playing "penny nap," — the height of schoolboy dissipation, — one who could have seen into his heart would not have despaired of him. It was something that he did not smoke, — not because of the harm which Bill French's cheroots might have done him, but because he could not forget that he had promised his mother not to smoke anything, be it rattan, sweet-fern, or tobacco; and to break his word, and most of all to break it to her, was synonymous in his mind, as it well should have been, with a very abandoned moral condition. And yet curiosity in part, and in part an unwillingness to be left behind in "knowledge of life" by the other members of his illustrious society, induced him to follow in whatsoever directions he was led, in spite of the fact that this new and daily more troublesome factor in his general make-up, his conscience, pricked him, and took away much of the satisfaction of his discreditable doings.

What would his mother have said if she could have seen him at one of these cunningly devised nocturnal parties? Her constant prayer has been that her innocent boy may not become prematurely old in the so-called ways of the world,—a knowing little gentleman, rotten before he is ripe, without enthusiasm, without heart, and without hope. Is there a parent who will not sympathize with this mother's petition to heaven? Civilization is regarding with increasing alarm the menaces of the uneducated poor; but its invocation rather should be, "God save us from the educated rich,"—educated and graduated in the sloth and vice which eats into the soul as no other canker can. Rich men's sons who do nothing for humanity but sneer, are a harder burden for Atlas to bear than all the host of the starving unemployed.

But even in his present stage, when it seemed as though Bill French's wisdom carried all before it in the councils of the Big Four, Jack much preferred the life of the border ruffian to that of the sly voluptuary. Bill's fun, though he had his part in it, appeared tame as compared with the ecstasy which proceeds from more obvious peril. To carry away a quart of lager under one's waistband, to go in debt to the amount of half a dollar if one's luck was bad, and to show up next morning sallow and watery-eyed, but very spruce and stylish as to one's collar and tie, proud as the distinction was, did not set Jack's-veins a-throbbing as he delighted to have them throb. If Bill had been consulted in the premises he would doubtless have maintained that his friend was not yet educated up to the point where he could appreciate at their proper value the advantages open to him. To this juvenile Epicurean the plots which the two more boisterous spirits were constantly unfolding involved a needless waste of vitality, from which he shrank more and more in proportion as the serpent's wisdom became his own. It was not policy, however, even if it were possible, to resist at all times the expressed desire of half the society. As a consequence, vitality ran riot in minor manifestations, such as the pilfering of neighboring hen-roosts, the sealing up of the lock of the schoolroom door, the firing of a tar-barrel in front of the Doctor's very window, and panted for more. Every one — by which is meant school opinion — was delighted, and with finger on lip whispered mysteriously, "Big Four."

As for Jack and Haseltine, they trod the earth with the demeanor of gods, and after dark put their heads together. Presumptuous youth is slow to be content with moderate glory. Had Phaeton escaped destruction he would have wearied of driving his father's horses in a fortnight, and been thirsting for a fresh exploit. Our heroes, who had up to this time escaped detection, were harassed by the feeling that authority took too little heed of the cuffs they administered to it. The bonfire had been put up with almost calmly. The next act of defiance should be such as could not be passed over without exposing their enemies to ridicule.

It was not altogether easy to hit upon a device worthy of their prowess and yet within the pale of permissible barbarity. For undoubtedly nihilistic as were Jack's and Haseltine's designs, there was a limit which they were not prepared to overstep. Although it might be that in the estimation of them both hanging was too good for the Doctor and his assistants, any plot endangering human life was, perchance regretfully, but none the less firmly, discarded. On the other hand, to burn the head master in effigy, a proposal which emanated from the seething brain of young Horton, struck the conclave as a superficial bit of mischief, which, however showy from its impertinence, would nevertheless inflict no real suffering on him at whom it was aimed.

Bill French, as was apt to be the case, even in matters outside of his own department, so to speak, settled the question finally.

"I say, fellows, I know what let's do," he said one evening, after they had been sitting silently racking their brains for a considerable time; "let's blow something up."

"Blow what up?" queried Jack, somewhat scornfully, thus showing that gunpowder and nitroglycerine had already entered into his day-dreams, but had been renounced for lack of suitable material on which to experiment.

"The tool-house."

"Great Cæsar!" ejaculated our hero with enthusiasm, "the very thing! Why have we never thought of it before?"

Whereupon Jack, by way of further ecstasy, began to execute a muffled clog-dance to a low whistling accompaniment.

"Sh! You'll have Sawyer down on us like a thousand of bricks if you don't let up," objected Bill.

The quarters of "The Big Four" were no longer in the lavatory, where their only light had been the proverbially capricious splendor of the moon, and where no whisper was too low for safety. At the beginning of this school year one of the studies occupied by the two upper classes, which had become vacant owing to the illness of its proprietor, had been boldly appropriated by the society. A piece of cloth over the keyhole and other appliances along the floor-line prevented the rays of the solitary candle which illumined their meetings from betraying them; and there they sat like four young ghouls, with masks upon their faces, or close at hand ready to be donned at the first signal of danger.

The tool-house referred to was a modest structure behind the gymnasium, which served Horace Hosmer for the use which its name suggests, and was besides a general storehouse in which to stow odds and ends out of place elsewhere. It stood in a position well adapted to shelter from discovery the mooted scheme on the fulfillment of which the energies of the Big Four were now resolutely bent. To obtain the needful ammunition required time; but on returning to school at the close of the spring recess the united accumulations of the conspirators' pockets were found to be two small cans of powder, a bunch of cannon-crackers, a piece of slow-match, and several fuses. The last-named were especially valuable for the reason that, to insure the safety of the society, a sufficient period must elapse between the touching off the mine and the explosion to allow those participating to cross the quadrangle and be hauled up again in the basket which was to be let down from the study where their meetings were held.

This does not look much like reform, Master Jack. Seeing you in such a guise at twelve o'clock at night — though no one would ever recognize you in your ferocious mask with the flowing horsehair mustache and your coat-collar muffled about your ears — makes one wonder whether you were really in earnest when you made your vow not to rest until you had defeated Tom Bonsall at the sculls. No use in our moralizing now, however, for wild horses would not keep you from your part in the tragedy. And indeed there is something rather winning, almost exculpating as it were, in the proud though mistaken consciousness of a righteous cause resplendent in your every movement and gesture. One sighs to see such energy and ardor of spirit expended in so mean a task. Even *you* would admit, if squarely taxed on the point, that you have no real grievance against the Doctor except that he is determined to make you study and to make **you** obey. "Yes, but that is the point at issue," you would doubtless answer. "We prefer idleness and insubordination. Why should we obey?"

On the night selected for the explosion, duly at the appointed hour the four boys crept on tiptoe from their respective dens in the large dormitory to the usual spot without disturbing anybody. Each brought with him part of the necessary paraphernalia. They proceeded immediately to draw lots to decide which two should perform the actual deed. The other pair were to remain behind to lower the basket down and pull it up again. It was solved by the process known as "freezing out." Each took a cent from his pocket and laid it on the table. There were three heads and one tail. Bill French's was the tail. He was therefore by previous agreement to be one of the home-guard. With trembling hand Jack deposited his coin for the second time. Not to be able to light the fuse himself would rob the affair of half its sweetness for him.

His was a head.

"A head," said Haseltine.

"So's mine," said Horton.

"No choice, then," said Bill. "Toss again."

This time Jack got a tail. He leaned forward feverishly and perceived that Horton had one also.

" A head," said Haséltine.

" You stay with me, then," said Bill, who was quick-witted in emergencies. "Let's get to work. Sooner it's over, the better."

Jack's heart gave a bound. It would have suited him to have had Haseltine with him, and he whispered in the ear of his favorite pal some words to that effect. It was everything, however, to be going himself, and he was well aware that Horton was no slouch on such an occasion.

It takes but a few moments to adjust the rope, and the two lads, after stowing the combustibles in their pockets, are ready to descend. Jack is the proud bearer of a small dark lantern, which gives him an additionally burglarish air. He flashes it once or twice playfully in Bill's face, much to that worthy's dissatisfaction, who is even more nervous than usual, going now and again to the door to listen after enjoining silence by an agonized "sh!"

But everything is as still as the grave. Being finally satisfied on this score, Bill proceeds with an air of gravity to uncork a couple of bottles of beer from which he fills four glasses, the property of the society and kept in a cupboard in the corner.

Each of the Big Four having doffed his mask lifts one of these from the table and surveys his fellow-members with dignity, waiting for the word of command from the Pater Primus, as the presiding genius is styled, before putting the beaded beverage to their lips.

"Brothers of the Big Four," begins Bill. "Once again we are met together to maintain justice and to resist tyranny. Here's success, and destruction to our foes."

"Success, and destruction to our foes."

As the voices echo his words the four glasses softly clink against one another. Then the heroes drink. It is a solemn rite to Jack. His blood is all on fire.

"We will die game," he utters grandiloquently, as he drains the last drops, and slips back his mask over his face much as a warrior would have replaced a helmet.

He goes to the window and tries the rope. It is strong enough for six times the necessary weight. He is putting one foot into the basket — a large clothes - basket filched the day before from Mrs. Betty's department — when Bill again enjoins silence and bends his ear.

"It's all right, Bill," whispers Jack.

"I don't half like it," replies the Pater Primus. "If we're caught, it means expulsion cock sure."

"Who's going to catch us? It isn't the time to squawk now."

"Who wants to squawk?" protests Bill.

"Lower away."

Down goes the basket slowly but surely with its living freight. Practice in former exploits has made the descent seem less ticklish than at first to the young aëronauts.

Jack and Horton having reached the earth in safety walk cautiously but rapidly across the part of the quadrangle which lies between them and the gymnasium, pass behind that building, and a moment later are in the tool-house. So far as danger to other property is concerned there is no reason why the tool-house should not be blown up: a reflection somewhat comforting to Jack, who in spite of his elation is conscious of a qualm or two as he realizes what he is about to do. No one can possibly be injured, he argues, and the tool-house is really of no use.

By the light of the dark lantern they arrange the cans of powder in such a manner as to be most effective, and lay the fuse. Then Jack, who has lighted a bit of slow match, after taking a peep outside to make sure that all is clear, sets fire to the train, which has been timed to burn for ten minutes, so as to permit every one to get back to bed before the shock comes. This done, the two imitators of Guy Fawkes slip out into the darkness and make a bee-line for home.

Somehow or other there is very apt to be some little flaw capable of ruining all, even in the most skillfully arranged plot, and, happily or unhappily, as you choose to regard it, the one in question proved no exception to the general rule. Moreover, it was through the carelessness of our friend Jack that matters did not turn out wholly as was expected. Although quite aware that Argus in the person of Horace Hosmer slept in an L of the gymnasium, the window of which commanded a view of the premises doomed to destruction, Guy Fawkes was rash enough not to close his lantern until just after stepping into the open air, so that a few rays managed to shoot themselves directly into the watch-dog's eyes with the effect of rousing the vigilant sleeper from his couch and inducing him to take a peep outside. . It was all dark now, but suspicion once awakened is not easily allayed in a faithful soul, and Horace's was of the faithful kind. Hastily pulling on a pair of boots and diving into an overcoat, he vaulted over the window-sill, and put in an appearance on the other side of the gymnasium before the boys were more than two thirds across the quadrangle.

Trepidation has eyes in the back of her head, as we well know. Consequently this new presence on the field of night was spotted by Horton even before Horace's well-known stentorian voice broke in upon the stillness with, —

"Come, now, what's your business?"

There was no time for parley. Increased speed had forestalled the bark of Argus, and increased speed answered it. The wings of fear vibrated fiercely in the darkness. The pursued had this advantage that they knew that unless they reached the basket in time to get clear of *terra firma* be-

AN ESCAPE.

fore the janitor was upon them they were "gone coons." Not a word was spoken by either of the terror-stricken incendiaries, but their flight was that of those who have but one hope.

Jack was the first to arrive. Happily for the hunted, their companions had not been napping, but were keenly on the watch for them. The basket was ready. Guy Fawkes leaped into it and squatted down, closely followed by his mate.

"Pull for all you 're worth."

Those above, quick to perceive that there was mischief in the wind, set themselves to their task with such good will that the aërial car fairly bounded from the ground in its ascending course. But none too soon. Hardly was it beyond the reach of a tall man when the cause of all this undignified haste came tearing round the angle of the dormitory. Horace made one desperate leap in the air, only, however, to scratch his nails against the bricks in falling back. By the time he had regained his balance the basket was at the top, and he could only catch a confused impression of grotesque faces surmounting youthful bodies before the masqueraders were safe indoors, and fleeing like stealthy deer to their respective quarters, where they lost no time in slipping off their clothes and getting into bed. So precipitate was their flight that they neglected to return the beer - bottles and glasses to the cupboard in which they were ordinarily concealed, an oversight which filled the nervous Bill with dismay when it occurred to him after his head was on the pillow. As for the basket, it fell backward from the window-sill the moment it was empty, almost on to the head of the astonished Horace, who examined it curiously.

" Well, well," he muttered, " these are fine doings. My eyes ain't what they used to be, but I 've a pretty decided notion as to who you are, my young masters, all the same. What in time were you up to, I wonder? Ha! what 's this? "

Horace, from a constitutional habit of thoroughness, had been passing his hand over the bottom of the basket, and his last exclamation was due to the fact of its coming in contact with a small article which on inspection proved to be a pocket-knife.

" H'm," he chuckled, " Heaven sends biscuit to them as has no teeth, as the minister used to say." After which pertinent observation the honest fellow slipped the treasure trove into his pocket and was taking up the basket again with a view to appropriating it as evidence, when a loud crash proceeding from the direction of the gymnasium awoke the echoes of Utopia.

"Holy Moses!" ejaculated the janitor, as he turned just in season to behold a column of smoke and rubbish rise in the near distance. Whereupon he started as fast as his legs could carry him to the new scene of action.

Needless to say, the four conspirators heard with mingled sensations of joy and anxiety the reverberation which informed them that their efforts had not been in vain. To Jack at least the noise, though clearly perceptible, was not so loud as he had hoped and anticipated. It had been his ambition to have not only the whole dormitory awakened, but authority itself startled from sweet slumber and forced to put its head out of doors in search of cause and effect. He experienced, therefore, some little disappointment from the fact that only two or three boys within reach of his own observation were awakened, and even they turned over to sleep again after listening for a moment for further developments. He was much too wide awake himself to sleep, but lay revolving in his mind the probable consequences of Horace's untoward interruption. Had Argus recognized them? That was the all-important point, uncertainty as to which was far from pleasant to Jack, despite his boasted indifference to authority. Visions of being dismissed from Utopia floated with disagreeable persistency before his mind's eye. What would his mother say? He might well ask himself that question.

Although the repose of authority was not disturbed, authority heard with amazement on the following morning the news which Horace had to tell it immediately after breakfast; and Jack could have no reason this time to complain that authority was slow to take notice, if the buzz of rumors floating about the school were any index of authority's state of mind. The impression produced on the youthful mind itself by the announcement of what had taken place was profound. There was an exodus at once to view the ruins, over which the faithful janitor was presiding with a sphinx-like grin that to Jack, who had strolled down with the rest to behold the result of his handiwork, did not seem reassuring.

At the first opportunity the guilty parties held a hurried consultation for mutual encouragement and the comparing of notes. Nothing was forthcoming except that the Doctor, after visiting the scene of the explosion, had granted an audience to Horace Hosmer, with whom he was still closeted. Meanwhile the ordinary school programme was going on as usual. Such suspense, though wellnigh unendurable, was relieved in due time. Late in the afternoon a summons came that French, Horton, and Hall were to go to the Doctor's room at once, but separately, and in the order named.

There was only time for a passing word between the trio.

"Mind we tell the same story and stick to it," whispered Bill in Jack's ear before he followed the messenger. "We never knew anything until we heard the explosion."

Jack stood watching the receding figure of the Pater Primus with a troubled air. The situation seemed decidedly perplexing. Authority, for some reason or other of its own, saw fit that those coming after should have no opportunity to hear what was in store for them from friendly lips. Consequently the third conspirator on the list was ushered into its injured presence without knowing what had been the experience of his predecessors.

Doctor Meredith, who was alone, greeted the culprit gravely and said, after a moment's hesitation, in a composed but serious tone: "During the last six months, Hall, there have been a number of very troublesome bits of mischief perpetrated in the school. The property of people in the neighborhood has been molested, fireworks have been discharged in the yard without permission, and a general disposition to break rules on the part of a certain number of individuals has been apparent. I have been very slow to take notice of this, hoping that the matters complained of were merely the result of the high spirits natural to boys. But I have been very much annoyed by it, for up to this time I have had to deal with nothing of the sort at Utopia."

During the pause which elapsed before he continued, Jack was able to congratulate himself that his previous endeavors had not been so much ignored as he had at one time feared.

" Last night," his inquisitor proceeded, still more gravely, "as you must be already aware, the tool-house was blown up by some malicious person or persons. Doubtless it was done as a practical joke, and I am willing to believe that whoever was engaged in the affair did not appreciate the serious character of the act committed. But all the same it was an abominable piece of mischief, and one which it is my duty and intention to investigate thoroughly, with a view to putting down, once and for all, the spirit of reckless insubordination which it is now evident to me has broken out here."

Once more the Doctor paused, as though he expected some observation from his auditor, who, having none to make, sought refuge from his own discomfort and his master's penetrating eye, by looking down at the floor.

" I have sent for you, Hall, to ask if you were concerned in the affair."

The room seemed painfully still to Jack, and the silence which followed this inquiry oppressive. How should he answer the question? If the Doctor knew all, why had he not taxed him directly with having blown up the tool-house, instead of asking him if he was concerned in it? The doctor evidently had suspicions merely, and was groping in the dark. What was there to prove his guilt except his own admissions?

During the brief interval in which these thoughts were passing through Jack's mind, he was conscious of his interrogator's eye bent on him searchingly — yet beseechingly, as it were.

"You have not answered me, Hall."

"Yes, sir; I was."

Jack was too self-absorbed to notice the sigh of relief which the Doctor gave vent to. One could have heard a pin drop.

"I am very sorry to hear it. You were not alone, I judge," added his master, after a moment.

"I lighted the fuse myself, sir," was the diplomatic reply.

"I see that you do not choose to name your associates."

"I have not said that I had any," Jack answered stoutly.

"I respect your views on that point, and shall question you no further in the matter. As for your own conduct, there is but one word to characterize it," continued Dr. Meredith, — " shameful. I do not understand what motive you can have had to destroy the property of the school. What *was* your motive?" Jack looked sheepish. " I suppose it was sheer love of mischief," pursued the Doctor, as though soliloquizing.

" Yes, sir."

" Have you not always been well treated here? Have you any cause of complaint?"

" No, sir."

" What in one sense is even a more serious matter, empty beer-bottles and glasses were found this morning in the vacant study. They belong to you, I take it?"

Jack bit his lip. This charge was harder to assume the entire responsibility for. But he was in for it now and must face the music.

" Yes, sir," he replied, rather dejectedly.

The Doctor was silent for a moment. " Hall, I am very much disappointed in you," he said, in a manner so unexpectedly genuine that somehow or other the words cut like a knife into the sensibilities of poor Jack, and in a sudden flash he saw his own conduct almost in its true light. " This is not the first time, by any means, that I have had occasion to be disturbed at your conduct. I cannot have at this school," he added, " boys who drink beer on the sly and blow up buildings. I have not quite decided what action I shall take in your particular case. You may go for the present. When I want you I will send for you."

Jack stood hesitating. " May I ask a question ? " he said.

" What is it ? "

" How were we found out? — er — that is, how did you know it was I ? "

" The janitor thought he recognized you ; but he was not sure. If you had seen fit to tell a falsehood you might have escaped. I thank God, my dear boy, that you had courage enough to resist that far worse fault than the faults you have been guilty of."

There were tears in the Doctor's eyes, and a strange tremor in his voice, that brought drops to Jack's own, of which he became conscious when he was outside the study-door. He had never felt so miserable in his life, and yet knew that he was proud of the course he had taken.

A few minutes later he was eagerly confronted by his associates.

"He does n't know anything, does he?" exclaimed Bill.

"What do you mean?"

"You did n't let on, of course? He asked me if I had anything to do with blowing up the toolhouse, and I told him no. So did Horton."

"But you did," said Jack.

"Do you mean to say you gave us all away?" shrieked Bill.

"Your names were n't mentioned. I was n't going to lie about it. The Doctor asked me if I was n't concerned in it, and I said I was."

"Hang me if you are n't the biggest flat I ever struck!"

"That's so," said Horton, who, as you must know by this time, was only an echo of Bill, which is a pretty feeble kind of part to play in life, as parts go.

"If you had only kept your mouth shut we'd have been all right. Horace only guessed at us," continued the irate Pater Primus. "I'd back you for a flat against the world."

" That 's so."

" Shut your head! " growled Jack. " I don't
want to hear any more guff from either of you.
I wasn't going to lie for you or any other fellow,
Bill French."

" We 'll kick you out of the society, see if we
don't. You 've broken the oaths, and you 'll be
mighty lucky if we don't vote to make cat's meat
of you," persisted Bill, who, when his imagination
got working, had a nasty tongue, as the saying is.
This last fling so enraged our hero — who has
become, I think, just a little bit of a hero in spite
of his shortcomings — that he made a dash at his
chief insulter with a view to slapping his face.
But the prudent William had made sure of his
distance before venturing upon so exasperating a
speech.

Jack was in no frame of mind to pursue his ma-
ligners. He felt very much down in the mouth.
Now that the prospect of being sent home in disgrace was imminent, the advantages of remaining
a Utopia boy seemed very great. He could not
bear the thought of being expelled, and yet he
knew that he could scarcely hope for any less seri-

ous sentence. The others would get off, and he would have to bear the brunt of it all.

In his agitation he started off at a rapid pace without heeding where he was going. Chance led him toward the lake, and a few moments later he was in his wherry pulling fiercely from sheer desperation over the tranquil water. There were not many scullers out this afternoon, but he recognized in the distance the shapely figure of Tom Bonsall, whose clean-cut, sweeping stroke it was not easy to mistake. Jack ground his teeth as he reflected not only that he and Tom could not at present be regarded as rivals, but that they now never could become so. Stung by the bitterness of the thought, he plied the oars savagely with a reckless expenditure of energy. When at last he gave in for a moment from sheer exhaustion, his shell shot close past another, narrowly escaping a collision.

" Whoa, there! Hold your horses!" cried a well-known voice.

It was Carlisle's. At any other time Jack would have been only too glad of his friend's company; now his inclination was to get away from everybody. Without remark he began rowing again with lightning speed, evidently to the surprise of Carlisle, who, after watching him for a moment, proceeded to follow in his wake, taking it quietly, but pulling a long, steady stroke. Jack was determined to throw him off, but though he struggled with all his might, his pursuer crept up on him inch by inch without seeming to make any special exertion. So frantically did he work to keep the lead that he soon began to splash, and finally, to his utter disgust, caught a crab just as Carlisle was lapping him. Before he could recover himself they were abreast.

"My dear youngster," began his friend without observing Jack's face, "you will never learn to row if you spend yourself so soon. You can't keep that stroke up. It's simply suicidal."

"Why can't you let me alone? What right have you to follow me?" was the fierce reply.

Naturally Carlisle looked completely bewildered. "No right, if you don't want me to," he said quietly. Then he added, with kind solicitude, "What's up, Jack? Are you ill, old fellow?"

Jack shook his head after a moment. He

was looking the other way to hide his welling tears.

"Tell me what's the trouble. Perhaps I can help you," said Carlisle presently.

"It isn't one thing: it's everything," sobbed Jack. "However, there'll be an end of it to-morrow," he continued enigmatically.

"What do you mean by that?"

"It was-I who blew up the tool-house last night."

"You, Jack!" Carlisle exclaimed, aghast. "How could you!"

Then realizing instantly that this was not the occasion for reproof, he hastened to ask, "Does the Doctor know?"

"Yes," said Jack, who had turned his face to observe the effect on his friend of the first announcement.

A few words made Carlisle familiar with the whole story. Jack did not hesitate to inform him just how matters stood, knowing that his senior would be in honor bound not to mention to others the conduct of Bill and Horton.

"There can be only one end to it," he said, in conclusion. "He'll make an example of me for the good of the school. Well, let him," he added, his voice again breaking, "*I* don't care."

"Yes, you do care. The cowardly sneaks!" ejaculated Carlisle.

"If they had owned up, there would have been three instead of one, that's all. It wouldn't have helped me any. I'm glad of one thing, Louis: Horace didn't spot Hasy."

The other was silent a moment. "It's all my fault," he burst out at last. "I ought to have protected you against that fellow. I marked him as a low-lived beggar before he had been here a week. The trouble is, I am so miserably selfish that I am taken up with my own affairs all the time."

"Indeed, that is not true, Louis. On the contrary, you've been at me all the time trying to keep me straight. It's no one's fault but my own. I see it plainly now. I've made an ass of myself, and the result is I shall break my mother's heart by being expelled."

"Time enough to talk in that style, youngster, when it happens. I'll see the Doctor myself," continued Carlisle. "Perhaps he'll be willing to

give you another chance. There's no harm in trying, at any rate. If he can be made to believe that
you're ready to turn over a new leaf, I know he'll
let you stay. But you must promise me, Jack,
that if he does, you will make a fresh deal all
round," he added, earnestly. " I'm slack enough
myself, Heaven knows, and not fitted to give advice to any one, but I've lived two or three years
longer than you; and have learned at least that a
fellow can't do everything that he wants in this
world. One has to recognize it sooner or later.
The trouble with you, as I told you once before, is
that you want the earth. You can't have it, and
the sooner you make up your mind to the fact the
better for you."

"I will do my best, Louis, I promise you. I
wish though I thought that there was ever a chance
of my being half so good as you."

"Nonsense, youngster. You've no idea," he
added, "of what a poor thing I am."

"You are looking in first-rate condition this
term," responded Jack, with a just perception of
how to please his friend. "I never saw a fellow
improve so in appearance as you have in a year."

"It's Dr. Bolles' lectures," said Carlisle, with a
gratified smile. "I owe it all to him."

"And if I ever improve," observed Jack quietly,
"I shall owe it all to you, Louis."

CHAPTER X.

UP-HILL.

THREE days later the whole school was called together directly after breakfast to hear a communication from Dr. Meredith. No one knew precisely what was in the wind, but all sorts of rumors had been floating about ever since the morning subsequent to the explosion. The only one of these that appeared to have substantial foundation was the report which had gained currency within the last twenty-four hours that Horton was to leave for good. The reason was not known beyond a general suspicion that his departure was connected with the destruction of the tool-house. When it was ascertained that he had actually gone early in the morning without bidding good-by to anybody, the excitement was at fever heat. What added to the mystery was that Jack Hall, whose confession of the daring deed had leaked out, still remained.

Utopia was puzzled, to say the least, and was

very prompt in filing into the schoolroom to listen
to the expected solution of the enigma. Thither
the Doctor came too, on the stroke of the hour,
looking sad, and accompanied by all the masters,
who ranged themselves about him as at one of the
school exhibitions. Before him on the desk lay a
suggestive ferule, the unaccustomed sight of which
caused expectancy to stand on tiptoe.

"Boys of Utopia School," said Dr. Meredith
with solemnity, "as you all know, an unpardon-
ably malicious piece of mischief was committed
against the school property a few days since. It
was the last and most offensive in a series of deliberate acts of insubordination which have caused me
much annoyance, and which I have put up with too
long, I am inclined to think, for the best good of
those concerned in them. By chance," continued
the Doctor, after a moment's delay, "suspicion fastened itself on certain members of the school, who
were sent for by me and questioned on the subject.
One boy confessed to having been directly connected
with the explosion; the others denied all knowledge of it. As it happened, the evidence possessed by us was not definite enough to convict as

against his own word any one of those suspected, with a single exception, and I will add that at the time I had no knowledge which of the boys summoned this exception applied to. The janitor who pursued the incendiaries on the night in question found in the basket, which was left by them hanging from the window, a penknife. This penknife," said the Doctor slowly, " was proved to belong, I regret with deep-sorrow to state, to one of the boys who had denied in unqualified terms any knowledge of the outrage which had been committed. That boy is no longer a member of this school. I have written to his parents to remove him, and early this morning he left Utopia.

" If there is anything that is odious to me," he continued presently, after the murmur which followed this announcement had subsided, "and which I am determined to root out of this school at any cost, it is falsehood. I made a point to caution each one of you against it, my dear boys, at the time you entered Utopia, and my constant prayer is that your souls may be kept clean from this deadly foe to character. What is most threatening to-day in the outlook for the noble develop-

ment of this great democratic country of ours is
the tendency to condone too easily embezzlement,
breaches of trust, bribery, and other forms of public and private dishonesty, the kernel of which is
deceit, and in the fostering of which lies national
ruin. If," he said, looking round the schoolroom,
" there is any boy here to-day who is so unhappy
as to have a lie on his conscience, I beseech him as
his master and his friend to let it be there no longer.
Any punishment that he may be called upon to
bear will be as nothing compared with the evil
which concealment will work upon his character
and life."

As the Doctor paused and seemed to be waiting
for some one to step forward, each boy glanced at
his neighbor, wondering for the most part who was
meant. Jack, who had been listening with fever-
ish impatience to every word, refrained from looking directly at Bill, but managed to take a peep at
him sideways. To all appearances the Pater Primus was completely at his ease and indisposed to
follow the hint thrown out to him. No one stirred,
and the silence, which became oppressive at last,
was broken by the master, who resumed rather
sadly : —

"When the boy who was manly enough to confess his wrong-doing left my presence the other day, I thought that it would be necessary for me in order to maintain the dignity of the school to inflict the most serious punishment in my power — that is expulsion. I should have hated to do so, for I like the boy, deeply as I deplore the rank insubordination and gross idleness of which he has been guilty since he came to Utopia. I am ready to believe that it will be more for his good to remain among us than to be sent away in disgrace; and I am heartily glad that the greater fault committed by another enables me to exercise leniency in his particular case. I have been given to understand by those interested in him," pursued the Doctor, "that he is sorry for his ill behavior and anxious to turn over a new leaf. I shall give him the chance to do so; but I am obliged nevertheless not to pass by without serious notice the wicked breach of discipline which he committed in wantonly destroying the property of the school. There was no excuse for the act whatever, and it was singularly unprovoked and impertinent. Therefore I am compelled to have recourse to a form of punishment which, except in the most extreme cases, should not be employed by a master. I am glad to say that never before while I have been at Utopia has it been necessary for me to whip a pupil. I am about to do so now because of the unusual nature of the offense of which he has been guilty. — Hall, you will come forward to receive a public whipping."

There was a painful silence, and then poor Jack, who had been sent for by the Doctor late on the previous evening and informed as to what was in store for him, arose and walked down the aisle. His blood was boiling with shame and anger, but at the same time he had made up his mind to submit to the flogging and to bear it without flinching, in acknowledgment of the kind words of encouragement and friendship which his master had spoken to him when he told him what his punishment was to be, — words which made Jack see more clearly than before how reckless and foolish he had been, and resolve with bitter tears before he went to sleep to try once more to resist temptation. Now, galling as was the ordeal, and though the tears of mortification welled into his eyes in spite of resolute biting of the lips, he walked quietly up to the desk.

Dr. Meredith had risen and stood ready with the ferule.

" Hold out your right hand, Hall."

Jack obeyed.

Down came the blows — one, two, three, four, five, six, seven, eight, nine, ten, eleven, twelve, thirteen, fourteen, fifteen ; — no love pats, but genuine hard stinging blows which were meant to hurt, and which did hurt.

" Now, the other hand."

Fifteen more followed no less scorching than their predecessors.

" That will do. You may take your seat."

Jack, whose only consolation at the moment was that he had not winced, got back to his desk somehow or other, and heard as in a daze the faltering voice of his castigator in conclusion : —

" I hope to heaven, my dear boys, that it will never be necessary for me to do such a thing again. I would much rather, believe me, that every one of those blows had been on my own hands. The pain would have been far less than what I suffered in inflicting them."

A moment later Jack knew that the school had arisen and was pouring out of the room. He had covered his face with his hands and bent his head upon the desk. Sob followed sob in quick succession, and his heart seemed to be bursting. Carlisle, who had remained behind, stood over him and stroked his head gently. After such an experience, a nature strong and virile as Jack's must needs find a vent for its pent-up anguish. But bitter as were his feelings, he knew in his heart that he had deserved his punishment.

It was many weeks before Jack recovered his spirits. At first he walked about with a crestfallen air, like one in disgrace. He kept apart by himself, and instead of the spirited leader of old, seemed subdued and unimpressionable. He did not enter for the spring events either at the athletic meeting or on the lake, and was judged by many to have lost all interest in sports. His changed demeanor gave a chance to Bill French to circulate the opinion expressed at the time of his confession, that he was a flat, and such is the tendency of boys to deprecate what they cannot understand that there were some who in their surprise at his apparent listlessness

adopted Bill's view of the case. Even Haseltine was
staggered at his friend's lack of enthusiasm over the
prowess of the school nine, which, under the captaincy of the "Kid," had been plucking unexpected
laurels from visiting and visited teams, and rallied
him on it. Hasy, by the way, had been very sore
at heart himself that Jack alone should have had
to bear the brunt of the tool-house escapade. Accordingly, after musing over the matter for a fortnight, he had gone one day to the Doctor, without
mentioning the matter to any one, and made a clean
breast of his own participation in the affair, with
the expectation and almost with the hope of being
made to suffer for it. But, quite to his astonishment, Dr. Meredith, after hearing his story and
thanking him for having had the courage to own
up, which was unquestionably the manly thing to
do under the circumstances, declined to take advantage of the confession further than to talk to him
kindly for half an hour on the desirability of a
little more steadiness and more interest in study
on his part.

"If only you felt half the concern regarding a
poor recitation that you do about muffing a fly,

you would be at the head of your class, Haseltine,"
the Doctor had said genially, — a proposition which
to his listener had seemed to border almost on the
ludicrous. As if, forsooth, comparison could be
made as to the relative importance of the ability to
hold on to a difficult sky-scraper and any excellence
in the class-room under the sun !

Hasy's opinion on this point was so unqualified
that a certain disposition to take his lessons more
into account, which Jack was beginning to show,
struck the young base-ball enthusiast as stronger
evidence than any other adduced of his friend's un-
natural condition.   Not that he for a moment went
over to Bill French's faction, — indeed, his contempt for that worthy's behavior had been quite in
proportion to Jack's, — but as he found it impossible to understand how his crony could derive satisfaction from this new habit of trying to learn his
lessons beforehand instead of letting them be ham-
mered into him in the schoolroom, he was naturally
puzzled and felt almost provoked.   Indeed, his dis-
approval of his friend's behavior was so sweeping that he failed to perceive that Jack in a quiet
way was getting into very good form on the river

by force of daily practice under the tutorship of Carlisle. Because Jack did not spurt, and appeared indisposed to tackle any and everybody, the impression was current that even in rowing, as in everything else, he was down on his marrow-bones.

So far as his own feelings went, it cannot be denied that Jack was far from cheerful during the weeks intervening between the date of his punishment and the end of his fourth-class year; and when vacation was at hand, he looked back on his efforts at improvement with a glum heart. Secretly and almost sullenly he had tried hard to redeem himself; but though others might see indications of progress, it seemed to our hero as though he was just as much in the slough as ever. He had always entertained the fancy that if at any time he should take it into his head to do well at his books and become a pattern of exemplary conduct, he would find it a perfectly simple matter to do so. Accordingly the poor fellow was now learning the lesson which so many have to learn, that continued neglect and frowardness can only be atoned for by humiliation and despondency.

These were principally experienced in regard to

his lessons, as he found slight difficulty in avoiding flagrant breaches of the rules now that the meetings of the Big Four were discontinued. The illustrious society had never been actually disbanded; but the transportation, so to speak, of one of its choice spirits, and the lack of cordiality existing between at least two of those remaining, had caused a hiatus in its proceedings which still gaped. An overture on the part of the Pater Primus to meet and talk matters over was rejected by Jack and Haseltine with scorn; and though Bill would have liked to get together by himself, as the saying is, and expel his mates with a view to reorganization, he probably had some doubts regarding the constitutionality of such a proceeding, or else was afraid of having his head punched, for he abstained from action in the matter.

But keeping up to the mark in his Latin and history and algebra was a very different affair, as Jack realized as soon as he tried to buckle down to work. He scarcely knew what to do in order to study, and it seemed at first as though he used to make a better showing when he trusted to luck, the prompting of those beside him, and the various other straws at which struggling dunces clutch when floundering in recitation. The exhibitions of ignorance which he made, now that he was bent on distinguishing himself, covered him with confusion in the presence of his instructors, and his hopeless attempts beforehand to compass the mysteries of irregular verbs, subjunctive clauses, and other grewsome obstacles in the pathway of learning, reduced him to despair. He detested study more than ever, and felt as though he should never be anywhere but at the foot of his class, struggle as he would. Pegging away seemed to make no difference. Could any one, he asked himself, tell from their respective showings in the schoolroom which had prepared his lesson in advance, Haseltine or he?

When a boy has acquired a reputation for idleness, it naturally takes time to convince those in authority over him that he is trying to do better. Some masters of course are quicker than others in noting the symptoms of change, which, as has been intimated in Jack's case, are not apt to be obvious at the start; and the masters at Utopia were no exceptions to this rule. Although several of them had discrimination enough to recognize in the poor boy's halting, blushing efforts the germ of awakened ambition, there were one or two who, with his recent whipping in mind, judged these signals of distress as indications that he was obstinately continuing in his old ways. Consequently his mistakes were treated by them with severity, which took the form, according to the disposition of the master, of stern reproof or of sarcasm. It was in vain that Jack's eyes filled with tears on such occasions, for his misguided tormentors saw in them merely the simulated grief of the crocodile or unrighteous anger.

The cup of his bitterness was filled to overflowing one day just previous to the end of the term, when Mr. Opdyke, his Latin master, called him up to recite in Virgil in the presence of some visitors. Mr. Opdyke, though ambitious that his class should make a good appearance, being also a very conscientious man, felt obliged to conduct the recitation just as he would have conducted it had no stranger been present, and consequently to call up a sprinkling of poor as well as of good scholars, in order to give a just impression as to the general average.

Jack trembled in every limb as he heard the unwelcome words :

" Hall, you may go on."

The class was reading the third book of the
Æneid, and the passage which had fallen to Jack's
lot began with the five hundred and sixty-first
line :

> " Haud minus ac jussi faciunt; primusque rudentem
> Contorsit lævas proram Palinurus ad undas;
> Lævam cuncta cohors remis ventisque petivit.
> Tollimur in cœlum curvato gurgite, et idem
> Subducta ad Manes imos desedimus unda.
> Ter scopuli clamorem inter cava saxa dedere :
> Ter spumam elisam et rorantia vidimus astra."

Jack managed to scan it through tolerably well,
and then began to translate.

" Not less than commanded they did " —

" Mind your tense, Hall."

" Er — do " —

" Go on. ' They do not otherwise than commanded.' "

" At first " —

" Well ? What does ' primus ' agree with ? "

" Palinurus," says Jack at length.

" Correct. ' And Palinurus was the first to turn,'
or, literally, ' Palinurus first turned.' What is
' contorsit ' from, Hall ? "

" Contorgo," essays Jack valiantly.

" Nothing of the sort. — Anybody ? "

" ' Contorqueo,' " cries a small lad, who has shot up his hand.

" Correct, Barrows. ' Contorqueo.' Go on, Hall."

" And Palinurus was the first to turn the rud- der " —

" Where do you find anything about rudder?" inquires Mr. Opdyke, with the irony of desperation.

" ' Rudentem.' "

" Indeed!   Barrows, tell Hall what ' rudentem ' means."

" A rope," suggests the youth named, too elated evidently by his first success.

" Timmins ? "

" Don't know, sir."

" Brown ? "

" Roaring."

" That 's right.   What part of speech is it ? "

" Present participle, accusative case, from ' rudo.' "

" Correct," says Mr. Opdyke.   " ' Rudens ' means ' a rope,' Barrows.   Some authorities ascribe its derivation to ' rudo ' on account of the rattling noise made by a rope.   Conjugate ' rudo,' Barrows."

"' Rudo, rudire ' " —

" Haseltine ? "

"' Rudo, rudare ' " —

" Brown ? "

"' Rudo, rudere, rudivi, ruditum.' "

" Correct; 'rudire, to roar, bellow, bray, rattle.' 'Rudentem proram, the hissing prow.' Quite the other end of the ship to what you thought it, Hall. You may continue."

There is an audible titter, which enrages poor Jack, who remembers that he had spent a good ten minutes the night before in trying to arrive at the meaning of "rudentem." He staggers on through the next line by dint of Mr. Opdyke's explanation that "remis ventisque" means "with oars and sails," and is a regular phrase for "using every effort." He gets a little heart by successfully conjugating "tollimur" and explaining the metaphorical use of "Manes," his knowledge of which is directly traceable to study, if his master did but know. He gets a cropper, however, in endeavoring to struggle with "desedimus," which he had looked for in vain under the heads of desedo, desedeo, and disedeo. When the omniscient Brown tells him that it is the preterit of desido, Jack is ready to kick himself in his disgust.

Only two more lines remain, over which Mr. Opdyke, believing, perhaps, that the context is a little difficult to master, is disposed to assist him, as, for instance, by explaining that "cava saxa" refers to "the rocks at the bottom of the sea," and that "ter spumam elisam," which Jack has not incorrectly rendered "the foam thrice dashed to pieces," is significant of the mariners' seeing the sky through a curtain of foam.

"By the way, Hall, give the principal parts of elisam."

Jack flushes proudly. Again hard work is its own reward.

"Elido, elidere, elisi, elisum."

Mr. Opdyke may be surprised, but he does not show it. He is the sort of man who expects his pupils to know their lessons, and displays emotion only when they fail. Besides, "elisam," though a revelation to Jack, had several times made its appearance before during the year. He merely says shortly,—

"Well, finish."

"RORANTIA ASTRA."

"We see," starts off Jack, with confidence, but
he is brought up short with another "Mind your
tense."

"We saw the foam thrice dashed to pieces and
the roaring stars."

"What?"

"The foam thrice dashed to pieces"—

"No, no; translate 'rorantia astra.'"

"Roaring stars," answers Jack, a trifle less as-
suredly than the first time. He had felt morally
certain when he was preparing the lesson that this
must be the meaning of the phrase from the look
of it.

"Indeed!" comes again with withering scorn
from his master's lips. "Did you ever see a star
roar, Hall? I have heard of boys roaring, but
never of stars."

A shout of amusement from the class, which Mr.
Opdyke is not very prompt to suppress, greets this
somewhat significant sally. When it has subsided,
poor Jack, who is scarlet with confusion, having
been told, "That will do," after taking his seat
hears Brown once more correct his error by explaining that "rorantia" is the neuter accusative plural

present participle of "roro," from "ros, dew," and that "rorantia astra" means "dripping stars"; as, to quote the after-remark of Mr. Opdyke for Jack's especial benefit, "any boy might have found out by looking in the lexicon."

Jack's heart, as he sat down, was sore within him. The visitors, smiling in spite of themselves, had evidently heard enough, for they now rose and began to thank profusely Mr. Opdyke, whose impassive calm boded no good, as the class well knew, to those who had been found wanting. In the midst of the leave-taking the bell rang, which was the signal for the close of the recitation, and a moment later the master turned and said, "Next time we will stop at line six hundred and eleven. I wish to speak to Hall a moment."

When every one else was gone Jack approached the desk with compressed lips and with every disposition to break down and sob. He had studied his Virgil hard, as he thought, and though the passage which he had been called upon to translate was the last in the lesson, he was not conscious of having shirked it. He had done his best, and what a pitiful showing his best was! However, although his doll seemed very full of sawdust, he was not going to give old Opdyke the satisfaction of perceiving his complete unhappiness.

Accordingly the Latin master, who believed himself an adept in reading youthful character, conceived the sullen air of determination manifested by the culprit before him as consistent with a purpose to remain a dunce, and, acting on this presumption, regarded the offender sternly, and said:

"My patience is exhausted, Hall. I have put up with your negligence until I can do so no longer with any respect for myself or regard for your good. I shall report your case to Dr. Meredith forthwith. There is nothing you can say which will alter my determination," he added sharply, as Jack seemed about to speak.

"Very well, sir," Jack answered.

Mr. Opdyke gathered up his books and was gone without bestowing a look on his unhappy victim, who, led by that which he had just heard to foresee his dismissal from school, went sadly to his room, bewailing his unlucky stars — "rorantia astra." The Doctor would surely take in very bad

part this report of neglected studies coming so soon
after his former disgrace.

In his unhappy plight he decided to go to Carlisle, to whom he told the story of his misfortunes
and from whom he obtained the sympathy he was
in need of. For Carlisle had not failed to observe
Jack's efforts to overcome the difficulties of the
Æneid in spite of his young crony's unwillingness
tò come to him for help, and was able with sin-
cerity to support the dejected lad's protestation
that he had really studied hard.

"Studied! You have studied like a Trojan,
Jack. It's an outrage in Opdyke to accuse you of
negligence. It serves you right, though, for not
letting me tutor you a bit. ' Rudentem, the rudder,' — and what was the other ? Oh, yes, —
' roaring stars.' Excuse my laughing, old fellow,
you outdid yourself."

"I don't care so much what Opdyke thinks,"
said Jack ruefully, " but I can't bear to have the
Doctor suppose I'm the same old quarter of a dollar. It's no use my trying to learn anything,
though. The harder I work the worse exhibition
I make. When you're gone next year, I don't
know what 'll become of me."

"But I shan't be gone. I 'm going to remain another year."

"Really?" exclaimed Jack jubilantly. "What has induced you to change your mind? When did you decide?"

"Only this morning. I 've been talking it over with Dr. Bolles, and he thinks it would be more sensible of me not to go to college for another year. There 's no hurry, for I 'm only seventeen, and though I 'm feeling first-rate he believes that by waiting I should build myself up completely. So I 'm to pass my entrance examinations this June and come back to the school as assistant in Latin next fall. It 's all arranged; and you 'll have to mind your P's and Q's, I can tell you, when you 're reciting to me, youngster."

These last weeks of the school year were always busy ones in every sense. Beside being examination time, at the close of which was the annual exhibition day when the parents and friends of the boys came often from a great distance to see their sons declaim or recite in public, they were busy also in an athletic way. On the morning preceding that on which the prize declamation was held it had become an established custom for the four eight-oared crews to compete together and subsequently for the best single scullers at Utopia to demonstrate by a two-mile contest which could pull the fastest. During the same week also the school nine endeavored to pit itself against the most formidable base-ball team that could be lured to Utopia.

This year, as you already know, Jack took no active part in either of the aquatic tussles. He saw, as was expected, the Mohicans again crowned cocks of the lake, chiefly owing to the dashing stroke set them by Tom Bonsall, and heard with a feeling akin to envy the statement go the rounds that Tom was to have a walk-over in the single-scull contest. There were no entries against him, and by paddling over the course he would have the right to claim the silver cup annually put up as a prize by a generous patron of the school. Somehow or other there was just at this time a dearth of fast scullers among the boys of the first two years, and here was a third-classer sweeping all before him without opposition even.

The single-scull race had been fixed for as late

as possible in the afternoon, in order to give any one who had taken part in the four-oared contest time to get rested. But, naturally, as few foresaw any amusement in watching Tom go over the course alone, interest in the event was very slight until the rumor got abroad shortly after twelve o'clock that Carlisle was going to have a try for the cup. It had already been announced early in the day not only that he had come out at the head of the school, but that his standing in the way of scholarship was proportionately higher than that of any previous Utopian. No one was surprised at this; but the news of his entry for the single sculls caused a veritable sensation, which found voice in a general prediction that he would be beaten. As for Jack, when he heard it, he waved his cap above his head and shouted himself hoarse. He had such faith in his friend's ability to do anything that he tried to do, that, as astounding as the announcement was, even to him, Jack would not permit himself to doubt the result. The odds were ostensibly against Louis, it is true, for Tom was the pink of condition and was open to slight criticism in the way of style, as Jack was very well aware, and I don't.

think our hero was quite able yet to appreciate
to the full the value in such an affair of steady,
systematic training void of splurge or notoriety,
although familiar with the fact that his friend was
in excellent practice.   And yet, notwithstanding,
Jack had a hope which from the first amounted
almost to conviction that Carlisle would win.

It was a great race — that battle royal between
Tom Bonsall and Louis Carlisle, and properly is
recorded among the famous rowing matches of
Utopia School. If this book was not devoted
chiefly to the experiences of another hero, I should
like nothing better than to describe in detail how
the two oarsmen, who were well matched in point
of size, pulled an even race to within a quarter of a
mile of the finish at a pace but little below that of
the best school record ; how the younger boy in his
desire to overcome his antagonist increased his
speed and gained a lead of half a boat's length, to
the delight of his backers, only to get blown and
yield his advantage, inch by inch, until the rival
shells were once more abreast; and how Tom in
his distress then lost his head and began to splash,
giving an opportunity for his senior's steady, thor-

oughly digested stroke to bring him to the fore and win the race with comparative ease amid the vociferous cheers of a rapturous crowd, among whom there was no one more wild with transport than our friend Jack. It was a fit ending to the victor's career at Utopia, — a career which had won him no enemies, and gained for him the respect and affection of masters and pupils alike, most of whom, however, as they admired him walking up to the boat-house, apparently still fresh and a picture of ruddy health, had but little appreciation of how largely he owed his great increase in vigor to knowledge of his own needs and to self-restraint — qualities whose value in the foundation of character it would be difficult to overestimate.

But for lack of space I might doubtless narrate also with abundant circumlocution, and not fear to tire those of you most fond of base-ball, how the Stars won a victory by a single run — a ten innings game — from the school nine in spite of the stimulating presence of applauding friends — some of them of the gentler sex — decked with the Utopia color; and despite, too, the fact that the "Kid" was in magnificent form, and our friend Hasy had been within a fortnight, on account of his brilliancy at the bat and in the field, made permanently a member of the team in the position of third-base man, which you will remember was the same proud position he filled when with the formidable Rising Suns. How the defeat came about it was not easy to explain, as every one had felt sure of the game, which suggests that we are very apt in this world to come to grief when we despise our adversaries. It was a good thing for the " Kid," however, and for Haseltine too, to have the conceit knocked out of them, as I have no doubt the Doctor thought also, seeing that the nine had carried all before it hitherto during the term. It does not do for boys, or for men either, who wish to hold their own and to go on improving, to get too cocky.

Notwithstanding these diversions, Jack could not help feeling very nervous in regard to the outcome of Mr. Opdyke's report to the Doctor, of which he had heard nothing, although a fortnight had now elapsed since his pitiful recitation in Virgil. Since then he had been in to the yearly examinations in the various subjects allotted to boys of his year, but without feeling much encouraged to believe that he had made a good showing. It was a new experience to him to be worrying as to whether or not he had answered this or that question correctly, and yet he was so wrapped up in trying not to be at the foot of the class that he could think of nothing else. It seemed to him as though he could no longer bear the thought of being regarded as an idle, lazy fellow.

Before breakfast, on the morning of the school exhibition, he received word that he was to go to Dr. Meredith's study, a summons which made him feel sick at heart, for he believed that he knew what was in store for him. Greatly to his surprise he was greeted by the head master with a pleasant smile, and could scarcely believe his ears as he listened to these words : —

"Hall, your work during the past term has been a great improvement on what you have done before. There is great room for improvement yet, my dear boy, but if you continue as you have begun there will soon be no cause to complain of you."

There can be little doubt that Jack went home for vacation with a light heart, especially when I add that he had the satisfaction of being assured by Carlisle, just before they parted for the summer, that if he would only stick to his present stroke and not try to get on too fast, he would certainly in time give that rising young oarsman, Bonsall, all he could do to keep his laurels.

"I've taught Bonsall a lesson, though, that he'll be quick to profit by, if he's the clever fellow I judge him to be," said Carlisle. "You've no child's play cut out for you, youngster; it'll be nip and tuck between you, and all I can say is, let the best man win when the time comes. I hope I shall be on hand to see the struggle."

CHAPTER XI.

NIP AND TUCK.

WITH the beginning of the third-class year Jack entered upon the second half of his life at Utopia. One day early in the new term he dropped into the more spacious study to which Carlisle, in his capacity of assistant in Latin, had been promoted, and falling into a chair exclaimed, "I say, Louis, I would like something to read."

"To read, my dear fellow? With all my heart. What shall it be?"

"That's what I've come to you to tell me. I've never read anything and I want to begin."

As you have doubtless noticed, Carlisle had hitherto in his intercourse with Jack kept in the background his most cherished tastes, and rarely, if ever, made allusion to books or other kindred interests, feeling sure that he would not find a sympathetic listener. But from this time forward the scope of their friendship was greatly widened. It was a simple matter for the older boy to gratify the desire of his interrogator, and before many weeks had passed by Jack had become an eager devourer of literature, held in check from proceeding too rapidly, however, by the injunction to digest thoroughly what he read.

" I only wish I had had somebody to impress the importance of that upon me when I started," Carlisle remarked to him early in their new intercourse. " I read everything I could lay my hands on as fast as I could see the words. Consequently I forgot half what I read."

" Were all these books given to you ? " asked Jack, indicating the modest little library of which his friend was the happy possessor.

" No, indeed. I purchased most of them with what I have saved from my spending money. Long before I was your age I used to save up every cent I got to spend in books. I shall never forget my delight when I was able to buy the copy of ' The Lady of the Lake,' above your head there."

Jack had never read " The Lady of the Lake." Indeed, he had never read any poetry in his life, and what is more, had in his ignorance cherished the belief that poetry was silly stuff, fit only for girls and milksops, and quite beneath the notice of a masculine individual like himself. This belief he was obliged to confess ill-founded after finishing the thrilling encounter between Snowdon's knight and the formidable Roderick Dhu. In fact, so great was his delight with both this poem and "Marmion," which Carlisle introduced him to immediately after, that he saw fit to learn passages from each of them by heart, much to the bewilderment and ill-concealed disdain of Haseltine, in whose presence he was disposed to rehearse them.

> "'Come one, come all, this rock shall fly
> From its firm base as soon as I,'"

he began one morning while they were dressing, assuming a martial attitude before the bath-room door, and armed with a base-ball bat.

"Oh, come off," said Haseltine contemptuously. "Quit that stuff!"

"It is n't stuff," expostulated Jack. "You ought to read it; it's immense."

"What is?"

"'The Lady of the Lake,' by Scott. There's 'Marmion,' too."

> " ' Charge, Chester, charge ! on, Stanley, on !
>   Were the last words of Marmion,' "

he added, waving the bat.

" Anything about base-ball in it ? "

" Of course not, Hasy.   It 's poetry."

" I don't see what difference that makes.   Any way, I guess prose is good enough for me."

" Will you read 'The Lady of the Lake' if I lend it to you ? " asked Jack.   He was genuinely eager to share the pleasure of his new discovery.

Haseltine did not commit himself on the point, but Jack left the volume in his crony's room, and experienced the satisfaction a few days later of hearing him ask, carelessly, —

" What did you say the name of the other book was ? "

" ' Marmion.' "

" I guess I 'll look it over now that my hand 's in."

This was scarcely enthusiasm, to judge by the mere words; but Jack knew well that Haseltine must have been greatly interested in order to have said even so much, an estimate which was confirmed a fortnight later, when the base-ball devotee accepted an invitation to read two hours in every week with him and Carlisle. This arrangement, which lasted through the year, soon became a source of extreme delight to both the boys, who listened with open ears to the various pieces of verse which their mentor selected for their edification. Carlisle took pains to explain that he was himself a mere student and beginner, and to encourage diversity of opinion, and consequent discussion, in regard to the merits of what was read. It must have been interesting to him to note the gradual change which took place in the tastes of his auditors, though be it said that Haseltine, to the last, refused to admit any, passage in the realm of verse to be superior to that which described the once sneered-at duel between the Scottish king and the Highland rebel. Both their hearts, and more particularly Jack's, were opened, however, to the beauties of more thoughtful poetry, which, and also the feelings and aspirations begotten by it, became new and working influences in their lives.

I am quite aware that this side of Jack's career cannot be made to appear so attractive to you boys by means of description as some of the more picturesque matters in which he was engaged; but if he

were called upon to-day to state what period in his
school life he looks back upon with the greatest satisfaction since going out into the busy world, I know
that he would specify that during which he acquired
his love of reading and interest in refined thought.
You remember that, though, when he went home
encouraged by Dr. Meredith's kind words at the end
of his fourth-class year, he was certainly entitled to
great credit for having made so determined a fight
against his inveterate habit of idleness, he was at the
time little more than a rough, harum-scarum sort of
a boy, — a plucky one, I admit, with plenty of good
stuff in him, — but nevertheless comparatively
thoughtless, and confined in his interests to the
ball field and boat-house. Before another year had
passed, while he was once more in excellent spirits,
there was something about his expression which
caused the other boys to speak of him as older-look-
ing. But Carlisle and the ever-observant head of
the school recognized with pleasure that his graver
countenance and less flighty manner were significant of more than seniority.

Our hero's prowess in the way of sport was
chiefly marked this year by his selection as one of

the Atalantas, in whose boat he was given the position of number four, and had the satisfaction of doing his best to make the crew formidable opponents
of the still victorious Mohicans. The Atalantas had
fallen to the rank of third on the lake in the last
race in which the four eight-oared crews had met;
but this infusion of new blood — there were two
other additions beside Jack — enabled them to come
in second in the spring contest, and not a very bad
second either. So fresh were they in fact at the
finish, that Tom Bonsall had to call on his crew for
an extra spurt when he supposed the race already
won.

Jack managed also, before another twelvemonth
had passed, to throw Carpenter flat on his back
and pin his shoulders to the ground in the middle-
weight spring wrestling, in retaliation for that athlete's victory over him when they were both classed
as feather weights. He wisely recognized his lim-
itations on the running track, however, which a gain
of ten pounds in weight had intensified, by not trying to compete with Jessup, who was still easily first
as a sprinter. If Hopedale, who, you will recall,
had beaten him twice in previous years, had been

still at Utopia, Jack might have found it difficult to
resist the temptation of making another struggle
for supremacy; but his old antagonist was no longer
at the school. It was a wise decision on his part,
for the champion succeeded in lowering Carlisle's
famous record amid tumultuous applause.

Jack's general reputation at this time was as a
good all-round man; a reputation which he was
urged to maintain by the intelligent superintendent
of the gymnasium, Dr. Bolles, between whom and
Jack there was mutual cordiality of feeling. Dr.
Bolles, as you will remember, had been pleased
by Jack's compact physique from the first day he
laid eyes on him, and had ever since lost no occasion to drop valuable hints as to how it might be
improved and taken care of. Jack had long ago
learned from this source the weak points in his
make-up, and was well versed in his instructor's
theory, that it was foolish for boys to cultivate
chiefly those parts of the body which were especially
well developed. In the opinion of Dr. Bolles, athletics were intended as a means for improving the
health and structure of the young, not as an end to
the pursuit of which they should devote their entire

energies; and he was emphatic in his cautions to Jack not to be led astray in this respect.

"Remember," he would say, "that however important it may seem to you to win this or the other match, the real object of exercise is to fit you for the serious work that you will be called upon to do as a man. The moment you sacrifice everything to sport, you are to all intents and purposes a professional, which is the last thing you were sent to school to become."

Although this view of athletics was novel to Jack, he was forced to admit to himself that it was in keeping with the other ideas regarding human duty and obligation which had suddenly been revealed to him as a consequence of his more sober life and the masterpieces of intelligent thought with which his mind was being brought in daily contact. He was able now to understand Carlisle's previous determination not to dissipate his energies in too many directions, and to pursue his training at the oar with the aim first of all of keeping in good condition so as to be able to fulfill his school work satisfactorily. Study did not come easy yet to Jack. Far from it, in fact. It takes a long time to recover lost ground and cover

new at the same time.   Often indeed he felt pretty
well discouraged and inclined to believe that he
should never do anything at his books.   Though by
no means dull, he possessed little more than average
brightness, which made the contrast which he could
not help forming at times between himself and his
mentor stand out with painful distinctness.   Carlisle
was so quick-minded, and acquired everything that
he undertook to learn so easily, that Jack could not
help expressing openly his despair of ever coming
within understanding distance even of his friend.

"Nonsense!" Carlisle would reply on such occasions; "you were a little late in beginning, that's
all.   Persevere, youngster, and you'll come out all
right in the end."

There was good advice in this, for though Jack
would never be likely through lack of natural abilities and taste to equal his senior in intellectual acu-
men, there was no reason why he should not become
an excellent scholar and graduate with distinction
by means of that very valuable quality — which is
too apt to be depreciated as a gift — known as perseverance.   Some boys will always be by disposition
quicker witted and more brilliant than their fellows,

but it does not follow by any means that the prizes of after-life fall to these " Admirable Crichtons." Stubborn, bull-dog, up-hill climbing and untiring determination to succeed will many a time win place and honor when easy-going talent goes to the wall. Don't let any one persuade you, boys, that you can equal all at once some companion who learns his lessons twice as easily as you do. God gives unequal gifts to his children, and if the one you have in mind is as resolute as you, no amount of industry will enable you to catch him. But, though your abilities may appear commonplace to begin with, you have no idea how many of those exasperatingly clever fellows you will leave safely in the rear before the race of life is over, if only you make the most of yourself by persevering unflaggingly from start to finish.

One day not long before the summer vacation Carlisle came into his study, where Jack who had the run of it happened to be pegging away at some lesson, and dropping into the window-seat began to look over the just issued copy of " The Utopian," the school paper, of which he had been an editor until he graduated, and to which he was still an occasional contributor.

"The Utopian" was conducted by a board of six taken from the three upper classes, who solicited articles and poems from the entire school, and was a breezy neat-looking little publication containing, beside local items of interest and detailed accounts of the triumphs and reverses of the nine, the fifteen, and the other athletic organizations, numerous imaginative pieces in prose and verse. Carlisle had for several years been one of its strongest supporters, and both in the capacity of "funny man" and poet had done much to keep its columns readable. Consequently he was familiar with the pseudonym and style of the usual contributors.

After reading out one or two stray bits of humor which he came across and over which he chuckled contentedly, and dubbing as "dishwater" a poem involving a love affair which doubtless he judged appertained rather to the mind's eye than to the experience of the narrator, he was silent a moment. Then he said:

"I wonder who 'Juvenis' is."

"Juvenis?" asked Jack, with apparent nonchalance, glancing at him furtively.

"Yes; there's a fellow signs himself 'Juvenis'

to some lines on the Ocean. It is n't a very original
subject, but whoever he is, he has seen the ocean
any way and knows what it looks like. It is n't
bad at all," he added.

If the ex-editor had chanced to regard his companion's face at the moment he must have obtained

an instant clue as to the identity of the unknown
rhymester. Jack was tickled to death, so to speak,
for this was the first information he had received of
the acceptance of his poem which he had inclosed
and addressed to the editors of the Utopian a fortnight before in the secrecy of his own room, and

with very little hope of its escape from the waste-paper basket. To have in addition to the conscious-ness of knowing that it was actually in print, Car-lisle of all men vouchsafe a word of praise in its be-half seemed to him like piling Pelion on Ossa. At least he felt as much up in the world as he could possibly have felt if standing on a pinnacle composed of those two mountains.

While he was deliberating whether or not to re-veal his authorship, Carlisle renewed the conversa-tion by asking to Jack's infinite amusement:

"Why should n't you try your hand at something of the sort, youngster? If poetry is n't in your line, write prose."

"What's the use?" responded our hero, with a well simulated attempt at indifference.

"What's the use of anything? In the first place, composition teaches you to systematize your thoughts and to express yourself with clearness. I believe, too, in cultivating the imagination. Of course every fellow who writes verse is n't a poet and is apt to be a fool if he thinks himself one, but his mind gets pleasure and profit out of the exercise. Take these lines I just spoke to you about," continued Carlisle, "they 're not much as poetry of course."

" Oh, no," interjected Jack, a little dolefully, off his guard.

" But the author must have derived a great deal of satisfaction from writing them, and can evidently do much better work with practice. If you ask ' what 's the use,' I can't express it to you in dollars and cents, but I 'm mighty certain that everything of that sort is good for one, and helps one to understand life better."

Jack began to laugh merrily. " That 's the best rise I 've seen for a long time," he said.

" I fail to see the rise."

" You will, though, when I tell you that I am the author of the Lines on the Ocean."

" You, Jack! Well, that 's a good one on me, I admit. You might have let me into the secret, I think," added Carlisle reproachfully.

" You see it was not a very original subject " —

" None of that, now. You may thank your stars, youngster, that I did n't pitch into your verses. I might have stabbed you to the heart unwittingly."

" In which case their authorship would have died with me. I knew you 'd feel obliged to tell me exactly what you thought of them if I showed them to you, so I kept mum."

" Well, you 've heard my opinion of them, and I
don't know that I have anything to add except that
for a first attempt they 're highly creditable," said
Carlisle.

Jack was excessively proud of his new accom-
plishment, and lost no time in showing the verses
to Haseltine, who, after reading them to the end,
observed laconically, —

" They 're not up to ' The Lady of the Lake.' "

Beyond this general criticism Haseltine did not
choose to commit himself, but being nowadays less
disposed than formerly to sniff at matters uncon-
nected with base-ball, he also abstained from any
observations in depreciation of poetry writing. But
though, as we have seen, not wholly unamenable to
culture, Hasy was true, heart and soul, to his first
love. No arguments had yet been able to shake
his unswerving allegiance to base-ball, and, as a
consequence, his daily increasing proficiency at that
game was giving him an enviable reputation on the
diamond, so much so, that it was universally con-
ceded that he would succeed the " Kid " as captain
of the school nine at the beginning of the coming
year. His fielding was really remarkable for so

young a fellow. He seemed to be in a dozen places at the same moment, and the batsman who dared to let anything drive within a wide radius of third base was sure to be discomfited. His base running was a marvel to behold, and his batting record by no means inferior. His most recent ambition was to pitch, and his twisters had already brought him into repute on the several occasions when he had been called into the box to relieve the " Kid." In his studies he managed to tag along just above the bottom of the class. A certain brightness, a clever knack of guessing correctly, it might be called, saved him from absolute disaster, and made him popular with his masters despite themselves.

With the opening of their second-class year both Jack and he found themselves among the leaders of the school. Its cock was now undeniably Tom Bonsall, who, in addition to being a member of the first class, stroke oar of the Mohicans, and champion sculler of Utopia, was justly entitled to be styled a rattling good fellow. Tom had, however, the air of feeling his oats, as the saying is, in spite of the lesson in humility which Carlisle had taught him, and, if he had a fault, was open to criticism on the score of vanity. What Tom Bonsall could not do was not worth doing, school opinion generally held, which was a sentiment full of danger to his career unless he chanced to possess an uncommonly level head.

Both Tom and Jack had filled out amazingly during this last twelvemonth. Tom was still the heavier of the two, and was a year older to boot; but his rival looked beefy enough and sinewy enough not to excite invidious comparisons. Indeed, if one had looked them in turn squarely in the face, I think he would, if a shrewd judge, have been struck by how clear Jack's eyes were and how fresh and free from pallor or staleness his complexion was, slightly to the prejudice of Tom, who, to tell the truth, had got a little into the habit of smoking cigarettes and being careless about his condition. It is pretty hard for a fellow as popular as Tom not to have to suit everybody more or less in order not to lose ground, and as Bill French and two or three others of the same stamp had a certain amount of influence in the school, he thought it good policy to keep on the right side of them, though disapproving of their general ways. This is a dangerous sort of game to play, and finer fellows at the start even than Tom Bonsall have learned it to their cost.

But little reference of late has been made to the wily Bill, for the reason that after the tool-house episode his intimacy with Jack perceptibly waned. But though he has not figured in these pages, it must not be supposed that he had ceased to be a potent influence at Utopia, or, alas! that he had changed in character. Bill's lie set an effectual seal on any budding virtues that may have been dormant in his soul and crushed them hopelessly, it is to be feared. Bill was not a villain, in the approved sense of the word. Quite otherwise, in fact. He had plenty of good points in that he was clever, entertaining, and, on the whole, amiable; but the trouble with him, as you have, I hope, appreciated, was that he was a coward. His tastes and impulses led him to avoid all that was open and above board, and to prefer just the opposite. You remember how he displayed these traits earlier in his career, and you will readily understand that now, instead of following any of the pursuits which the manly boys at the school took delight in, he found his chief gratification in posing as a flawless dandy, by which word

" flawless " I do not refer to his moral attributes but to his personal appearance. Bill and his set — for he had a number of more or less ardent disciples in this proclivity — aped with wonderful precision so far as they dared, and much further in secret than the laws allowed, the manners of weary men about town who think they know everything about life, and are tired of what they know. Even in the days of the Big Four this had been somewhat Bill's drift, but he had developed it latterly to perfection.

I bring him before you again that you may take one last glimpse of him and his ways, and form your own opinion regarding them both before he vanishes from our sight forever. I wish with all my heart that I were able truthfully to state that he came to grief before he left Utopia. To inform you that he was sent away on account of his evil example would be much more satisfactory from the point of view of romance and retributive justice, than to write as I am forced to do, that, although he was suspected and disapproved of by the masters, he managed to keep his ill doings so dark that he was never actually found out up to that time.

But we must take facts as they are, not as we would like to have them. I do not wish to give you the idea that Bill was hopeless, — though I regret to add that since he graduated from Utopia he has done little to encourage one to believe that he will ever be a useful member of society, — but it must be borne in mind in estimating character that the stereotyped villain such as was referred to just now is a. rare exception except in city slums, and that the sort of person most dangerous to the welfare of our community as it exists at present is not the cut-throat or burglar whom the policeman knows very well how to deal with, but the sneering advocate of licentiousness and self-indulgence and low standards of honor. Boys like Bill do not become thoroughly bad all at once. They deteriorate gradually. One thing leads to another, and though if no redeeming influence is brought to bear upon them in time their degeneration is wofully certain, there is often little about them to attract the unfavorable attention of those who do not know them well. Sometimes they are never found out at all by the world at large ; but you may be pretty sure that, as the years roll by, if they do not reveal themselves by their unworthy deeds or the expression of their faces, their hearts are sad and sore. Life has lost for them its savor even in an evil sense, and everything seems to them as the poet says, " weary, stale, flat, and unprofitable." But to be anxious that vice should be its own punishment, much less that wrong-doers should have strict justice meted out to them, is concern unworthy for thorough-going characters to entertain. Let the bad boys go their ways, and do not trouble your heads with wondering when and how they will be made to suffer for their unrighteousness. You will have plenty to do to guide your own footsteps and to steer clear of the pitfalls which have engulfed many a lad secure in the consciousness of his own power to resist temptation. For my part I pity Bill French and hope sincerely that he may yet turn out a decent fellow.

Meanwhile, with Carlisle away at college, where he had entered with flying colors, the new year saw Jack thrown on his own resources, which, though a doleful experience at first on account of his separation from his dear friend, was perhaps just what he needed to give force to his character.

He had become one of the older boys of the school, and instead of looking up to others was in a position to be looked up to himself by the lads in the lower classes, the consciousness of which was not slow to breed in him a sense of responsibility as to keeping an eye on youngsters who, like himself not so very long ago, were in need of a helping hand. He was now also one of the six editors of " The Utopian," an honor conferred upon him in virtue of several articles both in prose and verse which had emanated from his pen as a result of the favorable reception accorded to his Lines on the Ocean. His pseudonym " Juvenis" was well known in school circles, and his energy in securing both contributors and subscribers never faltered. He was the means of introducing a number of new features into the paper, most popular among which was a series of florid, but racy and pertinent observations on the national game appearing in every issue signed enigmatically " Third Base," which was merely an ostrich-like concealment of the identity of the captain of the school nine. Haseltine had regarded the proposition to become literary to this extent with favor from the very outset, and from the very outset also his lucubrations were so immensely popular that extracts from them found their way into the columns of the real press of the county, much to the satisfaction of their author.

But deeply in earnest as Jack had grown to be in his efforts to do his duty and to please his mother, which two ends not unnaturally were synonymous in his mind, and faithfully as he stuck to his school work during his year in the second class, he was looking forward with anxious but keen and determined anticipation to the day when he should have the opportunity to row man for man against his rival, to decide once for all which was the better oarsman of the two. It had become a matter of school knowledge and discussion that these two crack scullers — for they were now both recognized as such — were to settle this question at the spring races, and great was the difference of opinion as to the result. Each had his enthusiastic backers who believed in their champion's ability to leave his opponent far in the rear, and but little else was talked about out of school hours but the respective merits of Tom Bonsall and Jack Hall.

As Tom was to graduate this year, this was

Jack's last chance to prove himself his superior. Consequently neither of them allowed the other to outdo him in practice, and though apparently they both avoided testing each other's mettle in advance, their respective shells were visible at opposite ends of the lake at least once a day during the spring preceding the race.

Great preparations were made for the contest, and in order that the scullers might be perfectly fresh, the eight-oared race was fixed for the day after. But great as was the excitement, it was nothing compared with what it became when, a week before the important event, Dr. Meredith announced his intention of competing for the prize himself.

The report ran like wildfire through the school. "Have you heard the news?" every one asked his neighbor. "The Doctor is going in for the single sculls against Bonsall and Hall. He has n't rowed in a race, you know, since Whiteside crawled up on him so."

Whiteside's struggle was, of course, merely a tradition to five sixths of the boys, but it was one which had been handed down from class to class as an event yet without parallel in the annals of Utopia. The very fact that the Doctor had never entered a race since then had been tacitly accepted as proof that there were no longer competitors among his pupils sufficiently formidable to render a victory on his part otherwise than easy, and it is needless to state that the present announcement was regarded as a profound compliment to the condition of aquatics at the school. As to what the result of the race would be, few saw room to doubt. The Doctor was always in condition; the Doctor was always in practice; the Doctor was sure to win.

The opinion of the many was shared also by his two competitors, who discussed the matter from every standpoint. Neither of them could hope to beat the Doctor, but they were resolved that he should not carry off the prize without pulling for all he was worth from start to finish. So Tom and Jack vowed on the evening before the race as they stood side by side on the boat-house flat, watching their adversary shoot over the water in a final practice spin. If gritted teeth and determination could be of avail, the head of the school had no sinecure in the task which he had taken on himself.

The appointed day dawned bright and still. Jack, who had lain awake during the early hours of the night through excitement, was awakened from a deep, refreshing sleep by a well-known knock, which caused him to leap out of bed and open the door.

"Louis, where on earth did you spring from?"

"Jack, how *are* you?"

The two boys stood shaking hands and laughing delightedly for some moments before Carlisle — it was he of course — saw fit to explain in answer to his friend's question that he had run up from college on purpose to see the race. There was a leeway of three days, he said, between two of his examinations, and he had managed to get away.

"It was awfully good of you, Louis."

"Nonsense, youngster! I had promised to come if I could, you know, and I would n't miss it for the world."

"Have you heard whom I am to row against?" asked Jack feverishly.

Carlisle nodded. He had been told everything

by Horace Hosmer driving up from the station, it appeared, and been waylaid moreover by half the school, eager to know his opinion as to the result, and to give theirs.

"Have I any show, Louis, do you think?"

"You ought to know better than I, Jack. I have n't seen you row for a year."

"I can't bear the idea of coming in third. Somehow I feel as if I should have a better show if the Doctor were out of it."

"Too late to talk that way now," said Carlisle. "You must brace."

"Oh, I'm braced, never fear. It's merely like talking to another self to talk to you."

The race had been fixed for ten o'clock. The lake was reported to be like a mirror, and the day unexceptionable from an oarsman's point of view. Jack ate a fairly substantial breakfast at eight, and at Carlisle's suggestion remained quietly until nine in his own room, from which he emerged in an overcoat worn over his boating costume, a crimson and black striped jersey and crimson handkerchief, — the uniform of the Atalantas, — and a nondescript pair of trowsers. Haseltine was waiting be-

fore the door with a trap, borrowed from one of
the farmers, so as to spare his champion the un-
necessary fatigue of a walk, in which the three
bestowed themselves. Hasy announced that the
Doctor and Tom Bonsall had already gone down
to the boat-house.

The quadrangle, as they jogged through it, looked
completely deserted, and not a head was to be
seen in any of the dormitory windows, a condition
of affairs which was fully accounted for by the
appearance of the lake and its borders when they
arrived. Every boy who possessed a boat was out
in it, and the water was dotted with every variety
of craft from a Rob Roy canoe to the steam launch
recently presented to the school by a fond graduate,
which was occupied by Mrs. Meredith, the judges,
and some of the principal guests whom Founders'
Day — as the annual exhibition was called — had
brought to Utopia. The launch flew proudly the
school colors, blue and white, which properly were
worn to-day only by the Doctor, who was just
stepping from the float into his shell amid great
applause as Jack alighted from the vehicle. The
stand, which had been erected a few rods from the

boat-house, and which was just opposite to the finish, was crowded with visitors, many of whom were ladies in gay attire, and the members of the school, while the country people from miles around were ranged along the shore. It was a scene calculated to quicken the pulses of any one with a spark of enthusiasm. As for Jack, when he started to strip off his overcoat he was trembling all over, and could feel his heart going like a trip-hammer.

The course was to be two miles in all; straight away for a mile to a flagged buoy, and back again to another flagged buoy abreast of the boat-house. Two of the first class were to be judges, a third to be judge at the further buoy, and Mr. Percy had consented to act as referee in case of any dispute. Stoddard of the second class, and stroke oar of the Nimrods, was to send the contestants off by firing a pistol at the proper moment.

Jack was the last of the three to get into his boat.

"Is everything all right?" whispered Carlisle, who was bending over him holding the shell at the float. "Don't spurt until you have to, remember."

"O K," answered our hero.

"Let her go, Smith," said Haseltine jocularly. "Keep your courage up, old man," he added to Jack.

Carlisle shoved the shell out, retaining his grasp on the oar nearest him until there was clear water. Jack paddled a few rods and then shot off at a comfortable pace up the lake, followed by the wistful gaze of the spectators eager to gauge his powers. He caught a glimpse of Tom Bonsall, in a white shirt with a purple star on its bosom, and a purple handkerchief bound stylishly across his forehead, resting on his oars and watching him. Jack had no idea of wasting his energies by showing off. He had time just to warm himself up a bit before the signal to get into line. He pulled steadily and quietly for a few hundred yards, taking a last glance at his equipment to make sure that everything was all right.

He had scarcely turned to come back when the pistol sounded, and by the time he reached the starting line the Doctor and Tom were in position. According to the lots drawn that morning Jack was to be in the middle, with Tom inside; so he paddled in between them. Stoddard spent a few

moments in making first one and then another
retire or move forward a few inches, then asked
sharply, —

"Are you ready?"

Jack felt almost beside himself in the short interval that preceded the discharge, and his throat
seemed parched.

Crack!

The three pairs of blades flashed through the water at the same moment, and neither boat seemed
to gain any decided advantage as they bounded
away from the buoy amid the cheers of everybody.

"Hurrah for the Doctor!"

"Hit her up, Tom!"

"Bully for you, Jack!"

It took our hero some minutes to get his head
clear enough to be able to perceive what he was
doing, as compared with his opponents. He rowed
on and on excitedly without realizing anything.
He was conscious of rowing a rather quicker and
more jerky stroke than usual. His eyes were misty
and his throat drier than ever. The cheers of the
spectators were growing fainter, and he felt that it
was time to settle down to work. He made a gulp

THE BOAT RACE.

and looked about him. On his right was Tom pulling like grim death, at a rate which seemed to lift his boat almost out of the water. The stern of Tom's shell was nearly on a level with the back sweep of his own oars, which showed plainly that Tom had not far from half a length's lead on him. On the other side was the Doctor in his blue and white jersey, rowing steadily and smoothly as clockwork, neck and neck with him.

" Softly now," said Jack to himself. " This is too fast company for me. If Tom can keep this racket up he 'll get there first. My only chance is to let up a bit."

Accordingly he lessened the number of strokes to the minute by making each of them longer and more sweeping, with the immediate result that he felt in better shape, and that Tom had gained no further advantage on him. But there was no letup to Tom. He had the lead and was bent on keeping it.

They were too far off now for the shouts to reach them. Not a sound was audible to Jack but the slight plashing of the oars in the water. Over his shoulder Tom was struggling onward, and abreast of him, pulling with apparently no effort whatever and watching alertly the movements of his rivals, could be seen the dangerous Doctor. But Jack, too, felt calm now and fresher than when he started. He can even put a little more back muscle into his stroke, he thinks, as he feels his grip tighten on the oars with the consciousness of growing vigor. A few more sweeps like that will close up the gap between his out-rigger and Tom's.

But why does not the Doctor bend to his work to keep him company? The Doctor is pulling a waiting race evidently, and is going to let his rivals blow themselves against one another before he has an oar in the fight. Otherwise surely he would not have let Jack forge ahead so that he has to look round the corner now in order to watch him. The Doctor is an old hand and has seen many a race lost by too lively a pace at the start.

"Steady," reflects Jack, again trying to keep cool as he realizes that he has a lead over his most dangerous enemy. "Don't hit her up too lively." He appreciates the Doctor's tactics, and is not going to fall into the trap if he can help it, even though Tom, spurred on by swift pursuit, has put on more steam and is holding his own bravely. They are not far from the flagged buoy now. Jack can see it distinctly and has in mind that he must be careful to avoid a foul. They are likely to pass it in the order in which they are at present, about half a length apart, and Tom has the inside water. All three are pulling like well-oiled machines, and not a symptom of distress comes from either boat.

Tom turns first, and very cleverly too, close to the buoy so as to give no one a chance to cut in, and starts for home, but the others are at his heels and right after him. Jack in passing catches the eye of Sampson, the judge at the turn, and feels cool enough to nod in friendly fashion. Halfway, and he is still fresh as ever! He would like to try to press Tom, but for fear of the cool, deliberate Doctor barely astern. He remembers Carlisle's caution not to spurt until he has to, and only bends strongly and firmly to his accustomed stroke, which, however, is losing him no ground to say the least. Tom is evidently uneasy and is working to shake him off, forgetful, it appears, of his experience in forcing the pace a year ago. But Tom is a better oar than a year ago, and perhaps has taken that into account.

Ah there! The Doctor is waking up at last, and is putting in some stronger work; nothing very strenuous, but lively enough to warn Jack that he must have his head about him if he hopes to keep his lead to the end. One thing is certain now: Tom will have to row faster or give in; after which reflection Jack slightly quickens his stroke, and without actually spurting bends every muscle. Now or never! They are only half a mile from home, and a waiting race may be delayed too long. Already they are within ear-shot of the encouraging shouts of the crews and scullers on either side of their path, who have come out to meet them and are rowing back to be in at the finish. Now or never! Will Tom be able to quicken his pace? That is the question. He does quicken it, so much so that he is rowing desperately fast with short lightning strokes, which come so rapidly that it is difficult to note the interval between them. Brilliant, magnificent! "but," as some one who knew said of the famous charge of the Light Brigade, "it is not war." It is slaughter, my dear Tom, and simple ruination. You cannot keep it up. Even as it is, in spite of your splendid pyrotechnics, Jack's long steady swing is holding you, and what is more, pressing you into the bargain.

"Steady now," murmurs Jack between his teeth. He knows from Tom's exertions that his rival is spurting and putting all his vitality into his pace. A terrible moment of sustained effort follows, at the end of which the leader lashes the air with a misplaced stroke, the water splashes, and our hero's shell surging forward comes on a level with its forerunner, battles with it for twenty yards of struggling agony on the part of the doomed champion, and leaps to the front at last, just in time to meet the sweet music of the prolonged triumphant din of shouts and cheers sent down the breeze from afar by hundreds of voices. Jack is ahead, and only a quarter of a mile left!

Tom is beaten. And now for the Doctor. Where is he? What is he doing? No need to ask that question, friend Jack, if you lift your eyes. Tom is beaten, not only by you but by the Doctor also; and though your most dreaded enemy is still in your rear, the nose of his boat is almost on a line with your stern, and he is quickening at every stroke.

What a babel of cheers and exclamations bursts forth from the waving, transported crowd along the bank and on the benches of the densely packed stand! They begin to know who is who now, and can tell beyond the shadow of a doubt that the crimson and black and the blue and white are having a noble struggle for the lead.

"Jack Hall is ahead! Hall! Hall! No, he is n't! Hit her up, Doctor! Hurrah for Hall! Hurrah for the Doctor! Tom, where are you? Bonsall! Bonsall! H-A-L-L! Hall-l-l!"

The tumult is maddening. Can it be possible that Jack Hall, who, on the whole, before the race was rated lowest of the three, is going to break the school record and beat the invincible Doctor in one and the same breath? It looks like it, if he can hold his own for two hundred yards more. It looks like it decidedly, and there is plenty of clear water still between the winning goal and the foremost shell; and see, the Doctor is spurting with a vengeance — look! — look! — and is he not gaining, too?

"Doctor Meredith is ahead! No, he 's not — Hall 's ahead! Huzza! hurrah! Hall, Hall, hit

her up, Hall ! Look out, Hall ! The Doctor wins !
No he does n't ! Hall wins ! Hurrah ! Jack,
where are you ?"

The Doctor has crept up, no doubt about that.
The nose of his shell is now well beyond Jack's
out-rigger, and he is speeding like the wind. Jack
is feeling terribly tired, his throat that he thought
parched at the start burns as if it were on fire, and
his eyes seem ready to start out of his head. His
crimson handkerchief has fallen over his eyes, but
he gives himself a shake and it falls to his neck,
leaving his brow refreshingly free. He has vanquished Tom any way. So much to be thankful
for. Tom is a length behind, struggling still like
the man he is, but hopelessly vanquished all the
same. Jack turns his head, remembering to keep
cool if he can, and sights the goal. Not more than
one hundred and fifty yards left ! The reverberating yells and cheers are setting his blood ablaze.
He can scarcely see, but he knows he has not
spurted yet. He is neck and neck with the Doctor
now. There can be nothing to choose between
them.

"The Doctor wins !" "Not a bit of it; Hall

wins! Good on your head, Jack! Keep it up, Doctor! Go in, Hall!"

The time has come now, our hero knows, to put in any spurt that is left in him. Gripping the handles of his oars like a vice and shutting his eyes, Jack throws all his vital powers into one grand effort, which, to his supreme happiness, is answered by a great roar from the shore.

"Hall! Hall! Hurrah! Nobly done, Hall! Hall wins! Row, Doctor, row!"

The Doctor is rowing with all his might, you may be sure of that; but he has not counted on the staying powers of his adversary. He can do no more than he is doing, and this final spurt of Jack's, exhausting as it must have been were the race to be a quarter of a mile longer, will carry the day. The Doctor can hardly catch him now.

Jack has opened his eyes and takes in the situation. The din of applause is tremendous. If he can hold out for half a dozen strokes more, the victory is his.

One.

"Hall! Hall! Go in, Doctor!"

Two.

" Three cheers for Hall! One, — hurrah! —
Two, hurrah!"

Three.

" Three, — hurrah! H-A-L-L!"

Four.

" Hall wins! Hall wins!"

Five.

" Hurrah! Huzza! Hurrah! Hall! Hall!
Doctor! Doctor!"

Six.

Panting, breathless, and bewildered by the deafening cheers, Jack is made aware only by the sight
of the flagged buoy shooting past his oar-blade that
he has won the race and is champion of Utopia.
A second later the Doctor's shell glides beside his
own, and his master is the first to shake his hand
in hearty congratulation.

" You beat me squarely and fairly, Hall. It
was a grand race. You are the better oarsman of
the two."

Tom Bonsall, coming up on the other side, is
scarcely less generous, though he looks a little
sheepish, poor fellow, and winded and pale. Excitement keeps Jack up, and he paddles in gamy

fashion to the float, where he is welcomed by a score of hands and lifted on to the shoulders of his enthusiastic friends, who, cheering like mad, carry him up to the boat-house.

"Well, old man, you did it after all," said Carlisle, who was grinning like a Cheshire cat in his enthusiasm. "To tell you the truth, I did n't believe you could get away from the Doctor."

CHAPTER XII.

HASELTINE MAKES HIS CHOICE.

A YEAR has elapsed, and once more Founders'
day has come round at Utopia. The exercises of
the graduating class and the prize-giving have
taken place in the morning, and now every one is
digesting at leisure the excellent collation provided
shortly after noontime prior to repairing to the
quadrangle to witness the base-ball match which is
to conclude the day's entertainment.

In one of the studies in Fullham dormitory
sacred to the older classes two boys are seated engaged in earnest conversation. The room, a cosy
little den, owes evidently much of its comfortable
and somewhat artistic appearance to the good taste
of one of its owners, who, no other than our old
friend Jack, grown still more manly in figure and
with the same open countenance as when we saw
him last, is discussing with his chum Haseltine the
untoward news which the latter has received a day

7

or two before of his father's financial ruin. The
blow has fallen most unexpectedly on the poor fellow, and though the change in his plans which the
calamity must necessarily induce has given him but
small concern as compared with that which he has
felt for his father's unhappiness, it is important
now that he should think and talk about what he is
to do. He was to have gone to college, for which
he has been preparing himself with considerable
industry during the past year, but that is out of the
question now. He has his way to make in the
world, and the only point to be considered is how
he can best manage no longer to be a burden on his
family.

"The worst thing about it," Haseltine continued,
"is that I shan't see any more of you, Jack. I
don't care so much about the money on my own
account, but I should like to have spent four years
with you at Harvard."

"It'll spoil half my pleasure in being there to
have you away," said Jack. "We must manage
though somehow to keep up our friendship. We
can write to one another at least."

"I hate letters, — that is, writing them. My

spelling would shock you, Jack. If I were a literary character like you, now, it might answer."

" Don't talk nonsense, Hasy."

" Who 'd have thought three years ago that
you 'd have graduated third in the class and taken
a prize for a poetical translation from Ovid? If
only now I 'd followed suit," he observed somewhat
sadly, " I might have got the place of private tutor
to some rich swell or other, married my employer's
daughter, and rolled in my own carriage, while you
were still grinding at the university. As it is, I
shall soon either be breaking stones on the highway, or playing cash-boy in a retail dry-goods
store."

" I dare say," responded Jack, "the Doctor could
get you some place as tutor. A few months of
hard work would give you the necessary proficiency."

" But I want to begin work to-morrow."

There was a short silence, and then Jack said
slowly, " Of course, Hasy, I suppose you 've
thought of base-ball? You ought to have no difficulty in getting a salaried position in some club,
you know."

"I dare say I could," was the quiet answer. "How I should have jumped at such a chance a few years ago!" continued the school captain, tossing from hand to hand from force of habit the baseball which he held. He is in shirt and knickerbockers, ready for the game appointed to take place in half an hour between the school nine and one of the strongest professional teams in the country, which, on its way east, has been induced to stop at Utopia. "I was a foolish boy then, — and now, well, I'm foolish enough still, but I think I've learned something in these six years."

"Oh, Hasy, I'm so glad to hear you talk so. Do you know I lay awake all last night thinking about you, for I was afraid that with your fondness for the game you'd jump at the chance to become a professional. Forgive me, old fellow, I did you injustice."

"That's all right, Jack. No wonder you thought so, I'm such a base-ball crank. But I may have to jump at the chance notwithstanding. It may be the best thing I can do. Fifteen hundred or two thousand dollars a year is not to be met with every day in the week. It may be my duty to take such a place if it is offered, Jack," he said gravely.

"I think almost anything would be better as a profession than that."

"I can see that it would. Whatever I used to think, I recognize that to have to spend the best years of my life as a base-ball player would be a terrible misfortune. This school and the Doctor have taught me that there are more worthy ambitions than that, and though I have n't said much about it, I 've looked forward to something better. However, I must n't abuse base-ball, for it has been a good friend to me, Jack; and I believe that it has done me a heap of benefit not only physically, but in teaching me endurance and perseverance and the value of discipline. I feel as if I could take hold first-rate from the start of any business I entered, just because of my training at base-ball. And if it comes to the worst," he added, "I think I shall be able to make a good professional."

"I 'm sure you will, Hasy, if it comes to that. But something else will be certain to turn up, see if it does n't."

"It 'll have to turn up pretty soon, then, I 'm afraid," replied Haseltine. "It 's time to go," he continued, looking at his watch. "The game 'll be called in fifteen minutes. It may be my last for a long time, — at least as an amateur, — and I mean to give the Gray Stockings a hard fight to win."

The two friends proceed toward the quadrangle, where already a crowd is collecting in anticipation of the match. The large stand for spectators, which is one of the conveniences added to the grounds in Haseltine's day, is rapidly filling up, and just as the young captain arrives upon the scene the Gray Stocking team show signs of emerging from the tent erected for their comfort, where they have been dozing since dinner. The sight of them is sufficient to restore Haseltine's spirits, and almost to make him feel that he would be very well content after all to become one of them. They are strapping fellows certainly, and the way they toss about the ball during the few minutes' preliminary practice allowed them is very admirable.

And now from the main doorway of Granger Hall come out a large party intent upon being present at the game, consisting of Dr. Meredith and his masters, together with several patrons of the school and a number of ladies, who troop across the field

to seats reserved for them behind the wire screen
at the back of the catcher. The Gray Stockings
have won the toss and have sent the school to the
bat. The professionals, from their jocose demeanor,
evidently regard the affair in the light of a spree
or picnic; and the pitcher grins convulsively in
stepping into the box, as though the idea of playing
ball against a parcel of boys struck him as a colos-
sal jest.

The school nine looked like striplings certainly
when compared with their sturdy opponents, but
they are in the very pink of practice and condition,
and have moreover eaten sparingly of the good
things provided at the collation, so as to be fit as
possible for the match. A breathless interest per-
vades the audience. A game against a real professional team is something unknown in the annals
of Utopia.

" Three out, side out," calls the umpire, as the
third striker on the home nine knocks an easy
grounder to short stop, who pops it gayly to first
base.

It is now the visitors' turn at the bat, and all
eyes are bent on Haseltine as he plants himself

firmly to deliver the first ball. There has never been such a pitcher as he at Utopia. As compared with his curves, the once famous pitching of the "Kid" is remembered as second-rate. It has hopelessly baffled not only the pertinacious Stars, but other still more formidable clubs. It remains to be seen what these genuine ball-tossers will do with it.

"One strike!"

The captain of the Gray Stockings and one of the most prominent sluggers on the nine has swiped at the first ball and missed it, whereat his companions smile and one of them guys him with —

"Even money you strike out, Bill."

There is a hush, and then the umpire calls —

"Two strikes!"

Applause proceeds from the benches and titters from the visiting team.

"Three strikes — out."

The school is too much in earnest to regard the incident as ludicrous, and the crowd cheers rapturously to see the vanquished slugger retire from the plate; but one of the managers of the professional nine, who happens to be traveling with them and is sitting just in front of Jack, bursts out into loud guffaws of amusement, which are repeated still more abundantly when the next striker misses the first two balls and only saves himself from a similar fate by batting the third weakly into the very hands of short stop, who has no difficulty in disposing of him at first. The third man hits a foul tip which the catcher holds on to cleverly, and the innings is over.

"That's a great lad," exclaims the manager, who is in a bee line with the pitcher and so can judge of the delivery. "He can twirl the sphere like a good one. Backus and Lawson out on strikes! That's the best joke of the season." Whereupon he bursts out laughing again, so that his fat sides shake with merriment.

It would take too long to give the details of the great match, though indeed there is not much to be recorded in the way of run-making on either side. It is from first to last a pitcher's contest, and though the school can do nothing against the Gray Stocking battery, seven goose-eggs represents the score of the visitors at the end of the seventh inning. To the uproarious delight of all Utopia the heavy hitters of the professional team come to grief one after another in rapid succession, sometimes by striking out, and sometimes by knocking easy balls into the field, which are without difficulty captured by their opponents. No longer do the giants grin and turn derisive hand-springs. An air of serious devotion to business has come over them, and every nerve is being strained to save the game.

"Play ball — play ball," their captain reiterates with increasing vigor.

But it is in vain that he beseeches or commands. Somehow or other Haseltine's curves are too subtle for the visitors and they go down like nine-pins; and as in turn they sheepishly carry out their bats or return to home plate, the manager's derisive laughter adds a sting to their disgust.

Meanwhile, among the friends of Utopia, the young pitcher is the hero of the hour, and everybody is asking questions about him in the intervals of the frantic applause which rewards his successes.

" A right-minded, ingenuous, capable boy," responds Dr. Meredith, in answer to a query of one of the patrons of the school sitting beside him. " He has received sad news from home within the past few days, I regret to state. His father who was reputed to be a very rich man has failed, — disastrously though not dishonorably I am given to understand, — and the son will not be able to go to college as he had expected. There is a large family — seven beside this boy, I believe."

"Is he a good scholar?" asks the gentleman after a moment.

"To tell the truth, he is not very fond of his books, though he has done better at them during the last year. I think he would have been able to pass the college examinations, but it is by no means certain. He has plenty of ability though of the practical sort. I have often been struck by the energy and executive talent he has shown in relation to base-ball, which, by the way, almost amounts to a passion with him," says the Doctor, with a smile.

A shout of triumph interrupts their conversation. Another of the Gray Stockings — the first striker of the eighth innings — having in base-ball parlance fanned the air thrice in vain, flinging his bat angrily on the ground, walks back to his seat.

"H-A-S-E-L-T-I-N-E! Haselti-n-n-ne!" chants the whole school.

The manager slaps his knee. " I must have that fellow," he exclaims admiringly.

Jack catches the remark. He has heard also what has passed between Dr. Meredith and Mr. Holgate, the patron of the school, who are sitting on the bench immediately behind him, and while he is reflecting on the possible consequences of Haseltine's prowess, he hears Mr. Holgate say :

" I happen to know of a chance for an active young man who is n't afraid of work, on a railroad far West in which I 'm interested. I 'm inclined to think that as our base-ball friend has his way to make in the world and is not cut out for a scholar, it would be the best thing for him if I put him into the place, though if you say the word I 'll pay his way through college."

Jack's heart gives a bound. He cannot help listening, and he awaits eagerly the Doctor's reply, scarcely knowing what he wishes it to be; for deeply as he desires his friend's companionship at Harvard, he is able to appreciate the wisdom of Mr. Holgate's reasoning.

" I think," says Dr. Meredith slowly, " that you are right, on the whole. Haseltine will make an excellent business man. The position on the railroad will suit him best, everything considered."

" It is a place in which he will have an opportunity to make himself very useful, and if he does, promotion will be sure to follow," continues Mr. Holgate. " Holloa! that's the first square base hit I've seen to-day."

It is not only a base hit, but a two bagger in fact, which comes just in the nick of time to let in one of the Gray Stockings, who was on second when Captain Backus batted the ball with a vim born of triple humiliation. Twice before in the course of the game the visitors have had men on bases, but the terrible battery of the school boys has shut them out from a run. But now they are able to breathe more freely. The succession of goose-eggs is interrupted and the game theirs, if they can prevent Utopia from scoring. But the run has come only just in time as two of the visitors are already out. Lawson, however, not to be outdone by the Captain, follows with a terrible drive far over the left field's head, who is a no whit less clever fielder than Bobby Crosby used to be, which brings him and Backus both home, and makes the score three to nothing in favor of the Gray Stockings, which is all they get. The school nine amid intense excitement then go to the bat, and though they do their best to pound the ball they are whitewashed in one, two, three order, which brings the game to a close, as of course the Gray Stockings, being already ahead, do not need their ninth inning. It has been a plucky fight, though, and one which Utopia will remember with pride for years to come.

As Jack was about to mingle with the crowd with the view of being the first to hug Haseltine, he felt a hand on his shoulder and heard the Doctor's voice exclaiming, " Hall, I should like to introduce you to Mr. Holgate, who was one of our founders, you know."

Jack shook hands with the pleasant-featured gentleman, who said kindly :

" I saw you, Hall, if I am not mistaken, among those who received prizes this morning, as well as in the winning crew yesterday afternoon."

Our hero blushed with honest confusion. He was prouder of having won the prize for a metrical translation from the classics, however, than of having led the Atalantas to victory, for there had been no Tom Bonsall this year to dispute it with him, and every one knew in advance what the result would be. It had always been a source of keen regret to Jack that Tom's arm was so lame after the famous single-scull match that he had been obliged to stay out of the eight-oared race. He would have liked to have had one more struggle with his old rival just to prove beyond the shadow of a doubt who was the better man. But now Tom was in college, and there was no one left to dispute with him the supremacy of the lake, for the Doctor had openly confessed his own inferiority.

"It was a fine game, sir, wasn't it?" Jack said, with enthusiasm, as the three turned at the sound of the cheers which the Utopians were bestowing upon the victors. "Haseltine outdid himself."

"Hall and Haseltine are great cronies," observed the Doctor to Mr. Holgate.

"Your friend seems a fine fellow," said the gentleman.

"He's a splendid fellow, indeed, sir," answered Jack.

The Gray Stockings returned the cheers of the home nine and were preparing to get into the

vehicle which was to take them to the train, when
Jack, who had been looking through the crowd in
search of Haseltine, caught sight of him and the
base-ball manager in earnest consultation. There
was an expression in his friend's face that told
Jack even at this distance that the young pitcher
was fascinated by what was being said to him. Immediately Jack clambered down from the stand and
hastened toward them. As he came up to them
the manager was shaking hands with Haseltine, and
Jack heard him say just before he stepped into the
omnibus :

"Think it over and write me. The offer stands
open as long as you like."

After the omnibus had driven off followed by the
acclamations of the school, Jack threw his arms
ecstatically around his chum and cried, "You did
wonders, old fellow. It was glorious ! "

Haseltine made no response at first, and Jack
noticed that his eyes were full of tears.

"Jack," he said at length, — "he has offered me
the position of change pitcher on their nine at a
salary of two thousand dollars. It 's a big honor
for so young a fellow," he added, with an air of
pardonable pride.

"But you did n't accept, did you?" asked our hero excitedly.

"No; I told him I 'd think it over."

"Hurrah!" cried Jack.

"What do you mean?"

"No matter. Wait, that 's all. There 's better news for you than that, and you 'll think so too when you hear it."

Footsteps close at hand caused the boys to turn, and Haseltine's hand was cordially grasped by Dr. Meredith.

"You out-Haseltined Haseltine, to-day, Mr. Pitcher," the master said, then drawing him aside out of the hearing of Jack and Mr. Holgate, he informed him of the offer made by that gentleman, which I am sure you will all be glad to hear he accepted.

Five minutes later the head master and the two boys are walking slowly over the quadrangle toward Granger Hall, where they are to take tea with the Doctor, — their last tea at Utopia. As they reach the threshold, Jack stops and looks back for a moment over the playground where so many of his happiest hours have been passed, and says simply, —

" We shall miss the dear old school, shan't we, Hasy ? "

" Indeed we shall, Jack."

" And the school will miss *you*, my dear boys," answers the Doctor, laying a hand on a shoulder of each of them. " It needs the example of just such boys as you — East and West. God bless you both, and give you strength to devote your manhood to manly deeds ! "

www.ingramcontent.com/pod-product-compliance
Lightning Source LLC
Chambersburg PA
CBHW051519100726
47898CB00005B/1514

* 9 7 8 3 3 3 7 3 2 1 5 5 0 *